# FIGHTING LOVE

A Love to the Extreme Novel

# FIGHTING LOVE

## A LOVE TO THE EXTREME NOVEL

## ABBY NILES

Entangled Publishing, LLC
2614 South Timberline Road
Suite 109
Fort Collins, CO 80525
Visit our website at www.entangledpublishing.com.

Edited by Liz Pelletier and Nina Bruhns
Cover design by

Ebook ISBN 978-1-62266-046-9
Print ISBN 978-1-62266-047-6

Manufactured in the United States of America

First Edition December 2013

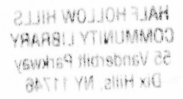

*To Heather, Camryn, Carrigan, Keaton, Scott, Storm &*
*Autumn*

*Three years together is drawing to an end. Thanks for putting up with my Jekyll & Hyde tendencies while I'm under deadline, especially this past year. Love you guys!*

# CHAPTER 1

ATLANTA, GEORGIA

What the hell did he give a woman for Valentine's Day when he no longer had connections?

Frustrated, Tommy "Lightning" Sparks increased the speed of his jog, his grip tightening on Warrior's leash as his feet ate up the sidewalk, his even breathing visible as it puffed up into the February morning air. The frigid chill stung his cheeks as he glanced down at the chocolate Labradoodle to make sure his agitation wasn't transferring over to his dog. Nope. As always, the animal trotted along beside him, happy as all hell.

He wished he could say the same.

What to get his best friend for Valentine's Day had worried the piss out of him for the last three weeks, and he was no closer to an answer. The damn holiday was tomorrow.

He always did something special for Julie to show

how much he appreciated their friendship. Last year, he'd arranged for her to meet her favorite country singer backstage after a concert. Easy enough to do, since the singer had been a fan of his, but Tommy didn't have that kind of influence anymore, did he?

Yeah, he was still Tommy "Lightning" Sparks. No one could take that from him, but the name was tainted now, didn't have the same punch behind it that it once did. Or the same pride.

And that fucking sucked.

Especially since it looked like the one person on the planet who meant the most to him was going to be stuck with a heart-shaped box full of chocolates for V-Day.

*To hell with that.* He wouldn't resort to such a lame present. Julie deserved more than some no-thought-or-effort-needed piece of cardboard with crap candy in it. He would just have to get creative.

He pounded on down the pavement, trying to come up with something. Suddenly, the acrid smell of burning hit his nose. Blinking out of his thoughts, he glanced around. Black smoke billowed high into the air, not too far in the distance.

*What the—*

The only things in the area were homes, and the amount of smoke he was seeing definitely did not come from a fireplace. He jogged around the corner. A group of people from neighboring houses had gathered in the middle of the street, some still in pajamas—in front of *his* house.

Breaking into a sprint, Tommy raced with Warrior down the sidewalk. The sounds of sirens blaring in the background let him know help was on the way. But the closer he got to the one-story vinyl-sided house, the more he had difficulty computing what he was seeing. Fire poured from the side windows, out the back of the house, up from the roof. What the fuck?

What. The. *Fuck*?

As he shoved his way through the crowd, he gaped wide-eyed at his house, dumbfounded. Everything he owned was on fire. Everyt—

Shit!

*My box.*

Panic compressed his chest. *No.* He thrust Warrior's leash at a lady standing next to him. "Take him." When she just stared at his hand, he yelled, *"Take him!"* With a startled jerk, she snatched the nylon rope. "Don't let him follow me," Tommy ordered her.

Just as a fire truck careened around the curve, immediately followed by a second one, Tommy darted for the house. A hand latched onto his forearm. "Dude, you can't go in there!"

*The hell I can't.* Yanking free, Tommy tore up the front porch and heaved a shoulder into the door. The wood gave instantly, and he stumbled inside. Smoke enveloped him, making his eyes water and his throat burn. Coughing, he covered his nose and mouth in the crook of his arm and looked around, trying to get his bearings.

Searing heat came from the engulfed kitchen; flames spread across the ceiling of the living room and hallway that led to his bedroom. Debris rained down from above. A glowing ember landed on the sleeve of his black fitted running jacket. Knocking it off, he hurried across the living room, hunching over, low to the floor. Not that it helped. The thickening smoke filled every corner. One end of the couch suddenly lit up in flames and ignited the curtains behind it. As the fire crept up the wall, the room brightened.

*Get the box and get out.*

He moved forward. The intense heat was unbearable. Sweat rolled down his face. Flames shot out from the hallway into the living room, driving him back. Fury made him bellow as he surged forward into the hall.

He couldn't lose it. Everything that meant anything to him was in that box.

Two beams crashed to the ground a few feet from him. Orange embers swirled toward him. Once again he was forced back. His lungs burned, his eyes watered, his throat felt scorched. He desperately needed air.

But he couldn't give up. Not yet.

Just as he was about to push forward one last time, two arms locked around him and dragged him backward. Instinctively, he yanked against the hold. Then he saw the bedroom, and the fight left him in one defeated *whoosh*. The room was immersed in flames. The wall, the ceiling, the bed…and the closet…a fiery hell.

The box was gone. And Tommy felt as if he'd just lost a part of himself.

As the two firemen pulled him outside onto the lawn, fresh air greeted his starving lungs. He inhaled a greedy breath, which had him rolling onto his side, coughing.

"Is anyone else in the house?" a fireman yelled at him.

Finding he couldn't speak, Tommy shook his head between hacking coughs.

When a couple of paramedics tried to put him on a gurney, he sat up and waved them away, rasping, "I'm fine."

The female EMT wrapped a blanket around him. "I have to check how much carbon monoxide you've inhaled. You'll need to come with me."

Considering his lungs felt really heavy, he probably shouldn't argue. As he sat down in the back of the ambulance, Tommy glared at his house. *Former house.* And once again he felt his world close in on him.

When it fucking rained, it poured.

He stared at the flames licking over his front porch and engulfing the entire front of his house and garage. Fire poured out the side windows, out the back of the house, out the roof. Everywhere.

He'd gone for a run. A goddamn run.

Yanking off his beanie, he knotted his fingers in his dark blond hair and stared at the fiery mass that had been his home. He'd only been gone for a little more than an hour.

Hell, why was he thinking about time? Shit happened. Hadn't he been riding the shit-happened roller coaster for months now?

A bubble of laughter threatened to explode out of him. After everything that had come down on him over the last four months, of course *this* would happen. It had to. It was the next logical sequence of events. He'd fucked up. Lost his title. Got his ass ousted from MMA. So, to make money he'd essentially sold himself to the highest bidder.

*Of course* his house would burn to the fucking ground.

The EMT placed something against his lips. "Breathe

into this until I tell you to stop."

After he did, his lungs rebelled and he coughed hard.

"CO detected, but low." She held up a clear plastic mask. "Sir, I need you to put this on. It's oxygen. It will help get the carbon monoxide out of your body."

He pressed the mask over his nose and mouth and inhaled the crisp, pure oxygen. Another cough erupted out of him, but he continued to inhale deeply as he watched his life go up in smoke for the second time this year.

"Sir, does anything hurt?"

Years gone in fucking seconds.

"Sir? Are you hurt?"

Annoyed, he shook his head, said, "No," and tore his attention away from the house, the lost memories, to survey the chaotic scene around him.

By now fire trucks and police cars littered the road, lights flashing. Two firefighters manned a hose, shooting a powerful jet of water at the front, while two others concentrated on the side. He didn't know what was being done about the back. If anything. The fire looked out of control.

He watched another flame erupt from a different portion of the roof. Still, when it came right down to it, nothing in that house mattered except that damn box.

Hell, he'd had no idea how important it was until he'd realized he was about to lose it. And now it was too late.

Fuck!

A whine came from beside him and he scratched the top of Warrior's head. The chocolate Labradoodle looked up at him, tongue hanging out.

"It'll be all right, buddy."

At least he always took his dog with him on his runs.

"Are you the owner?" a firefighter asked as he walked up.

"No. The renter."

"Does anyone else live here?"

"No, just me and my dog."

"I need to ask you a few questions." When Tommy nodded, the man flipped open a notebook and asked, "Name?"

"Tommy Sparks."

The man, who had been concentrating on writing, glanced up sharply. "Tommy *'Lightning'* Sparks?"

Fucking great. An MMA fan. "The *former* Tommy 'Lightning" Sparks." Just like his house, his career had gone up in flames four months ago. "It's just Tommy Sparks now."

He hoped there was enough edge in his voice to get across he was in no mood to take a trip down memory lane.

Apparently there was, and the dude went back to his twenty questions. "When did you leave?"

"A little more than an hour ago."

"And you went where?"

"For a run."

"Do you smoke?"

Hadn't he just said he was a runner? He squinted at the man, trying not to lose his patience, when he knew the man was just doing his job. "No."

After a series of more questions that all ended with the answer no, the firefighter asked, "Have you been noticing any electrical problems?"

Now they were getting somewhere. "A light switch has been on the fritz. I reported it to my landlord about six weeks ago, but he hadn't fixed it yet. I don't use it, though."

"Where was the switch?"

"In the kitchen."

The firefighter closed the notebook. "I hate to say this, but the house is going to be inhabitable."

*You think?*

"Do you have anyone to call?"

Tommy nodded. His landlord, for one. Let him know what was going on. Then he needed to figure out where he was going to stay tonight. Hell, more than tonight. It would take him a while to find a place to live. So he'd have to impose on someone for more than a few nights. Even if he found a place, he didn't have a bed or a couch…or even a spoon. Man, the only clothes he had were what he was wearing.

The enormity of what had happened hit him, leaving him as dazed as he'd felt after he'd regained consciousness from Ricky Moon's knee to the face during the championship fight.

He'd lost everything then, too.

Thankfully, this time insurance would replace everything that had just burned to a crisp—except for the few things that actually meant anything.

Since nothing would ever replace the contents of that box, there was only one other thing he needed. Or rather, *who* he needed.

He needed his best friend.

• • •

Julie Rogers turned her Prius onto Tommy's road, passing the lines of ranch-style houses in the modest neighborhood on the outskirts of downtown Atlanta. When Tommy's house came into view, her mouth dropped open on a stunned gasp. *Good lord.*

The front was charred beyond recognition. On the sides, the windows were shattered and blackened. The beige vinyl siding that remained was covered in black soot and the roof had huge, gaping holes. When Tommy had called her twenty minutes ago, his detached, emotionless tone had worried her. He'd simply said, "My house just went up in flames. I need you." Then he'd hung up. A part of her had hoped he'd been exaggerating. He hadn't been.

Where was he? She scanned the area. When she finally spotted him sitting between the back doors of an ambulance, a blanket wrapped around his broad shoulders, holding an oxygen mask to his mouth, his other arm draped around Warrior as he stared at the ruins, her heart climbed into her throat. After throwing the car into park, she shot out and raced toward him, her black heels clacking hard on the pavement. "Tommy!"

His head snapped in her direction and relief shone bright in his green eyes. When she reached his side, she grabbed his face between her hands, gaze frantically traveling over his soot-covered skin. "My God, are you okay?"

Other than the grime and the holes in his clothes and on the black beanie on his blond head, nothing seemed injured. He lowered the mask. "Yeah. They want me to do this for a few more minutes as a precaution, and then I can go. I wasn't in there long enough."

She stared at him a moment. Then she threw her arms around his neck, hugging him tightly. When his lips immediately grazed the side of her head, an action he'd done since they were teens, and he whispered, "I'm okay, Julie," tears burned the backs of her eyes.

This man meant the world to her. More than he would ever know.

She pulled back to look at him. The pensive expression twisting his handsome face made her heart clench. He'd been through so much lately. Yeah, some of it was his own doing, but this…this wasn't. She wanted to cry at the lost look in his eyes.

Tommy always acted like nothing fazed him, as if he didn't have a care in the world, which she found both admirable and infuriating. But this moment of vulnerability he was displaying threatened to bring forth the emotions *she* kept under lock and key. So, as she'd done for the past twenty-three years, she pretended they didn't exist and went to him as his best friend.

"What happened? Were you asleep?" God, what if the smoke had gotten to him before he'd woken up? The thought had her hugging him tightly again. "Did Warrior wake you?"

"No, we were out for a run."

Confused, she jerked back and stared at him again. Yes, he definitely looked like he'd just emerged from a burning building. "Then why—"

"I ran in to get something."

She gasped. "You did *what*?" Then she slapped him on the arm. Once wasn't enough. She smacked him again. "Are you insane? You could've died! I could be standing here sobbing because I lost my best friend for being an idiot!" She shoved his shoulder, then walked a couple of feet away, rubbing her forehead. "Jesus, Tommy. What the hell was so important you would risk your life over it?"

"It doesn't matter now. It's gone."

"*What's* gone?"

He glared at her. "I need *you*, Julie. Not a lecture. Drop it."

He was right. This wasn't the time. All that mattered was he was safe, even if he had made a reckless decision, which wasn't surprising anymore. Over the last year, Tommy had made many of those. "What happened?"

"They think it started in the kitchen. It was that damn switch. I'd been after the landlord for weeks to change it."

Julie glanced back at the charred house. All that remained of the garage was a few scorched beams, half a wall, and the blackened skeleton of Tommy's cherry-red Corvette. She grimaced. "Oh, Tommy. Your car."

"It's insured," he said, shrugging.

"What about rental insurance?"

"Have it." He sent her a lopsided smile. "Maybe I'm growing up after all."

At those words, she flinched. He was trying to be humorous, bring a little lightness into the moment—she got that—but she didn't like him using the words *she'd* yelled at him four months ago to go about it, especially after something like this. Losing his home to a fire was something he had no control over. The night she'd told him he needed to grow up, well…she'd meant it.

Having to bail Tommy out of jail for brawling at a bar had been the lowest point of their friendship, and she'd been furious. Not to mention the fallout from the MMA scandal of the century—Tommy being banned from his coach's training facility hadn't been the only consequence. Ethan Porter, the president of Cage Match Championship, had banned him from the cage, too. Thankfully, the brawling charges had been dropped, so one night was all he'd spent in jail.

"You know I said that because I was pissed, right?" she said softly.

He shrugged. "There was some truth to it."

Yeah, more than some, actually. She let her silence speak for itself. Tommy knew what it meant.

One of the EMTs came over and had Tommy breathe into some contraption. After the woman looked at the reading, she nodded. "You're good. If you start having any nausea, lightheadedness, or any other symptoms, go straight to the ER, but you should be fine."

After that, a firefighter came over to speak to him for a few minutes, then told Tommy he was free to go. He stood and stretched his six foot three inch frame then ruffled Warrior's head. "Let's find us a place to crash. What do you say, buddy?"

"You can stay with me." At the suggestion, his nose curled in distaste and she swatted at him. "Hey! What's the problem with staying at my place?"

A chuckle came out of him as he slung his arm around her shoulder and dropped a kiss on top of her head. Even in three-inch heels her, she fit easily under his arm. "It's not you, doofus." When she raised a doubtful brow, he laughed outright. "Okay…maybe it is you. Julie, you're my best friend. But we haven't done close living quarters since we used to sneak in and out of each other's bedrooms when we were kids. What if we end up killing each other?"

The memory made her smile. "Well, if all else fails, I guess we can make up over walkie-talkies."

"Ah, shit, I forgot we used to do that." He sighed, hugging her closer to his side as they walked toward her car. "I appreciate the offer, but I don't like imposing on you. I'll find something."

"Have it your way."

He always did.

When they reached the car, Tommy let Warrior in the backseat, then climbed in himself. As she started the engine, he said, "I really need to feed Warrior. I always give him a big bowl of food after we run. Can we stop at a store?"

"I have some food at my house."

Again with the nose curl. God, that drove her nuts.

"My dog will not eat that foo-foo shit you feed Lucy. He eats manly dog food, isn't that right, buddy?" He scratched the dog behind the ear and earned a lick across the cheek.

"You do know your face is covered in soot and you smell like a campfire, right?"

"I could give a rat's ass what I look like right now, Julie. Besides, I don't have anything to change into anyway." When she glanced over at him, he had the oddest look on his face, a mixture of disbelief, amusement, and confusion. "Jeez, I don't even have a toothbrush."

When he turned and stared at her with the same strange expression, she worried the reality of what had happened was about to truly hit him. The man had just lost everything he owned.

"You okay?" she asked.

"Yeah. The unimportant shit is starting to pop up. Like the rib eye I bought last night." He shook his head. "Why that would even cross my mind, after losing..." He inhaled deeply.

She took one hand off the steering wheel, reached over, and squeezed his hand. "It'll be okay."

He clasped it and squeezed back. "Yeah. It's like, for a moment I forget, and nothing has changed. Then it hits me like a ton of bricks again. Kinda like it did after..."

"You lost the title," she finished gently.

"Yeah. I guess it's natural, right? I thought some weird-ass stuff after Mike booted me out. Every time I thought about heading over to the gym, I had to remind myself Mike had banned me, and why. I had to do that for weeks before the new routine finally took over and I stopped thinking about it. I can't believe I'm having to do this all over again."

"Well, at least this one isn't your fault."

He let out a shocked laugh and shook his head. "*Ow!* Damn, woman."

She shrugged. Though she'd hated that Tommy had been banned from the cage and even his training facility, this was all part of the growing up he needed to do. As he'd gotten older, instead of settling down like most men eventually did, Tommy had only gotten wilder.

The man did love his women. As a consequence, he'd never had a serious relationship. In fact, in the twenty-three years she had known him, she couldn't remember seeing him with the same woman twice. Well. She had seen him with *two* women at the same time, but, again, the actual girls never stayed the same.

Then there was his attitude. Thankfully, that had never been directed at her. He'd always stayed the same with her, but everyone else—including his training posse, especially after he won the Middleweight championship a little over a year ago—yeah, she understood how it had been easy for Mike to tell him to get the hell out.

Fighting hadn't changed Tommy. He'd fought his way up since he was twenty. But the lifestyle that came with "hitting it big" had. The parties, the cockiness, the women, all of it. The man had become so wrapped up in everything and everyone else around him, he had completely ignored Julie. Hell, he hadn't even noticed when she'd left.

She really didn't ever want to meet that man again.

She just hated that his blindness had cost him the cage. And brought him to this.

No career, no future. And now, no home.

• • •

Tommy tucked a long yellow envelope under his arm as he walked out of the post office exit. Julie had been awesome, as always. She'd chauffeured him around all morning, stopping to let him buy some necessities. Thankfully, when he ran, he always carried a debit card, his license, and some cash, along with his phone, in his wrist wallet. That habit had kept him from being completely without access to money.

Too bad money wasn't finding him a place to stay. A pet-friendly hotel was an option, of course, but he didn't like the idea of his dog being cooped up in a hotel room for God only knew how long before he found a new place.

But Julie didn't need him underfoot, either.

He had to see if he could make other arrangements. Unfortunately, only one other person came to mind, and he knew it would be a long shot. He dug out his phone, thumbed through his contact list, then hit the call button.

Dante "Inferno" Jones had been a good friend of his for a couple of years now. "Hello," Dante answered.

"Hey, man. It's Tommy."

"Tommy! It's been a while. How've you been?"

"All right. Keeping busy."

There was a moment of silence. "So what's up?"

Tommy rubbed the stubble on his jaw. He had never been big on asking for help. "Uh, yeah…I had a fire at my place. Looks like I'm going to be out somewhere to live for a bit, so I was wondering if I could crash over at your place." He left out how bad the fire actually was, not wanting Dante to feel obligated.

"Fuck, Tommy, I'm sorry. Of course you can stay here. I'm warning you, though, this place will be a madhouse for the next two weeks. We've got family coming in who decided to make our wedding a vacation trip. On top of that, Caitlyn is on edge. She's pushing me to elope and call off the wedding. She's so over the planning." He chuckled softly. "But you are more than welcome to stay."

Tommy grimaced. Yeah, he wasn't doing that to Dante. "You know, don't worry about it; you have your hands full now."

"Are you sure?"

"Certain."

"Well, just know the offer is open if you want to crash

here."

"Will do. I'll talk to you soon."

He went to hang up when he heard Dante's, "Tommy. Wait a sec," and he brought the cell back to his ear.

"Yeah?"

Muffled mumbling came across the line. He figured Dante had put his hand over the speaker. Then Dante came back clear. "Caitlyn just reminded me you never responded to the wedding invitation. She needs a final head count. Are you coming?"

Tommy grimaced. A wedding. The last place in the world he wanted to be. But Dante had always supported him, so he needed to return the favor. "Yeah, I'll be there."

"Are you bringing anyone?"

"Julie, probably."

There was a moment of silence, where Dante's mumbling came through again. "Are you her extra, then?"

"What are you talking about?"

"She's already RSVP'd and checked the extra person."

Tommy blinked. She hadn't mentioned that to him.

"Well, put me down as attending."

"And a date?"

He was sort of in between women right now. Not from lack of interest from them, just on his part. He wasn't too worried about it. He figured he was still adjusting to the changes from the fallout. He'd get his groove back. "Nah. Just me."

"All right, then. Looking forward to seeing you, buddy. Been too long."

"Yeah. Me, too."

They said their byes and hung up.

While Dante might be happy, Tommy knew his buddy's wedding was going to be a bitch to face. He'd see people he hadn't seen in months, which was why he hadn't answered the invitation yet. He actually kept going back and forth about it. He'd been planning on bringing it up to Julie this week, but apparently she was already going, and with a date.

Good for her. The woman worked too damn hard and didn't play enough.

It'd do her good to let loose a little.

After he returned to the car, he climbed in, tossed the envelope on the dashboard, and said, "Well, you're stuck with me."

She narrowed her eyes. "What are you talking about?"

"I gave Dante a call to see if I could stay with him and Cait for a while. He said yes, but things seemed pretty chaotic with the wedding and all, so I figured I'd better not add to it." He sighed. "I'd do a hotel, but—"

"Shut *up*." She groaned as she shoved her fingers into her thick brunette hair. "I already said you could stay with me. As long as you want. So just. *Shut. Up.*"

"It could be a few days. Weeks, even."

"What part of 'as long as you want' don't you get?"

He smiled. Okay. He'd just try not to be in the way. "Dante told me you had a date."

She sort of jerked back and peered at him. "A date?"

"For the wedding. I was going to ask you to go with me, but, you know, if you can get a little—" He waggled his eyebrows.

She shoved him, laughing. "Jesus, Tommy."

"What? I can't be excited about my best friend getting

some action?"

As far as he was concerned, she needed to get more of it. With her long, dark hair, expressive, hazel eyes and easy smile, Julie was a beautiful woman. He had little doubt men lined up to take her out. Her problem was her inability to freaking relax.

"Unfortunately, I'm not getting any action. My date fell through."

"Well, that's a bummer." He winked. "I won't be as *exciting* a date, but you can go with me."

She studied him for a minute, then shrugged. "You'll do, I guess."

He feigned hurt. "That was bitchy."

"You said you wouldn't be exciting, so what did you expect?"

Laughing, he leaned over and kissed her cheek. "I'll still make sure you have a great time. Promise." He sat back and put on his seat belt. "You know, this does beg the question of dating."

She shot him an uncertain look. "Dating?"

"With the fire and all, I'll probably be too preoccupied to fool around with anyone, but you… Well, just because I'll be staying with you, don't think you have to be home every night with me. I want you to continue on like I'm not there, okay?"

Something flashed across her eyes that he couldn't decipher. "Yeah. Sure." She glanced out the windshield, and when she glanced back, the look was gone and mischief sparkled in her eyes. "But when I am home and I cook, you eat."

"Woman, I just lost everything I own. Are you trying

to take my life, too?" She just stared at him in that impish way he loved, and he started to laugh. "Fine. I'll scarf down that god-awful crap you like to call food."

"As long as we're clear." She cranked the car.

"Yep." It wasn't the perfect solution, but at least the only thing he'd have to worry about while he got himself resettled was a possible case of food poisoning. The less drama he had right now the better.

And Julie never came with drama.

# CHAPTER 2

Tommy scowled at the one-story light blue vinyl-siding house as Julie parked her car in the driveway. Man, he was in a dick mood. None of it was Julie's fault. She was just trying to help out a friend, but four hours ago he'd had his own place. His own possessions. His own life, dependent on no one. It'd been nice. His. And now it was all nothing but ash.

Hell, he'd even lost the hat— "Fuck," he muttered.

"Tommy?"

"Hmm?" he murmured.

"Will you please tell me what you went back into the house for?"

Damn it. Leave it to her to pick up on the only thing that came close to making him want to break down. He refused to cry like a fucking girl in front of Julie.

"It's gone now, Julie, so it doesn't matter." He cursed the hoarseness in his voice and fumbled with the handle.

Her hand clamped down on his arm. "It matters to me. Warrior was safe. I can't imagine what else would've pushed you back into the house."

Groaning, he closed his eyes and leaned back against the seat. The joys of having an almost quarter-century friendship with someone? She was way too comfortable pushing shit because she knew he'd fucking tell her. "It was my box."

"You can replace that. I can't replace *you*."

"Yeah. The box. Not what was inside it." Opening his eyes, he turned his head. "The Atlanta Braves cap you gave me for my sixteenth birthday was in it."

Shock widened her eyes as she placed a hand to her mouth. "You still have *that*?"

How could she think he'd get rid of it?

"Jesus, Julie, I have everything you've ever given me, including that horrible mix tape of Vanilla Ice and New Kids on the Block. It was all in that box."

"You ran into a burning building to save the cheesy presents I've bought you over the years?"

He scowled at her. "They weren't just presents. They're memories. Our memories, Julie. You're the only family I have. That box meant a lot to me."

"Oh, Tommy. I-I…" She paused, brows pulling together in thought.

Ah fuck, she was going to say something to make this worse. Before she could find the words she was searching for, he waved his hand. "It's gone now. Let's just leave it at that."

Out of everything he'd lost, that hat had hit him the hardest. Which was crazy, really. He never went into the box of mementos he kept of his and Julie's decades-long friendship. But knowing it was gone, it felt as though someone had torn his guts out.

Grabbing the envelope, he opened the door and moved to the back of the car. Thumping the top of the trunk, he waited for Julie to pop it. After he grabbed the shopping bags, he strode up the walkway.

When it came right down to it, Julie was his family. His only family. He didn't have any siblings. Had no clue who his father was. His mom had been worthless—an alcoholic who'd marched men in and out of the house like it was the Macy's Thanksgiving Day parade. The only good thing that woman had ever done for him was rent the house next door to the one Julie's family moved into.

Julie was all he had. And he'd just lost every single memory of their friendship that he'd kept buried in the back of his closet like a goddamn treasure chest. Fisting his hands around the shopping bags, he shook off the thought, focusing on reaching the front door and not the torrent of emotions that was threatening to take him down.

The house was small, as was the front yard, and it was perfect for Julie. In the spring, the now-dead garden beds in front would no doubt overflow with colorful annuals that she'd plant when she got spring fever—which she got like clockwork each April. She'd sit on the swing hanging on the front porch reading a book, sipping a glass of Merlot. She'd mow the lawn in her ratty tank top, cut-off jeans, and the MMA baseball cap he'd given her a few years ago. A small smile came to his lips.

Maybe being here wasn't such a bad thing.

Warrior raced past him up the stone path to the front

door, not even needing a leash to keep him headed in the right direction. The dog was probably excited about their new living arrangements. Tommy spoiled that dog rotten, but the one thing he didn't have was a doggie door. Julie did, and even though her pup was miniscule in comparison to his, she'd bought a larger opening so Warrior could follow Lucy around since they spent so much time over here. Now his dog would be able to run around the spacious fenced in backyard whenever he wanted.

As he climbed the steps to the entry, he heard Lucy yapping and clawing at the door on the other side. When Julie unlocked the door, the white fur ball bolted through, and she scooped the Pekinese up in her arms.

"Someone's glad to see you," Tommy said.

She smiled. "She's always happy to see her mommy. Aren't you, sweetie?"

The tiny tongue flicked out across Julie's jaw. Then Lucy noticed Warrior. She struggled against Julie's hold, and when Julie placed her on the ground, the two dogs danced around, pawing playfully at each other. It always amazed him how well those two got along, considering the size difference. The way Warrior towered over Lucy never intimidated the little dog. She gave as good as she got.

Just like Julie.

As she started to walk into the house, he grabbed for her hand. Squeezing her fingers, he said, "Thank you…for letting me stay."

Her eyes softened. "Anytime, Tommy. Really."

After a quick squeeze of her own, she released his hand and waved him and the dogs inside. When he crossed the threshold into the living room, he stopped. The house overwhelming him in a way it never had before, reminding him that he now owned nothing but the few shopping bags he gripped in his hands. The living room was completely decked out. A matching sage couch and loveseat with plush striped pillows sat before a brick fireplace. In the corner was a large flat-screen television sitting on a light oak entertainment center that matched the hardwood floors.

Pictures in black frames of her parents, sisters, and him hung on the wall. His heart tightened as it always did when he saw his picture included as part of her family.

Proof that he was just as important to her as she was to him. Thank God for that. He wouldn't know what to do without this woman.

A gentle touch landed on his bicep. "You okay?"

He blinked and looked down at her. "My photos are all gone, too."

"Tommy. I'm so sorry."

"All I can do now is move forward." He nudged her with his shoulder. "A wise woman once told me that."

"Don't think you're going to get out of dinner with flattery."

He grinned. She always knew the right thing to say. "Not working, huh?"

"Nope."

"It was worth a shot."

She shook her head. "I'd show you to your room, but you already know where it is. So I don't see the point. You know where everything is. Make yourself at home."

Home.

No. This wasn't his home. It was Julie's. The entire

house breathed her.

He left her standing in the living room and strolled down the hall, past her room, then into the guest room. Now, his room. Dropping the bags on the bed, he glanced around. This room wasn't as decorated, at least. Didn't feel so much like Julie as every other room in the house did. The walls were light beige and went well with the white and blue paisley comforter. Two glossy black end tables matched the head- and footboard of the bed.

Another flat-screen, though much smaller, sat on top of the dresser.

She appeared and leaned against the doorjamb. "Good thing I bought that TV a few months ago when Mom came to stay, or you'd be SOL. I don't share the remote."

"I don't mind suffering through your shows."

"Really? You'd watch *Real Housewives* with me?"

He grimaced. He'd forgotten about that one. Julie was a reality TV junkie.

She snickered at his expression. "I may just make you watch it with me now."

"My worst nightmare."

"Unpack," she said, nodding toward the bed. "I'm going to throw on some dinner. How's spaghetti sound?"

"Trying to ease me in lightly, huh?"

"Don't get used to it." She pushed off the frame and turned to leave. "Tomorrow's meatloaf."

"Ugh." Julie's meatloaf was horrendous.

The twittering of her laughter followed her down the hall. She knew she sucked at cooking. Problem was, he wasn't any damn better. He lived off take-out and protein shakes.

He sighed. *Unpack*. His gaze landed on the envelope. First he needed to make sure he had everything he needed to file his claim. Taking a seat on the bed, he opened it and withdrew the contents. An inventory checklist he'd made just a few months ago, along with photos, and a flash drive that had a video of everything he owned. Had owned.

Oddly, he hadn't bothered to get rental insurance until after he'd been kicked out of CMC. He figured his sudden dip into Responsibility Land was mostly thanks to Julie's "grow up" comment, which had really kicked him in the teeth at the time. Even so, as he'd taken the photos he'd felt kind of stupid, thinking he'd never need them. Boy, had he been wrong.

Maybe there was something to this growing up thing, after all.

He set aside the flash drive and started to leaf through the pictures. And froze. A thousand emotions bombarded him. Remorse. Anger. Resentment. Longing.

The photo had been taken right after he'd won the championship. Drenched in sweat and blood, he held the gold belt raised above his head in triumph, his mouth wide open with a yell. *Damn*. The pain of loss slashed through him like a sharp knife.

His gaze strayed to the woman standing beside him, grinning up at him with the soft glow of adoration in her eyes, and his chest tightened with affection.

Julie.

God, she'd been so proud of him that night. Who would ever have guessed that, just eight months later, the night he'd defended his belt for the first time—and lost— she would end up at the jail, waiting in the pickup area with arms crossed tightly across her chest, disappointment etched on every inch of her face as a guard escorted him out of the cellblock. Even now, four months after her scathing, "You really need to grow up," those words still rang loud and clear in his ears.

He leaned his head back against the headboard with a sigh.

Maybe it was about time he took them to heart.

• • •

Julie held a pot under the running tap until it was three-quarters full. After she placed it on the stove, she wiped her hands across the sides of her jeans and sighed. A weird current had buzzed through her ever since Tommy walked through the door. One she couldn't exactly explain. It wasn't unease…more like tension.

Crazy. He'd been here many times since she'd moved in two years ago, and she'd never felt like this. But it was different this time, wasn't it?

He wouldn't be leaving after dinner to go home. He would be staying overnight…for a while.

Which meant she would have to deal with the constant ups and downs she had with Tommy. The ups being when she was completely in the "friend" zone and just laughing and having a great time with him. The downs were when she was overly aware of him in a way a best friend shouldn't be. Those moments were not his fault. They were hers alone, and she did her best to keep them under control.

Unfortunately, she was on a high-speed, belly-lifting downward plummet right now. The only thing that was going to cure it was getting used to Tommy being here all the time.

"Need any help?" he asked as he stepped into the kitchen.

Her heart stopped for a second, then started to beat erratically. *Jesus*. He'd showered. The soot had been scrubbed off his handsome face. Freshly shaven cheeks showed off the strong curvature of his jaw and his full masculine lips. Loose fitted jeans rode low on his hips, but the damn shirt had to be a size too small, hugging every freaking muscles of his upper body, from his ripped biceps, to his broad shoulders, to the wide expanse of his chest. Thankfully, the material loosened around his waist. Why? Because she knew everything was tight there too. Damn him. *Got to get used to him being here, girl.*

"Not really." Everything was either frozen or from a jar. She spotted the portabella mushrooms sitting farther down the granite-topped counter. She always added extra to the sauce. She pointed with her knife. "You can cut those up."

"I'm on it."

He slid behind her, hands resting on her hips, chest grazing her shoulder blades. Closing her eyes, she gritted her teeth, almost groaning when the front of his jeans brushed the back of hers.

*Damn small kitchen.* She should've bought a bigger house. A mansion, maybe.

Yeah, right. That still wouldn't have been enough room.

"Need something to cut with," Tommy said, not moving away.

"I got it!" Quickly leaning over, she grabbed the entire

butcher's block and shoved it toward the mushrooms. He quirked a brow at her but remained silent as he finally stepped past her and withdrew a knife. *Thank God.*

She knew she was acting weird. She couldn't help it. His presence dominated the kitchen, made her very aware of how close he was standing while he chopped the mushrooms.

How they were now—oh my God—*living together.*

No, no, no. Not living together. Tommy was just *staying* here. Big, big difference.

The rest of the cooking didn't get any easier. A lean forward as he grabbed the oil brought focus to his strong arms. An accidental brush of his hand against hers as he dumped the mushrooms into the sauce while she stirred sent a rash of goose bumps over her. Then an intentional electrifying touch as he took the wood spoon from her and told her to sit down in the living room.

Julie didn't argue. The kitchen was getting way too hot to handle.

By the time he handed her a plate with a heaping portion of spaghetti and a slice of garlic bread, she was ready to shatter. She grabbed the glass of wine she'd placed on the coffee table and took a long gulp.

A draft swept through the room, and she shivered. Without thought, she picked up the remote to the fireplace and clicked it on. As soon as the flames ignited, she realized what she'd done.

Stupid. Stupid. *Stupid.*

She was wound tight enough without setting the freaking mood.

She shot a peek at Tommy, who was shoveling

marinara-coated noodles into his mouth.

Not that he was conscious of it. She was alone in her acute, painful awareness of him and the awkwardness of her inappropriate feelings, while he chowed down on spaghetti, completely oblivious to her torment.

And why was *that* surprising? Hadn't the man already encouraged her to freaking *date* while he was here? Not that she had any plans *not* to date. Her unanswered attraction was the bane of her existence. She tried to date as much as her schedule would allow her to, hoping to find the guy who would make her forget Tommy Sparks. So far, she'd either not met this fantasy man or he didn't exist.

Wonderful.

She refused to believe the latter. She was *not* destined to be in love for the rest of her life with a jerk who waggled his eyebrows in encouragement when he talked about her having a date with another man. No. Way.

"What's on TV tonight?" he asked, yanking her from her thoughts.

Silently thanking him for the distraction, she said, "It's a channel-surf night, actually. You don't have to sit with me. It's okay to eat in your room."

He paused with the fork halfway to his mouth. "Is that what you want me to do?"

"No…no." *Yes.* But she couldn't actually say that, or she risked setting a very bad tone for this new living situation. "I didn't mean it like that. I just don't want you thinking you have to keep me entertained."

She mentally cringed at her word choice. Thankfully, he didn't notice.

"I don't. I'm right where I want to be."

"Good." She forced a cheerful smile. "Good."

*So not good*.

For the next twenty minutes, they ate in silence while she flipped through channels, finding nothing, absolutely *nothing*, to take her mind off the man sitting beside her. Every time he shifted on the couch, she wanted to bolt from the room and lock herself away. Tormented by the wish that he was really shifting toward her to throw his arm around her and not because he was grabbing a napkin to wipe his mouth or placing the plate on the coffee table.

God, she *hated* when she got like this. For the most part, she had a pretty damn good hold on her attraction to Tommy. Being best friends for all these years, they had developed a certain routine. When he put his arm around her and kissed the top of her head, it was the equivalent of when he used to put her in a friendly headlock as kids. He told her he loved her so often it was nothing more than a, "Damn, you're awesome." In those moments, he was just a friend to her — a best friend. Her *person*. As she was his.

But every once in a while, like now, she became hyperaware of the man. How close he was. Every movement. And that gnawing need she'd lived with for so many years started to drive her insane. The need to be with him as a woman. To touch him. God, the dirty things she would gladly do to this man when she felt like she did right now…

All he'd have to do was give her one of those smoldering looks she'd seen him send other women, and she'd be across this couch in less than a second.

She actually wanted to laugh at herself. As much as she talked a big game in her head, she really didn't know how she would react if Tommy ever did look at her like that. Probably slap her palm across his forehead to make sure he didn't have a fever.

Finally admitting defeat, she clicked off the TV and dropped the remote beside her. "Nothing's on."

As he took a chug of his soda, he shrugged. "TV's overrated."

"Says you."

"I think we can find something else more productive to do."

So could she, but she highly doubted she was thinking what he was thinking. "Like what?"

"We could talk."

"Talk?"

He smiled, a stupid half-lifting of one side of his mouth that made her heart slam against her chest. "Yeah, you know, put words into sentences."

"We talk all the time, Tommy." She hated the way her voice had a breathless tinge to it, hated how he made her feel butterflies with one damn look.

Seriousness stole away his lighthearted expression. "Not lately. You've been working a lot of hours and I've been shooting the fall catalog for Athletic Life." He scowled. "I never imagined I would be making a living modeling in catalog spreads for a small sporting goods store. Earlier this week we were shooting the fishing poles." He rolled his eyes to her. "*Fishing poles*, Julie. I hate fishing."

"Did they make you wear those rubber boots that come up to your hips?" she asked, trying to get back the lighthearted way they'd been all afternoon.

"Yes!"

He shifted his body toward her, bending a leg onto the cushion so it almost touched her thigh as he propped an elbow on the back of the couch and leaned his head on it. She swallowed, her gaze straying to the masculine knee so freaking close to hers. Mere inches. Not nearly far enough.

So much for trying to keep it light.

*Where are the dogs when you need them?*

As if she'd somehow telepathically summoned them, she heard the flap of the doggie door and eight paws racing toward them. Lucy jumped onto the couch and curled up on Julie's lap. Warrior, tail wagging, tongue lolling out of his mouth, eyed the space between Julie and Tommy.

Tommy laughed and scooted back, allowing the dog to settle between them.

*Thank you, animals.* The physical barrier she needed to keep her cool.

She gave both mutts a good head-ruffle for their unknowing cooperation.

"How are things at the vet clinic?" he asked.

"Good. Busy. But I'm not complaining. I know I was resistant to hiring help, but Melody ended up being an excellent addition." Julie was a veterinarian, and her practice was just starting to thrive.

"See? If you'd just listen to me more often."

She lifted her hands in a sign of concession. "You were right."

"Holy shit, say that again."

She suppressed a smile. "Don't push it, bub."

Tommy had been the one to urge her to hire a second vet, flat-out stating she was working too fucking much and needed to make time for fun. Considering the fact she had been watching him play too much and not work nearly enough, she hadn't fully appreciated the advice at the time.

But she'd ended up realizing if she kept going like she was, her body was going to make her stop from sheer exhaustion. So she'd hired Melody, and the woman was as dedicated to animals as she was, and had helped take the clinic to the next level.

He stroked the dog's fur, studying her with an indecipherable look.

"What?"

"The whole reason I wanted you to hire someone was so you could go out and have some fun. Have you?"

These little reminders of how unbothered Tommy was with her dating other men were always welcome, though each one came with a little pinch of hurt. They kept her from pining away for the man, waiting for him to open his damn eyes. She didn't want to be that woman. She felt *sorry* for women like that. Women who refused to let go of men who didn't return their feelings. Julie wanted to marry, have kids. Tommy had no interest in those things, and most likely never would.

"Been on a few dates," she said with a shrug. "I still work a lot, Tommy. So it's hard meeting someone."

"Tried the dating websites?"

"With disastrous results."

"Maybe we should go to the club. It's a great place to meet people." His ideal place for partner shopping.

"That's not my scene anymore. You know that. I hate going to those parties after a fight."

"I also know you need to relax and let your hair down."

"I can let my hair down without resorting to something I did in my early twenties."

His jaw clenched, and she shook her head, silently cursing her snippy comment. She'd pretty much told him, *again*, he needed to grow up.

Hell, not her business. It was *his* life. Her priorities were different. They had been since she returned to Atlanta four years ago and opened her practice.

"One day you're going to open your eyes and realize you've worked your life away, Julie."

"Yeah, and the flip side to that coin, Tommy, is that one day you're going to open *your* eyes and realize that you had a career but lost it because your ego got too big and you were always searching for a good time."

Which was why she and Tommy would never work. As friends they were great. That way, the stuff he chose to do didn't affect her personally. He unknowingly hurt her feelings on occasion, but that was more her issues than his. However, if they were together, as in sharing a life together, she would never tolerate some of the crap he pulled that she did as his friend. Then she'd lose far more than just a relationship—she'd lose her dearest, most treasured friend.

So, Tommy not feeling for her the way she felt for him was actually a *good* thing. Now she just had to convince her damn heart.

"That was a cheap shot, Julie."

"Was it? You know I love you, and we have always been straight with each other. But you were screwing up. Sure, you loved to party before you won the championship, but there was always some sort of balance. After you won, hell, I don't know what happened to you." She shook her head. "Watching that cop handcuff you and put you in the police cruiser—that was absolutely one of the worst moments of my life. And it was because of *your* actions."

Anger burned bright in his eyes as he glared at her. He had never told her the reason he'd punched the son of the CMC official who controlled his ability to enter the professional cage, he'd just said the punk had deserved it. As he leaned forward, she knew she was about to find out.

"You want to know why I hit him?" His teeth clenched. "Because of you."

She jerked back. "Me?"

"He hit on you, didn't he?"

"Yeah, he was past drunk. I told him to get lost."

"Yeah, I've seen you do that. Icy eyes, frosty tone, superior expression. He let me know how much the stick you had up your ass pissed him off. Let me know in graphic detail what he'd do to you to make you regret rejecting him." His face transformed into the murderous scowl he got when he entered the cage. "And sitting here today, knowing the consequences, I'd hit the fucker all over again for even *thinking* of laying a hand on you." He shot off the couch, and a few seconds later, the door to his bedroom slammed.

Stunned, Julie stared at the empty space on the couch across from her. Not that Tommy defending her was any surprise; he'd done so before. What filled her with horror was how grossly wrong she'd been about the events of that night, the things she'd so easily believed of him, that had led her to yelling at Tommy that he needed to grow up.

A few hours earlier, he had lost the championship belt—just two minutes into the first round. Ethan had chewed him out for his crappy performance, which really had been terrible. Surly, and being a total son of a bitch, Tommy had been knocking back shots at the bar. For once, she'd been glad he was ignoring her.

Ethan's son approached him and they started talking. Next thing she'd known, Tommy had busted the guy's nose and taken out the two friends who'd tried to defend the kid. Tommy was left standing in the middle, a quivering mass of rage.

Cops were called. He was arrested. Mike refused to coach him any more. Ethan banned him from fighting in CMC. And Julie had bailed him out of jail.

This entire time she'd believed he'd thrown a Hulk-sized temper tantrum because he'd been sitting there sulking about losing the title and Ethan's son just happened to say the wrong thing to trigger the explosion.

But that had never been the case. He'd been defending *her*. And as a thank-you, she'd freaking told him he needed to grow up.

How the hell did she make up for *that*?

. . .

Tommy sat in an uncomfortable plastic chair as a giggling woman put some kind of makeup shit on his face in the stockroom of Athletic Life. He'd called a car rental agency first thing this morning and had them deliver a sedan so he could get to work on time. He hated every second of this job, but it was a well-paying gig that didn't take up too much of his time. Just a few hours a day for a few weeks, while the Athletic Life marketing suits took photos of specific gear and equipment they wanted showcased on an actual human in the catalog. The job would be wrapping up soon, and it couldn't come soon enough as far as Tommy was concerned.

However, today he was in a crappier mood than he usually was when he was here. He hadn't slept well, had tossed and turned most of the night, remembering Julie's criticism and how it had hit him right in the chest.

What sucked was that she was right. He *hated* when she was right. Over the last four months of soul-searching, his former out-of-control ego and constant partying were two things he looked back on and regretted. Maybe Mike, and possibly even Ethan, wouldn't have been so quick to cut him off if he hadn't been fucking up so badly for months.

Being a career fighter had always been Tommy's dream. He'd busted serious ass to be recognized by CMC—the largest, most respected MMA organization in the world. CMC only hosted the highest-caliber fighters, and being offered a contract to fight for them was like being offered the Holy Grail of fighting. And he'd had it.

He'd pinpointed the start of his downfall to a little more than a year and a half ago when he'd won the fight he needed to be a contender for the belt. At his victory celebration that night, he'd partied hard. That win had also come with a hefty paycheck and winning bonus. For the first time ever, he didn't have to worry about money.

He'd started spending more time at the bars and clubs. It didn't faze him to walk into a place alone because he knew he'd be surrounded in no time. Men wanted to be his friend, and the women… He'd never lacked for willing, gorgeous women, but after that win, they all but begged to be with Tommy "Lightning" Sparks. And he'd been all too happy to oblige.

All that attention had gone to his head and he'd turned cocky, which had morphed into arrogant asshole after he won the belt from Griffin. He'd started skipping practice, staying out late, blaming everyone else when he had a bad practice. He'd totally lost control. And what had happened? The first time he defended his title, he'd given the poorest showing of his entire MMA career.

Then he'd punched the president's son.

Still. That he would *never* regret. He'd told Julie the dead honest truth. Even knowing what was going to happen, he would hit that motherfucker all over again.

"Is he ready?"

Coming back to the present, Tommy glanced over his shoulder to see Bonnie, the photographer, standing inside the door.

"Yep." The makeup woman dabbed one more of something on the corner of his nose and straightened.

He pushed out of the chair and ambled over to the photographer he'd been working with the last couple of weeks. She was attractive. Tall. In her spiked black heels, she was the same height as his six-three, which meant she was probably around five-ten in bare feet. Bright, wavy red hair reached the middle of her back, and she had green eyes that were too green to be real. Her outfits were on the tight side and showed off her tiny figure. She had a sexually deviant vibe about her, which usually turned him on. But nope, he wasn't feeling her.

She was too aggressive for his taste. She'd made it clear that she wanted to tie him up and do dirty things to him. Maybe the offer would have been more intriguing if she'd offered to let him tie her up, though he doubted it, even if he did get turned on by being the dominant one.

*No one* was turning him on lately. He didn't know what the fuck was the matter with him. He loved women, but ever since the night he was arrested—the *only* time in his life restraints had been put on *his* wrists—he hadn't had any fun at all.

And it always came back to Julie's expression that night after he was released. Her disappointment had killed his libido. Except…

No. It wasn't Julie. Yeah, he'd let her down, and if there was one person he hated letting down, it was his best friend. But if there was one person he hated letting down even more, it was himself.

*He'd* killed his own damn libido.

"Okay, Tommy, today we're going to do the MMA portion of the catalog. We'd like to get a picture of you in front of one of the bags Athletic Life offers."

He'd known this was coming, and he hadn't been looking forward to it. Even though he'd had a bag set up at his house, still jumped rope and tried to keep to some of his conditioning routines, he hadn't posed as an actual fighter since he'd stepped out of the cage after his mortifying loss to Ricky Moon.

Bonnie glanced at the group around him. "We want it to look like he's been working out *hard*. So make the man *glisten*." She sent him a sidelong look with an inviting purse of her lips.

And again, there was nothing. Not even a twitch.

A pair of boxing shorts was shoved at him with an order to put them on. Dropping trou right there, he shed his jeans and tugged the shorts over his boxer briefs, then yanked off his shirt. The group attacked with baby oil first. Once that had been rubbed on his skin, they spritzed him with water until he looked like he'd been working out for hours.

After they wrapped his hands—which they did a shit job of—and put the gloves on, he was moved to an area that had been cleared out in the back of the store for the photo shoot. A white sheet hung as a backdrop. Later, Bonnie would Photoshop a gym into the background.

As Tommy squared off with the red hanging bag, nostalgia hit him hard. Lowering his hands, he straightened, staring moodily at the piece of equipment that had been such a huge part of his life. Until he'd fucked it up.

"Tommy, are you okay?" Bonnie asked.

He turned to stare at her.

*One day you'll look back and realize you had a career but lost it.*

The hell he would.

"Yeah, I'm fine. Just realizing I have a few wrongs to set right."

Starting with his best friend.

# CHAPTER 3

Julie stood outside Tommy's bedroom door, fist raised to knock, but she couldn't gather the courage to make her knuckles meet the wood. Wasn't he making it clear he wasn't ready to talk? That he was still furious over last night? Sighing, she lowered her arm.

It was Valentine's Day, and she hadn't seen him all day. She never *didn't* see Tommy on Valentine's Day.

Scratch that. Two hours ago, she *had* caught a glimpse of him as he'd stormed past her sitting on the couch, and he'd gone straight to the bathroom for a shower—without so much as a glance in her direction or a hello tossed her way. He'd never returned to the living room.

She was desperate to make amends with him, but plainly, Tommy wasn't ready. And if he wanted space, she had to respect that, especially now that he was living here. The last thing she needed was to make him feel like she would push her presence on him even when he was giving a clear "not ready for this" sign.

She went back to her room and closed the door, then walked over to her dresser. She picked up the gift she'd wrapped for him in shiny red paper, feeling stupid for being hurt that he'd forgotten Valentine's Day. But this was the first year since they were ten they hadn't exchanged presents, and damn it, it hurt.

She'd never forget their first year. While all their other classmates had received those cheap paper character Valentines, both of them had gotten a "special" real card for the other. The one he'd given her had the cutest puppy on the front of it, and inside it said, "Will you be mine?" Her child's heart had almost exploded with happiness, just as her adult heart expanded at the memory, because she knew now what Tommy had done to buy that card. His drunk of a mom had begrudgingly bought the other Valentines but refused to buy Julie's. For a week, Tommy had walked up and down the streets collecting bottles for the deposit until he had enough money.

After she put the present back on the dresser, she slipped between the covers, leaned over, and shut off the light. She'd just stretched out and put her head on the pillow when a loud static sound came from under it. She shot straight up and gaped at it.

"Green Knight to Lady J."

*He didn't!*

She hadn't heard those nicknames in forever. After introducing himself as the Green Knight the day they'd met, he'd coined her Lady J when he learned her name was Julie. He'd called her Lady J until he outgrew his knight-and-castle phase a little over a year later.

To keep a peal of laughter from erupting, she pressed the back of her hand to her mouth. Grinning, she shoved her hand under the pillow and pulled out the walkie-talkie. "Lady J, copy."

"Emergency meeting in the dungeon. Meet me in five. Green Knight out."

"Copy that."

Pushing back the covers, she jumped out of bed and rushed for the door, assuming the dungeon would be the living room. As it squeaked open, static screeched in the room.

"Retreat! The infidels are watching. You'll be discovered! You must use our usual method of movement."

Her gaze strayed to the window. Was he serious? "Tommy. It's thirty degrees outside."

There was a moment of silence, then, "Live a little, Lady J."

The walkie-talkie went dead. A soft scoff escaped her mouth as it hit her why Tommy was always telling her to relax. While he was trying to recreate their childhood, she was worried about the cold. Wow, she really had forgotten how to relax and just go with it. Maybe she needed to listen to him more.

After she pulled on some thick socks and her Uggs, she yanked on her white fur-lined winter jacket, wrapped a scarf around her neck, and pulled on a plaid knit hat. At the last second, she snatched up the present and zipped it inside her jacket.

When she lifted the window, an icy breeze smacked her in the face and she shivered, but she climbed through the opening. Once she dropped to the ground, she paused.

As kids, these emergency calls had meant meeting at the tree house in her backyard to play video games because Tommy had needed to get out of his house and away from his mom. There wasn't a tree house here, but she still had a backyard.

As she made her way down the side of the house, an orangey glow appeared, growing larger the closer she got to the backyard. When she rounded the corner, her unused fire pit had a roaring flame and the temperature went up about ten degrees. As she spotted Tommy standing beside a blanket he'd spread on the ground and the TV from his room sitting atop it, a bubble of laughter shot past her lips. He was wearing a long-sleeved green shirt and dark brown slacks with a black belt low around his hips—with a wooden sword hanging at his side. An almost exact replica of the outfit he'd changed into daily after school to become the Green Knight when they were kids.

Happiness filled her chest as she walked toward him. *He hasn't forgotten.* And this was the best gift he'd ever given her—memories.

When she reached his side, he kissed her cheek. The touch of his lips on her skin burned, but she didn't have it in her to be upset by the reaction. All of this was just so sweet.

"Happy Valentine's Day, Lady J." As he placed a crown made of aluminum foil on top of her head, love filled her chest to overflowing, just as it had the night he'd done this so long ago. Hours after they'd met, a ten-year-old Tommy had tapped on her window with a set of walkie-talkies and a crown exactly like this one. After giving her one of the walkie-talkies, he'd set the crown on her head and said,

"From this day forth, I dedicate my life to protecting you, Lady J."

And he had never broken that promise.

"I don't think you've called me that since right after we turned twelve, Tommy."

He held up a finger and gave her a stern look. "It's Green Knight tonight."

He had given her a lot over the years. The more money he earned, the more extravagant the gift—but this one beat them all. Because it was from his heart.

"This is fantastic."

"I have more." He motioned for her to sit and she saw the Super Nintendo set up in front of the TV.

"Are you serious!" She turned an excited smile to Tommy, who was grinning ear to ear. "What game?"

"Which do you think?" Before she could answer, he said, "We're going to get it on like Donkey Kong tonight."

Even the double entendre didn't faze her. All she could do was laugh at the length he'd gone to recreate this. She sat down on the blanket and took a controller in her hand. After he dropped down beside her on the blanket, he dug around in a backpack that was set off to the side and pulled out two Yoo-hoos.

At the sight of their favorite childhood drink, she threw her head back and laughed again. "Oh my God. You pulled out all the stops, didn't you? How many of these did we guzzle growing up?"

"Between the two of us, I think we kept them in business." He turned the bag upside down, pouring out all kinds of snacks from when they were kids. Airheads, oatmeal cookies, Doritos, Sugar Babies.

He'd done so much. Remembered so much. And the happiness filling her became overwhelming. Tears pricked her eyes as she gazed at him.

His expression turned from smug to horrified in a second. "Shit. I won't ever do anything like this again if you cry."

She gave a wobbly smile. "This is just so wonderful, and you did it even after everything that happened last night. Tommy, I just feel horrible about what I said. It's your life. It's not my place to judge it."

He gave a dismissive shake of his head. "I was judging *you*, wasn't I? Telling you that you'd look back and see that you'd worked your life away. You were just being honest in return. Look at the difference between us, Julie. Because you've worked hard, you have a successful business and you own a beautiful home. I've played hard, and I don't have a damn thing to show for it. In fact, I've lost everything I *had* worked for. What right do I have to be mad at you for telling me the truth?"

"It's my fault that Ethan and Mike fired you."

"Come on. You know better than that. That punch was the final straw. Nothing more. If it hadn't happened, I would have done something else to justify my release. Either way, maybe this needed to happen." He nudged her shoulder with his. "You're right. I *do* need to grow up."

Guilt churned her stomach. "Oh, Tommy."

"Would you stop being so damn somber? I'm messing with you." Then he gazed off into the distance. "Besides, when everything is taken away, you start to realize what's really important. I miss fighting. And because of my choices, I won't step foot in a CMC cage again. That's humbling, you know?" Glancing at her, he sent her a tight smile.

"Yeah, I can imagine it is."

The silence that fell between them was thick. Wanting to get back to the carefree way they had been moments before, she unzipped her jacket. "I got something for you, too."

The corner of his mouth quirked up. "Really?"

She withdrew the present and handed it to him. After he ripped open the wrapping and lifted the lid, he froze for a moment with a breathed, "No shit." He snapped his head over to gape at her. "Where did you find this?"

His amazement made her bite her lip to keep from grinning like a fool. "There's a memorabilia sports shop in downtown Atlanta. I went over on my lunch break today and they had it."

Awe etched on his face, he turned the baseball cap over in his hands. "Jesus, Julie. This is better than the first time you gave it to me, and it was pretty damn awesome then."

Tommy had always been a huge Braves fan. That hat was the first big present she'd given him after she got her first job.

"There's one more thing in there."

He peered inside. "My iPod?"

"Yep."

After he put an earbud in and hit play, his laugher finally made her grin break free. "Are you kidding? New Kids?"

"It's not a tape, but I thought it'd work as a replacement."

For a long moment, he studied her. As his gaze moved over her face, his delight faded to a seriousness that was so unlike Tommy it made her shift uncomfortably.

"Thank you," he finally said with a grittiness to his voice she'd never heard before. He leaned over and kissed her cheek, whispering against her skin. "Best Valentine's Day ever."

"Yes, it is."

As he leaned back, their eyes met and something odd happened. The air went suddenly still. Her heart skipped a beat and a crackle zapped between them. Clearing his throat, Tommy reached over and ruffled her hair the way he used to do when they were kids. "You're awesome, Lady J. Think I'll keep you as my BFF for another couple of decades." He twisted open his Yoo-hoo and took a long swallow.

Julie blinked. Had she imagined all that sizzle?

God, she didn't know. She wasn't one to read into anything with Tommy because he was usually pretty straightforward and easy to read. Especially for her. But this was the first time she had ever felt what could possibly have been a *mutual* moment of attraction. Had it really been attraction, though? Definitely on her part. She wasn't so sure on Tommy's…

It easily could have been an emotional moment for him. She *had* given him two presents he had been very upset about losing yesterday. That had to have brought on some overwhelming feelings. Which definitely made more sense than the attraction thing.

She studied him now. Shoulders relaxed, face the same. He looked back at her with his usual casual smile.

He shook an Airheads packet and tossed it to her. "Here. I know how much you loved these."

Yeah, she'd definitely imagined it.

. . .

Tommy rolled over and cracked his eyelids open to check the alarm clock to see how much longer before he had to get up.

Six forty-five.

He shot straight up in bed. That couldn't be right. He snatched the clock off the nightstand and groaned. He'd set the alarm for the correct time; he just hadn't set it to go off. *Damn* it. He was supposed to have been up thirty minutes ago, and out of the house by now.

He blamed Julie. She'd fucked up his head after she'd given him her present, and continued doing so long after they'd parted for the night and gone to bed. Shoving the covers aside, he stalked across his room to the door.

There had been a freaky weird moment last night. Jesus. He'd almost *kissed* her. And not the way he usually kissed her—a peck on the cheek. He'd wanted to *really* kiss her. How nuts was *that*?

After tossing and turning most of the night, he'd finally found peace by connecting the ridiculous impulse to the emotions he'd been feeling at the moment—the overwhelming awe and affection he'd felt for her when he'd opened that gift had left him stunned. When he'd looked at Julie, the feelings had only quadrupled as he'd realized how much she listened to him, understood him, and was always there for him, no matter what.

Because she was his *best friend*.

He strode down the hall. When he reached the bathroom, he grasped the knob, pushed inside, and instantly felt like he'd been hit with the stupid stick.

With her back to him, fresh from her shower, Julie was completely nude as she ran a comb through her hair. The wet brunette strands reached right below her shoulder blades, gently caressing her skin and introducing him to an hourglass figure and a flawless, apple-shaped bottom.

His gaze locked there. The rounded cheeks were cock-hardening perfect. A woman's ass had always been his weakness, but Julie's? Fucking hell. He'd never wanted to get his hands on a butt more.

"Tommy!" She twisted toward him, covering herself with her arms, but not before he saw the enticing swell of her breast. As she squatted to snatch a towel off the floor, he still hadn't moved. "Get. Out!"

What the hell was he doing? He shook his head, backed out, and slammed the door. "Sorry!"

Taking deep inhales, he collapsed back against the wall. Out of everything he could have seen on Julie's body, why did it have to be her ass?

He shook his head sharply, trying to dislodge the image. The tempting perfection of it refused to vanish. Even worse, his dick was raring and ready to go from the replay.

No. Oh, God. *No*. This was so wrong on so many levels. Julie was his best friend. He'd never once thought of her in a sexual way. But he'd had no clue she looked like *that* under her clothes.

The bathroom door slammed against the wall and a furious Julie emerged, wrapped in a robe. She shoved him and he lifted his arms to ward her off. "What the hell, Tommy! Knock before entering."

Angry that she'd made him see something he could never unsee, and finding that he *liked* it, he yelled back, "It's called a lock! You don't live alone anymore, Julie. Lock the goddamn door." Just to get it out there and remind himself more than anything, he added, "I do *not* need to see someone I consider my sister naked." He pointed at her. "Don't do that to me!"

He stalked back to his room and slammed the door. Shoving both hands in his hair, he fisted his fingers and tugged, letting out a long, frustrated yell as he paced the room.

Last night he'd wanted to kiss her, and now she had a perfect ass. *Fabulous.*

God, he wanted to throttle her.

Hell, she'd probably throttle *him* if she knew what he was thinking about her.

Thankfully, there was a way to fix this. He'd been out of the game too long, that was all. His body was wacked out. Not used to going this long without a woman. There was an eager and willing woman at work who was more than ready to help get him back in the game. He just had to convince her it would be much more fun if *he* tied *her* up.

• • •

Unfortunately, nothing had gone the way it was supposed to for the rest of the day.

It was all Julie's fault.

And Tommy was seriously pissed.

As soon as he walked into the photo shoot that morning, he'd started putting the moves on Bonnie. She very easily allowed him the lead, which was the way he liked it. But there hadn't been even one little shimmy of anticipation in his pants. Why? Because Julie's ass kept teasing him. Thinking of *that*, his pants had felt a whole lot of action.

The pending "date" had sat like a rock in his stomach all damn day. He *never* dreaded spending time with a woman. He fed them and then they had an excellent time between the sheets. At the end of the night, they parted ways with full bellies and sated bodies. Perfect for everyone.

But that's not what had happened tonight with Bonnie.

The truth was, he'd had no urge to take the woman to dinner, much less take her to bed, because that beautiful ass was tormenting the ever-loving hell out of him. The more it kept popping into his mind, the more he wanted to direct his attention toward *that* source of lust. A very dangerous thought.

But a date was a date. So when they'd finally called a wrap on the shoot, he'd driven Bonnie over to a nice restaurant. Only, the more she'd talked, flirted, and made blatant comments about phallic-shaped objects, the more he'd wanted to get up and leave.

He wanted to be with Julie. Not her ass. But *her*.

Which was why he now found himself in his car, alone, driving home well before midnight. And hating life.

Since when did he *ever* want to sit around the house watching TV and eating popcorn instead of going out and having fun?

Never, that's when. And yet, he'd begged off a night with a gorgeous, more-than-willing woman, using the lie that the food hadn't agreed with him. A damn *stomachache*? Seriously?

It was Julie's fault. All her damn fault.

And he intended to give her a piece of his damn mind.

• • •

After a solitary dinner, Julie leaned back on the couch with a glass of Merlot. Earlier this afternoon, Tommy had sent her a text saying he wouldn't be home until late, so don't wait up.

Code for he'd met a woman.

Considering he'd been pretty damn horrified at seeing his "sister" naked this morning, he was probably in someone else's arms right now, trying to banish the image from his mind. The thought made Julie's stomach twist. She took another long swallow of her wine. Not that she'd ever thought Tommy would see her naked, but having him blurt out the sibling comment verified everything she'd always known.

Tommy would never see her as anything more than a sister figure.

Somehow she had to start thinking of him as a brother and get rid of all that other stuff. She'd been truthful with him about dating. She did date. Just not as much as she'd like to. She'd also been truthful that her schedule kept her from meeting many eligible men, and the few she'd met online had ended in disaster.

Every once in a while she'd meet a guy, though, and they'd start dating. Sometimes it didn't work for her and she ended it, but more often than not, the guy ended it. Mostly after meeting Tommy. She used to always be upfront that her best friend was Tommy "Lightning" Sparks, and the guys always thought that was *so* awesome…until they met him. Then they seemed unable to handle the pressure of dating a woman whose best friend was an MMA super-fighter.

Some hung around for a few more dates, some called it off that same night, and others just never called again. The ones who gave her a reason said they weren't looking for anything serious, and men didn't fool around with girls who had a best friend who could put them in the hospital. Now she kept Tommy to herself, hoping some guy would fall for her and not be intimidated by the other important man in her life.

She was a good woman. She worked hard. She was attractive. Independent and loyal. Any man would be lucky as hell to have her, if she did say so herself. And if Tommy Sparks didn't want her, somewhere out there was a man who *would* love to have her.

The front door opened and she was surprised to see Tommy storm in and slam it shut. What was he doing home so early? He stalked into the kitchen and started making a racket, slamming cabinets and the fridge. The lid of a beer bottle popped off.

She started to rise, to go and ask him what was wrong, but when he came to stand in the door of the living room, he glared furiously at her, as though she'd done something wrong.

Immediately, she was on the defensive. She sat down again. "What's crawled up your ass?"

A snarl came from him as he stalked into the living room. He slumped on the other end of the couch and stretched one arm across the back, staring straight at the wall in front of him, jaw clenched. Then he guzzled the beer.

"I've had the mother of shit days. The worst ever," he finally muttered.

Since his freaking house had burned down a couple of days ago, she'd disagree with that assessment, but Tommy tended to see things differently than she did.

"Want to talk?" she ventured.

"Nope."

"Are you going to be a douche for the rest of the night?"

"Most likely."

*Okay then.* She took a sip of her wine. She'd seen Tommy in many frames of mind, and after more than two decades with him, she'd believed she'd seen them all, but this was a new one. He had completely shut her out. He never shut her out. "Then how about going to your room to sulk?"

Slowly, *very slowly*, his head turned toward her. Anger had made his green eyes darken to a moss green. "I'm not sulking. I'm trying to wrap my mind around the fucking unimaginable."

She couldn't tell if he was angry at her or at whatever had happened. It was the first time in a very long time she couldn't read Tommy at all. And it left her feeling very unbalanced.

"Is this what you do every night, Julie? Come home, sit on the couch, drink some wine. Watch TV? That's it?"

Were they going to have this argument? *Again*?

"No. I do go out. Melody comes over. You come over all the time."

He scowled at her. "I'm not some kind of stand-in boyfriend, am I?"

Her mouth dropped open. "Where the hell did that come from?"

The scowl deepened. "You don't date. In fact, have you ever even been in a relationship? Any guy I've met, I haven't seen him a second time."

She ground her teeth. "That's *your* fault, asshole. You try being a woman who is best friends with a professional fighter, and see how many men are willing to stick around. Besides, you're one to talk. You jump from woman to woman like you're terrified you'll die if you stop."

"Not terrified, Julie. I do it because I enjoy every fucking second of it." There was a nasty edge to his voice she'd only heard when he was really furious. "You're like a damn spinster. When's the last time you were actually *with* a man? Maybe if you'd let a man at you, you'd relax some."

Her jaw dropped nearly to the floor. Then *she* got mad. *Really* mad.

Shaking with fury, she shot to her feet. "I don't know what your fucking problem is or why you're being so goddamn mean, but *screw you*."

# CHAPTER 4

This house was not big enough for the both of them.

Julie shoved a spoonful of oatmeal in her mouth and tried to concentrate on the taste of cinnamon and apple, pissed that she was even aware of the sounds of the shower running in the background. A hot, steamy spray that would hit a naked masculine chest, plastering those fine blond chest hairs to Tommy's skin as the water rolled down his body.

Especially after what he'd said to her last night.

*Spinster.*

What was this, the freaking 1800s?

"Good. I'm glad I caught you before you left."

She jerked her head up.

*Oh. For the love of God.*

He stood in the doorway, a towel wrapped low around his waist, still damp from his shower. Her belly twisted painfully with the need to touch the man, and not in a best-friend way. Which pissed her off even more.

"What?" The bite in her tone came through loud and clear.

He grimaced. "Yeah, okay, I deserve the anger. I was an asshole last night. I'm sorry."

Striving to be civil, she wrangled her fury with him. "Where'd that even come from? Do you have an issue with our relationship you're not telling me? I've never made any demands on you other than as a friend."

She'd made damn sure she'd only done that because she'd always known Tommy was incapable of giving her more.

He slid his hand through his wet locks, something she knew he did when frustration was getting to him. "Julie, I love you and I want to see you happy. It bothers me how alone you are."

"Why? It doesn't bother me."

"I just want to be sure I'm not somehow filling the man role in your life and it's making you complacent."

Of course. Since every other woman he came across took any scrap of attention he flung her way, his best friend *had* to be completely satisfied with the excessive Tommy time she received, to the point that she didn't need another man. Wouldn't his ears burn if he knew how much she'd give to move past him? "You're not," she deadpanned.

He swallowed, then gave a jerky nod. "All right, then. I won't say anything more about it."

"Good. Because I'm getting really sick of hearing your opinion of my love life." She shoved back her chair and picked up her plate. "I have to get to work. I'll see you tonight."

After cleaning up and grabbing her things, she hurried to her car.

Numb.

That was how she felt. That had to be progress. It showed that she'd made some kind of disconnection within herself that was rewiring to see Tommy in a different way. Thank God.

Twenty minutes later, she pulled into the vet clinic's parking lot. As she walked in through the back entrance, her partner, Melody, frantically motioned to her from the front desk. "Come here. You've *got* to see this."

The other vet was usually much more controlled with her emotions. The barely restrained eagerness rolling off her took Julie slightly aback. "What is it?"

"Come. *Here.*" Her waving increased. "Your nine o'clock is already here. You're not going to believe what you're about to see."

Curiosity piqued, Julie cautiously stepped around the reception desk that was separated from the waiting area by a glass window. Her mouth dropped open.

"I know, right!" Melody said, awestruck.

There, stuffed in one of their tiny waiting room chairs, was the biggest, most ripped man she'd ever seen. Rippling muscles strained beneath a tight shirt, the sleeves of which had been cut to make room for his bulging biceps. But it wasn't the man alone that made her hottie meter go off. It was the way he was cooing at the white Persian kitten he held in his huge arms.

"My word," Julie breathed, thoroughly captivated by the sight.

"To say the least," Melody said. "Have you ever seen

anything so sexy?"

Unfortunately, she had—the man who'd stood in her kitchen this morning in only a towel, worried out of his mind that he was her stand-in boyfriend. She really needed to put his mind at rest. "Not lately," she said thoughtfully.

"Do you know him?"

Julie knew why Melody was asking her the question. The man had the telltale signs of a cage fighter—the little injuries their bodies seemed to carry at all times. "No, he doesn't look familiar, but I can't see his face." The man's dark head was bent low over the kitten as he used one of his fingers to rub the fur between its pointy ears. "Besides, just because I'm friends with Tommy doesn't mean I know all the guys on the circuit."

"You know a lot of them, though."

She couldn't deny that. "What's his name?"

"Brody Minton."

Brody "The Iron" Minton. No, she didn't personally know him, but she'd seen him fight. He was in the heavyweight division, which explained his build. Those fighters ranged anywhere from two twenty to two sixty-five. Some of them even had to cut weight before a weigh-in to make the weight limit. It also explained why she didn't really know him. Tommy was middleweight and kept to a svelte one eighty-five.

"Yeah, he's a fighter."

"You think Tommy knows him?"

"Probably. If I'm not mistaken, Brody trains at Tommy's old gym. What's he here for?"

"The kitten won't eat."

Julie nodded, pushing aside her awe and donning

her vet cap. "Can you go ahead and get him situated in a room?"

"Oh, it'd be my pleasure."

Chuckling, Julie hurried to her locker and tugged on a white lab coat, then stepped into the examining room. "Good afternoon, Mr. Minton. And who do we have here?"

"Uh." He shifted before red crept up his neck to his cheeks. "This is Princess."

Normally she didn't react when she heard a pet's name, having heard some doozies over the years, but his deep voice saying such a feminine word had her stumbling to a stop. "What was that?"

He grimaced. "My three-year-old niece named her. I didn't realize how embarrassing it would be to say the name outside my own home."

Julie smiled. What a wonderful uncle to let his niece name his cat, and then stick with it in public. "Well, I think it's perfect."

She ran her hand down the kitten's soft fur. "I see she's only a few weeks old."

"Ten weeks. I've had her for two."

It was so odd to see such a huge man have such a small pet. He seemed like the type to walk a Rottweiler on a thick chain. But the worry in his caramel-colored eyes as he reached out to pet Princess, his hand engulfing the kitten as it slid down her fur, let Julie know he didn't care that a cat wasn't the animal most people would envision him having.

"What's the problem, Mr. Minton?"

"Brody, please. I hate being called by my last name.

I'm not that formal."

"Okay, Brody, what's going on with Princess?"

"She won't eat. She was doing fine, but about three days ago, she just stopped, and she keeps pawing at her face." His eyes lifted to meet hers, and she was struck by how handsome he was. "I've tried to look in her mouth, but I can't see anything."

"What do you feed her?"

"Dry cat food." He winced. "I occasionally give her wet. I know it's not good for her, but she loves it, and when she stopped eating that, too, I knew something was wrong."

"Sounds like she may have something stuck somewhere on the way down. Let's have a look in her mouth." She went to the door and asked Melody to assist her.

While Melody held the kitten, Julie looked inside with a penlight, checking every crevice she could see. Sure enough, something was wedged between her back teeth. "Has she been chewing anything lately?"

"She's into everything, but most recently she chewed through a cardboard box."

Yeah, that looked about right. Julie took a pair of tweezers and tugged out the foreign object. "I think we've solved the mystery, Brody." She held it up. "It's tiny, but this wet bit of cardboard would've been enough to make her mouth feel uncomfortable enough to not want to eat."

He released a breath. "Really? That's it?"

"Yep. I'll go ahead and prescribe some antibiotics just in case, but I think she'll be fine now. If she still isn't eating in a few days, come back and we'll do further tests, okay?"

"Thanks, doc."

He scooped up the kitten, but then hesitated as he looked at Melody and Julie. The giggle that came from the other vet as she hurried from the room made Julie blush. "Was there something else?"

"Yeah, I was wondering if I could take you to dinner, as a thank-you."

The blush scalded her face. "That's not necessary."

"Then how about as a date? Unless, of course, your boyfriend would mind."

She blinked.

Not unless a stand-in boyfriend counted.

Tommy's words echoed in her head. *Spinster, eh?* Was Brody a sign?

"No. No boyfriend." She gave him what she hoped was a dazzling smile. "And yes, dinner would be great."

He smiled, and she found she liked it. It didn't have her melting to the floor or anything, but it was warm and friendly, and he seemed really nice.

"You have plans tonight?" he asked.

"Unless you consider sitting on the couch watching TV plans, then no, I don't."

"Hey. I love a great night in, kicking back and relaxing after a hard day. I swear sometimes there is nothing that beats it."

Her smile stretched into a full grin. "*Exactly*. But tonight I think I'd like to go out."

Someone who actually got it! Tommy just stared at her like she was speaking gibberish when she tried to explain why she liked to stay home.

"I'm very happy to hear that. Can I pick you up at eight?"

After she gave him directions, she smiled. "I'm looking forward to it."

And she actually meant it.

• • •

Smoothing down the fabric of her blue wrap dress, Julie walked into the living room. She'd changed her outfit five times. Casual. Dressy. Seductive. Until she'd finally settled on a combination of all three.

The dress stopped about four inches above her knees and had a deep V-line down the front that created an enticing display of her cleavage. But the three-quarter sleeves kept the dress modest. Sort of. She'd slipped on a pair of black heels and curled her dark hair so it was full and bouncy instead of straight like she usually wore it. And she'd chosen to go with the smoky-eyes look.

She looked hot. More important, she *felt* hot.

One last thing, and she'd be ready for Brody to pick her up. Where had she put her purse?

Spotting it on the couch, she leaned over the back and reached for the strap. A noise that sounded like someone choking came from behind her. Glancing over her shoulder, she saw Tommy standing in the kitchen doorway, a sandwich held in his hand, scowling at her.

When she straightened and turned around, his nose crunched up in distaste. "Where are you going dressed like that?"

"I have a date."

If his head had jerked back any farther it would've snapped right off. "A date?" Then his gaze roamed over hers again and his scowl deepened. "That outfit."

He vigorously scratched the back of his head. "Yeah. I wouldn't wear that."

"Why not? This dress is hot." She held her hands out in front of her breasts. "I'm showing them off. Isn't that what guys like?"

If anything, Tommy blanched even more as his throat convulsed on a swallow, his gaze straying down before he jerked it back up and over her head. Good lord, the man even refused to admit she had boobs.

She put her hands on her hips. "*You* may see me as a sister, Tommy, but let me assure you I am a red-blooded woman. And no matter what you think, I *am* fuckable to other men."

His eyes snapped to hers, something dangerous darkening their green depths as he took a step closer. "Is that what you want, Julie? To be fucked?"

Having Tommy ask her such a bold question left her completely breathless, and all she could do was gape at him as he took another step toward her.

"I don't think that's what you're looking for. So you need to change." He said the last sentence slowly, calmly, but his face was anything but. It was tight—except for a vein pulsing in his forehead.

"Oh, no you don't." She shook her finger at him. "You are *not* going to pull the big brother act on me, Tommy Sparks! Last night you were all worried about how much I stayed in, and now you're pissed because I'm going out? I don't think so."

"Is that what this is about? Did you ask the first guy you saw this morning to go out because of last night? I am not okay with that."

Her mouth popped open. "I don't *care* what you're okay with. And for the record, I didn't ask him, *he* asked *me*, and I thought he was pretty damn hot, so I said yes."

"Going out with strange men isn't very smart."

She shook her head. "Oh my God, you're driving me crazy. Besides, you know him, so he's not a stranger."

"What do you mean, I know him?"

The doorbell rang. "You're about to see."

She hurried to the door and opened it. Brody wore black slacks with a deep purple silk button-down shirt. His longish dark hair was combed and styled away from his face. Deep caramel brown eyes gazed down at her as a low whistle came from his chiseled mouth.

Could the man be more opposite of Tommy, who had done everything *but* give her a compliment? Jerk.

"You look gorgeous," Brody said admiringly.

She smiled. "Thank you. Pretty damn hot yourself."

A low grumble came from behind her and she shot Tommy a withering look.

"Brody." Tommy came to stand directly behind her, his chest pressing into the back of one of her shoulders. She sent him another glare.

"Tommy." Brody glanced between the two of them before he offered his hand, which Tommy took, albeit reluctantly. "Been a while. How have you been?"

"Just peachy. You?"

Brody was either oblivious to the snarky tone Tommy was using or chose to ignore it, because he simply shrugged and said, "Can't complain." He cleared his throat. "What exactly are you doing here?"

"I live here." He placed an arm around her shoulder in

that familiar brotherly way he did, and she rolled her eyes.

"He lives here temporarily." When his fingers bit into her skin, she jabbed him hard in the stomach. She wouldn't tell anyone about his house. That was his business. Not Brody's. "He's getting some remodeling done and needed a place to stay."

"Well, that's nice of you."

She smiled at Tommy through clamped teeth. "There's nothing I wouldn't do for this man. We've known each other forever. He's like a brother to me."

*Ow!* Jerking out of his grip, she rubbed the top of her shoulder where he'd pinched her and glowered at him. He scowled back just as fiercely.

"So. You ready to go?" Brody asked uncertainly.

"More than ready." She sent Tommy one more scathing glance before heading down the steps with Brody, determined to enjoy her date.

• • •

Brody "Goddamn Perfect" Minton.

The Golden Boy. Mr. Goodie Two Shoes. Mr. Wonderful.

And a totally perfect match for Julie.

The idea seriously chapped Tommy's ass.

Hell, his ass had already been chapped before he'd learned who she was going out with. That dress hugged every delicious inch of her body, making him all the more aware of the desirable woman she was.

Making him disturbingly aware that another man, at this very moment, was enjoying every tempting curve of that damn dress and what it revealed. Probably keeping tabs on the gaping neckline in hopes of getting a peek of her abundant breasts.

Fury shafted through him and he increased the speed of his pacing. Where the hell were they? It was a fucking work night!

The fiercely protective big brother part of him had roared to life as soon as she left, and he'd paced the living room for hours now, it seemed. As the time ticked by, he realized he was way more jacked up than a brother should be about his "sister" being out on a date with another man. Way more furious about that man seeing her in that sexy dress. And to make matters worse, Tommy had also noticed way too much about Julie's body in that dress.

What the hell was happening to him?

He didn't know *what* he was feeling. He'd never felt anything like it before.

Jesus H. Christ. Had she ever wore her makeup like that around him?

Nope. He would've noticed. Because it invited sex. Smoky, mysterious. Fuckable.

She'd used that word, and goddamn it, it was a statement of utter truth.

The woman had been downright take-me-up-against-the-wall-right-now sexy, and he'd been more than happy to oblige.

And it freaked him the fuck out.

He turned at the wall and paced back across the living room again, stopping briefly to peer out the window into the darkness. Nothing. Not a headlight in sight.

He didn't know what to do with this overwhelming lust he was suddenly feeling for her. Hell, he couldn't remember the last time his dick twitched at just seeing a woman bent over. Sure, he usually felt arousal at such a blatant display of femininity, but it generally took a little friction for his cock to get involved. Not with Julie. He'd wanted to come out and play immediately.

And that freaked him out even more.

He stalked to the kitchen and whipped open the fridge, searching for something to eat, then slammed the door again. He so wasn't hungry. What he needed was a stiff drink.

He dropped his forehead against the freezer door and bounced it against the cold metal a few times, trying to knock some sense into his head.

Julie wasn't some woman he could just fuck and move on. This was *Julie*. His best friend! The crying little girl he'd comforted twenty-some years ago, the one who'd changed his life forever. He'd made a vow to protect her that day.

Which meant she needed protection from men who thought a relationship was the equivalent of being handed the death sentence. Men like himself.

But she wasn't out with a Tommy, was she? She was out with a Brody—one of the good guys. The kind of man a woman would be proud to take home to her daddy, a man who had a list of accomplishments a mile long, who dedicated his time to the needy, who fed starving children, helped old ladies cross the road, and saved animals from burning buildings.

A real fucking superhero.

The kind of guy who, two days ago, Tommy would've been thrilled to see with Julie.

But when she'd opened that door and he'd seen

Brody—all he'd seen was red.

It was one thing for Julie to date—Tommy encouraged that; he wanted her to go out and have fun. But *not* with another fighter.

In all the years he'd been in MMA, she had never gone out with anyone from the industry. Not once. If anything, she'd seemed determined to stay far away from the whole scene, unless an event involved him or he asked her to come with him.

He'd liked that. He did *not* like the thought of her cheering for another fighter the same way she did for him.

She was *his* cheerleader; she stood on *his* side of the cage, not someone else's. And he didn't give a flying fuck if Brody was in a different weight division. He'd take on Brody in the cage any old day, and he'd show the asshat who Julie would always cheer for.

Except…he wouldn't be able to issue a challenge like that, would he?

No, he wouldn't, because he wasn't a Brody. He was a Tommy, and Tommys made rash fucking decisions that got them banned from MMA.

Julie was dating a fighter while *he* was no longer a fighter, and that thought drove him mad.

Time to fix that.

He'd made the decision to start righting his wrongs, and he'd started with Julie. He'd enjoyed the hell out of planning his Valentine surprise for her. The second wrong on his list to right had been Mike…but he'd gotten a little distracted from his goal when he'd seen Julie's naked body and realized how very much he liked it.

*Hell.* He needed to get refocused. Forget about Julie.

Find a way to make amends with Mike. Yeah. That's what he would do.

The twitter of Julie's laughter suddenly sounded from just outside. Muffled voices came through the front door. Tommy stiffened and glanced at the clock. Before he could stop himself, he rushed over to the window and peered out.

Good thing he did, too. They were just in that awkward first-date moment of kiss-or-don't-kiss. Standing in front of each other. Close, but not too close. A bit of weird tension buzzing between them. Brody had his hands shoved in his pockets. Julie had her fingers twisted together in front of her.

There was no way in hell that man was going to kiss her.

Tommy flung the door open, causing them to jump apart.

Fighting a satisfied smirk, Tommy leaned a shoulder against the doorframe, crossing his ankles. "Hey guys, have fun?"

Brody's brows drew together then arched up. "Uh. Yeah."

"Good." Tommy sent him a tight smile. "Glad to hear it."

Both of them stared at him, but he just cocked his head to the side and stared back, not moving.

"Brody," Julie said. "I had a great time tonight. Thank you."

"I did, too. I'd like to do it again."

Tommy really had to work to keep a scowl from forming on his face, especially as Julie looked at him with an expression that clearly said, *Get lost.*

Not fucking happening.

When she saw he wasn't going anywhere, she blew out a breath and glanced at Brody. "I'd really like that. Call me?"

"You can count on it."

As she brushed by Tommy, she pursed her lips at him in a very Julie way of showing annoyance. He almost chuckled, but thought it best not to. Once she was safely inside, he stepped back, preparing to close the door as he held the other man's gaze. "Later, Brody."

The amusement in the man's eyes took him aback. "Sure, Tommy."

As Brody turned and headed back to his car, Tommy frowned. He really didn't care for this guy. Closing the door, he turned to find Julie with her hands on her hips. "What was that all about?"

"What?" he asked innocently, trying to keep his eyes on her face and not on the breasts the blue fabric was hugging, the way he wanted to.

She waved her hand toward the door. "That! You were the one who said you wanted me to continue with my social life as if you didn't live here. That was *not* letting me continue like you didn't live here."

"Considering it's only ten o'clock and you're already home, I assumed the date didn't go well. Thought I'd help end it a little more smoothly."

At least that sounded plausible enough. Right?

"The date *did* go well. I like him. We have a lot in common. And not that it's any of your damn business, but I'm home early because I have to work in the morning. I can't stay up all night and be able to do my job the next day. So the next time you decide to play big brother... just...*don't*."

Spinning, she marched down the hallway to her room, leaving Tommy with two very different emotions warring for dominance from her parting words.

First was her offhand comment that she couldn't stay out all night. A direct slam at his tendency to do just that, and how he'd messed up because of it. He doubted she was even aware of how it had hit him. But damn, the difference between him and Julie couldn't be clearer. And it seriously bothered him.

Which led to the second thing.

After that first kick of desire he'd felt for her days back, he'd reached over and ruffled her hair as he'd done countless times when they were kids. Then he'd made sure to throw around the word "sister" a lot. So he was the one who'd set this up. He *did* get that. But three times today she'd tossed "like a brother" at him—three times!—and each time his body had rebelled at the words coming out of her mouth.

If she said it again, he feared he was going to show her just exactly how much of a brother to her he *wasn't*.

• • •

Staring at the ceiling, Julie lay in bed as she absently stroked Lucy, who'd started scratching at her door the moment she'd slammed it shut. When she had opened it back up, the dog immediately sprang forward and jumped on the bed. She welcomed the company.

She hadn't lied to Tommy. The date with Brody *had*

been nice, and they did have a lot in common. But there hadn't been any kind of spark.

And that sucked, because Brody was perfect. They liked the same shows—sans *Real Housewives*, to which he'd had the same reaction as Tommy, which of course she'd immediately thought of as soon as Brody had scowled. He loved animals and did volunteer work at a local no-kill shelter. Even though he did on occasion go out to the local country bar, The Boot Scoot, after training with the guys, he wasn't into the club scene like Tommy was, and he never stayed long.

The man was completely opposite of Tommy.

And yet Tommy refused to leave her mind.

The walkie-talkie screeched to life. "Julie?"

Turning her head on the pillow, she stared at the yellow-and-black device. Why had she left it on? *Ignore it. Pretend you're asleep.* But she reached for it anyway, cursing her weakness for this man. Pressing the side button, she said grumpily, "What?"

"Do you remember the day we met?"

Her heart caught. She stilled for a moment, her annoyance notching down a fraction. "Of course. Could never forget it. What brought that up?"

"I was thinking about it earlier today."

He was thinking about it? That was so...sweet. Though it didn't make up for him being such a butthead today. "Wishing we hadn't met? That why you've been so obnoxious lately?"

"Very funny. No, I'm serious. Remember?"

She couldn't stop a small smile as she recalled the ten-year-old boy with shaggy blond hair and green eyes, a wooden sword hanging from his belt, who hadn't even introduced himself to her, he'd just put his arm around her and placed a kiss on top of her head—just as he still did. "You were so gallant that day."

"A fair maiden weeping for her lost puppy. What was a young knight to do?"

She chuckled. "You were so into knights and dragons back then."

"I found your puppy, though. Do you remember me bringing him to you?"

"Posey was trying so hard to get free."

She'd been sitting on her front steps, sniffling over losing Posey. She'd only had the pup a week—a present from her parents because they'd had to move to a different state due to her dad's job transfer. Tommy had come walking up the path, carrying a wiggling, excited puppy in his arms. When he reached the bottom of the steps, he bowed, held out the dog, and said, "For you, m'lady." And she'd fallen head over heels in love at that very moment.

Unfortunately, she'd never fallen out again.

Tears burned the backs of her eyes.

"Sometimes I wish we could go back to being kids," he said wistfully. "It was so much easier then. So straightforward. Why do things have to change?"

She had to take a moment to speak. "Adulthood sucks."

"Yeah. Messes everything up." There was a sigh, then, "Good night, Lady J."

She had to swallow the lump in her throat. "Good night, Green Knight."

As she placed the walkie-talkie back on her nightstand,

she brushed away a tear that slid down her cheek. It had been a long time since she'd cried over Tommy. When she was in her teens, crying had been a constant as Tommy had started dating, never once looking at her the same way he had other girls. She'd been desperately hurt when he asked other girls to the prom or homecoming. Then she'd gone off to college and he'd gotten started in fighting.

The separation had done her good. She'd dated and come into her own as a person, separate from him. They still talked and hung out together when she was in town, but she'd realized her life wasn't over just because he didn't return her feelings.

When she moved back to Atlanta four years ago and opened her clinic, she had hoped enough time had passed that any childhood feelings she'd had for her best friend had only been a childhood crush. They hadn't been.

If anything, those feelings had blossomed into an adult yearning that left her feeling overwhelmed at times, angry at others. But she'd kept her mouth shut about how she felt, believing that somewhere she would find the *actual* man who was meant for her alone. Because it *wasn't* Tommy. It couldn't *be* Tommy.

They were too different. She was wine and a quiet night home. He was shots of tequila and thumping music in a club. She was planning. He was chaos. She wanted a future. He was firmly planted in the right-here-right-now.

But he was also the boy who'd found her puppy. The teenager who'd bloodied Bruce Coleman's nose for refusing to respect her "no" and taking a kiss anyway. The man who'd held her after her dad had died from a heart attack. Who'd dropped everything every time her car broke down. Worked tirelessly to help her demo the clinic and renovate it. Then helped her move in and paint her new house. He had always been there. No matter what.

He had always been her hero.

And *that* was the man her heart firmly refused to let go.

# CHAPTER 5

When Tommy walked into the kitchen the next morning, Julie was standing in front of the counter. A gray long-sleeve workout shirt clung to her breasts while a pair of black Capri running pants hugged her thighs and butt. When she shifted to scoop a spoonful of protein powder from the container, one toned ass cheek bounced up.

He fisted his hands to keep from going up behind her and taking both cheeks in his palms, while he buried his head in her neck. The desire to do it was so strong he barely kept himself in check, that devilish side of him wanting desperately to know what she would do if he brushed up against her. He'd done it so many times in the past and never thought a thing about it, but now…

Damn it, he had to know.

He stepped forward. As he slid behind her, he put one hand around her hip, a little farther than was appropriate for just a friend. When she stiffened, a smug smile tried to emerge. He brushed the front of his pajama bottoms across her ass and bit back a groan, having to quickly move away as his cock immediately started to stiffen. But he didn't miss her quick inhale.

A part of him scolded himself for his dirty tricks, but the other parts egged him on to do more. And right now he wanted to do so much more.

He leaned in close, pressing his chest into her shoulders. "Whatchya making?"

As she glanced up at him, brows raised, she leaned away. "What does it look like?"

"It looks like you're attempting to make a protein shake, but you're doing it wrong." He closed his hand over hers, shaking the protein mix back into the container. Her gaze shot to their hands, then up to his eyes. "Let me show you," he offered.

Brushing behind her again to go to the fridge, he watched her for any sign of awareness. Her fingers closing into fists was a dead giveaway. When he came back, he casually asked, "Peanut butter?"

She pointed to the cabinet on her other side. When she started to move to get it, he again latched his hand on her hip, staying her. Leaning across her, he pressed his chest into the length of her back as he reached to open the door and grab the jar. He felt a quiver run through her body.

He pulled away, staring down at the back of her head. The urge to yank her around and do some very non-friendly things to his best friend ripped through him. From the way she was responding, he had a feeling she might not object, and that made the desire even harder to ignore.

He was playing with fucking fire. He knew that.

And this fire had the potential to destroy more than just mementos from his past. It could destroy the one person who meant more to him than anyone on the planet. And destroy a friendship he didn't think he could live without.

That thought knocked him back to his senses.

"You know," he said, then stopped to clear the huskiness from his throat. "It's getting late. Why don't I finish this while you go shower?"

"Great idea!" She was out of the kitchen in an instant, without a backward glance.

A few moments later, he heard the shower start. A picture of her pulling the tie out of her hair so her long brunette strands flowed free over naked shoulders formed indelibly in his mind. He squeezed his eyes shut, shaking his head as he adjusted his pajama bottoms.

Damn, he need a shower himself. A long cold one. Unfortunately, that wasn't going to help. It had been a while since he'd had a little him-time. And he *needed* it right now. Maybe using some of the images that were torturing him—like Julie bent over with him rocking behind her... His cock immediately sprang to full attention. Hissing between clenched teeth, he leaned his elbows on the counter.

This was fucking *insane*. He was a grown man. He should have better control of himself. But he'd never actually denied himself a woman before. Was that the problem? Was that why he was wound so tightly? Because he was refusing to act on such a natural impulse?

Considering the way he loved women, it made sense... and it made him want to be sick.

The idea of any part of his player ways being directed at Julie was unforgivable—the titillating seduction, the sweaty night in bed, then him leaving in the morning before she was even awake. Hell, he'd kill another man for even thinking it about Julie.

"What are you doing?"

He glanced over at Julie, who stood in the kitchen doorway, wearing only her red silk robe that hit her mid-thigh. His gaze slipped to the deep V that displayed the enticing shadow of her cleavage. The wet strands of her hair fell around her shoulders.

"Nothing." He straightened, realizing he hadn't done shit with her shake since she'd left. "Head started hurting."

Which was the truth. Just not the one on his shoulders.

"Want me to get you some Tylenol?"

"Already took some, but thanks." He quickly added skim milk, a tablespoon of PB, and some protein powder, then cut on the blender. After it was mixed, he poured it into two cups, shoved a straw in one, and handed it to her.

As she took a sip, her eyes closed and she moaned around the straw. His gaze fell to her mouth sucking on that thin tube, and his grip tightened around his own cup. God, this woman was going to be the death of him. "Mmm. Tommy, you really do make a yummy shake." She opened her eyes and smiled. "Thank you."

Nanoseconds from pouncing on her, he quickly turned his back. "Don't mention it."

"I just have to blow-dry my hair and get dressed, then I'm off to work. I won't be home tonight, so you're on your own for dinner."

Frowning, he spun around. "You won't? Where are

you going?"

"I've got plans," she said, and left him standing in the room alone. "See you later."

His stomach sank. One guess as to who those plans were with.

And he was stunned at how much it pissed him off.

• • •

Julie locked the back door of the clinic. Before she'd left for work, she'd brought her jeans and red blouse with her, not wanting to go back to the house to change. Sad to admit, but it was the truth.

She wanted to avoid Tommy. At all costs.

If she was really smart, she'd start eating take-out and buying pre-made protein shakes for the duration that Tommy was in her house. Because every time they were in that tiny kitchen together it became too hot for her to handle. *Especially* today. Holy Mother of *God*. The touching, the brushing...he'd had her nipples puckered into tight peaks, her clit pulsing in need. All she'd wanted him to do was press behind her, take both her breasts in his hands, and tweak those stiff tips, then slide one palm between her legs and rub away the ache there.

She'd had to play that fantasy out in the shower. Why? Because, as always, Tommy was completely oblivious to the raging lust he was igniting in her.

As she turned around, she tossed her keys in her purse and wrapped her green peacoat tighter. Brody leaned against the side of his navy Mercedes, wearing a leather jacket, his arms folded across his chest, his jean-clad legs crossed at the ankles. She didn't feel so much as a flutter, much less anything remotely like what she'd felt in the kitchen this morning.

How unfair was that? Brody was a good-looking man. She had tons in common with him. She laughed and felt comfortable around him. And yet it was Tommy, who was completely wrong for her, who lit up her damn body like she was drunk on a binge, with the freaking aftereffects to match.

*No.* Not fair. She had to give Brody a chance. Just because he hadn't made her melt on the first date didn't mean he wouldn't. She needed to give it a little more time.

He pushed off the side of his car and walked toward her. "Gorgeous as always."

"Thank you," she said, smiling.

After he opened the passenger door, she slipped inside. "So, am I going to have you all to myself today, or is Tommy going to make an appearance?"

"I'm sorry about last night. He keeps a very different schedule than I do, so when I was home by ten, he thought the date had gone badly."

Brody gave her an odd look she couldn't decipher before he closed the door and rounded the front of the car. After he buckled in and started the car, he glanced over at her. "How long have you two known each other?"

It surprised her that anyone who was familiar with Tommy didn't already know the answer to that. "How well do *you* know him?"

"Not that well. I joined Greg's gym right before he moved to Mike's. I've watched him fight, seen him at a couple of fighter functions, even talked a few times. But that's about it."

"I don't remember seeing you at any fighter functions."

"Ouch, that hurts, because I sure remember seeing you. I knew who you were the moment you walked into the room at the vet clinic. I've seen you on Tommy's arm on more than a few occasions. At first, I assumed he was your boyfriend, but then he'd show up with another girl while you were there."

*Thanks for that reminder.* One of the many things about Tommy's after-party lifestyle that had hurt. "Yeah. We go way back. Tommy is like my…brother."

Why did she have a hard time saying that to Brody? It'd come out pretty easily to Tommy last night. Maybe because he had no issue calling her his sister.

"That's good to know." The charming smile Brody sent her should have melted her insides. Unfortunately, no puddling was happening. Damn it.

"So where are we going this afternoon?" she asked.

"I was thinking simple. It's warm for the end of February, so how does grabbing some food and eating at the park sound? We still have about an hour of sunlight left."

"Sounds wonderful."

After they stopped at a greasy diner for burgers and fries, they made their way to the park.

It was packed full of people taking advantage of the warm day. This winter had been mild in comparison to last year. Today was relatively warm at sixty, but the breeze kept a slight chill in the air, making it clear that winter hadn't fully left yet. As she waited for Brody to get a blanket out of the car, she scanned the grass for a sunny spot, seeing that everyone else had the same idea. Luckily, there was an area in the center of the field where they could settle in.

After Brody spread out the blanket, he motioned for her to sit, which she did, then he situated himself beside her as he dug into the bags and handed her the food. Silence descended between them. She watched the runners, the mothers pushing their babies around the walking path, the toddlers squealing as they ran through the fields. No words were needed between her and Brody. They could just sit by each other and enjoy their surroundings.

She liked that.

What she didn't like? That she wasn't completely aware of him. When Tommy sat beside her, she was in tune to every shift he made. If he moved closer to her, her heart would stutter. If he shifted away, she'd anticipate the next time he would come near her again.

Why couldn't she be more aware of Brody?

Did she need to try harder?

Maybe that was it. She scooted a little closer to him. When he followed her lead and slid next to her, bracing his arm behind her so his body cocooned her, she waited to feel something. Anything.

There was nothing.

She blew out a frustrated breath.

Then Brody motioned with his cup to the other side of the park. "Well. Look who we have here. Seems Tommy pops up wherever we are."

"What?" Julie whipped her gaze toward the area where he was pointing.

There *was* a guy with a ball cap on over there with Mac Hannon, about half a football field away, in the middle of lowering his body into a plank position. When the guy launched his body off the ground to land on his feet and then jump up in the air, she gasped.

Tommy—and he was wearing the hat she'd bought him.

Sweat sleeked his skin. When he dropped back into plank, his arms flexed, displaying the always impressive muscles in his biceps and shoulders. She caught her bottom lip between her teeth.

God, he was the sexiest man on earth.

"My God, what's he doing?" she whispered.

"Burpees."

She rolled her eyes. "I *know* that."

Brody chuckled. "Figured you might, but wasn't sure how to answer the question."

"I meant why is he with Mac?" As far as she knew, he hadn't really talked to anyone from the training facility except Dante since Mike had told him to get out.

"Looks like they're doing a conditioning session," Brody said.

And Mac didn't seem like he was close to letting up, either, with his stopwatch out. Even though she couldn't make out the words, she could hear Mac yelling at Tommy. Not like that was anything new. Fighters all seemed to yell at each other when they trained, especially the coaches.

But what did this training session mean? Had Tommy decided to try to get back into MMA? Would he even be able to? For his sake, she hoped so. She knew how much he loved fighting. But MMA also came with a lifestyle… one that had changed him. For the last four months he'd been away from it. What would happen if he stepped back into that life?

She shook her head. It was *his* life. As his friend, all she had to worry about was being supportive.

Worrying about those other things was girlfriend stuff. And that was not her place.

. . .

He felt fucking alive.

Tommy had been taking a run in the park when he'd bumped into Mac doing the same. They'd started bullshitting, and one thing led to another, and the next thing he knew they were both headlong into one of Mike's conditioning sessions. One of them would stand with the stopwatch, barking orders, while the other busted serious ass to get as many completed as he could before time ran out. It was something Mike had set up because every damn one of the guys was so competitive.

By the end of the session, they'd had a killer workout of sprints, burpees, push-ups, and squats.

Tommy's muscles quivered as his fingers bit into the grass for one last plank. His hands shook. He was breathing hard. Adrenaline pumped through him. He'd been working out solo for so long, he hadn't realized how much he missed the rush, the high that came with competition, of having someone yell at him to move faster.

"All right." Mac clicked the button on his stopwatch. "I think we've about killed ourselves today."

Chuckling, Tommy pushed up from plank and brushed off his hands. "Damn, man, that was awesome."

"Yeah, I'm glad I ran into you. I needed the extra training."

Mac "The Snake" Hannon had come into the professional MMA scene about three years ago, much later in life than most fighters, but just as impressive. His refusal to give interviews had given him a mysterious edge that had made the fans salivate. Despite the pressure from the media, all Mac wanted to do was fight and go home. And that was exactly what he did, only emerging from his apartment for training or a scheduled fight.

Because of his recluse-like tendencies, no one really knew much about him, other than he used to be a chef and he'd lost his wife before moving to Georgia and joining Mike's gym. Even though he kept his distance, Mac was always supportive of his peers, and, occasionally, even cracked a smile.

"Got a fight on the horizon?" Tommy asked.

"Yeah, the end of March."

"Ah." Tommy worked his neck. "That's the middleweight bout, isn't it?'

Mac grimaced. "Yeah, Moon's defending the belt against Dolven."

"Hope he does a better job than I did at defending it."

His friend studied him for a minute. "You could always win it back for yourself, Tommy. Shut up all the naysayers calling you a fraud."

"Really? A fraud?"

"You expect anything less with some of the crap you pulled? Those of us at the facility knew how good you were, how great you could be." He shrugged. "You chose a different path. Those on the outside think you only won the title out of sheer luck, and that's why you lost it so quickly."

"Fuck that. I busted ass for that title."

"You didn't bust ass to keep it, though."

Tommy ground his teeth. No. He hadn't.

"I'm just saying," Mac continued. "Maybe you need to get out there and show them where they can shove their opinions."

"And how am I supposed to do that? Mike has barred me from the gym and Ethan won't let me near a cage. I punched his son…in the face. I broke his nose."

"Yeah, you did. And so did Pete Randolph Saturday night in Montreal."

Tommy's brows shot up. "Holy shit." Pete Randolph was a newer fighter in the light heavyweight division. He only had two professional fights under his belt. "How quickly did he get shafted?"

"He didn't. In fact, Ethan banned Junior."

Tommy blinked. "Are you kidding? Why?"

"He came on to Pete's wife hardcore. A lot of people witnessed what happened. A few more fighters came forward, saying they'd had some issue with the jackass. Ethan confronted his son, threatened to cut him off completely if he didn't tell him everything." Mac scrunched his face. "Word's spread, Tommy. We know what happened with Julie and what he said to you afterward. Why didn't you speak up?"

"What would have been the point? I'd been screwing off bad before that even happened. Just a couple of hours before, I'd lost the belt in a pathetic showing in the cage. Mike was already livid. Ethan had already gotten in my face and threatened my contract. Once I threw the punch, my fate was sealed."

"Well. I think Mike would be more willing to listen to you now."

Tommy sighed. "I've been planning on talking to Mike—I owe the man an apology. I guess there's a part of me that's ashamed, so it's hard to face him. If there is a slim chance that he'd actually take me back into the fold, I'd prefer to face him in tip-top shape." Tommy sent his friend a pointed look.

Mac's eyes narrowed. "Proceed."

"What do you think about having a training partner? You'll get in some extra training for your fight and I'll get in some practice with a live person. I haven't grappled in months."

After a moment of hesitation, Mac nodded. "Sounds like a fair deal. How about the same time tomorrow? Plan for three hours?"

Tension whooshed out of him. With Mac, the answer could've gone either way. "Sounds great. We can do it over at Julie's. She's got a big backyard. I'll buy a mat and some gear tonight."

"Julie's? Why not your place?"

"We're living together now," he muttered, distracted by making a mental list of stuff he needed to buy.

When Mac clamped him real hard on the shoulder, he almost face-planted on the ground.

"Congrats, man! It's about damn time. I was wondering when you'd come to your senses and snatch that woman up."

What was he—? *Oh, shit…*

"Uh…no, it's not what you think. My house burned down. Lost everything. I'm staying with her until I can get resettled."

A grimace crossed his friend's face. "I'm real sorry to hear that. But I'm even sorrier to hear you're still as dumb as a pile of rocks."

"What the fuck, man?" Jeez, Mac had a reputation for being blunt, but damn.

His friend didn't appear the least bit apologetic for his comment. "If you're not careful, some other man is going to come in and sweep that woman right off her feet. Guess what you'll be then?"

When Mac paused, Tommy just stared at him, which made his friend shake his head and grunt with disgust.

"You'll be second in her eyes. Right now, you're first, and you've *always* been first. How's it going to feel when you're not the most important man in her life?"

He didn't want to fucking think about that. "Jesus, Mac, why would you even encourage something like that? You know my reputation. Would you want your daughter dating me?"

Tensing, Mac squinted off into the distance for a minute before looking back at him. "Nope. If I had a daughter and saw you get out of the car to pick her up, I'd load the shotgun."

"Then why—"

"We're not talking about hypothetical daughters. We're talking about Julie. And you would die before treating her like one of your flavors of the day. I'm just telling you, man, life's short. What's here today might not be here tomorrow." The muscles in his face tightened and he started backing away. "I'll see you later." He turned and jogged off.

Knowing he was thinking of his wife, Tommy let him go. *What's here today might not be tomorrow.* That was his biggest fear. That he'd lose Julie. Not in the way Mac lost his wife, God forbid. But because of his actions, because he'd hurt her.

While he appreciated Mac's faith in him, Tommy wasn't convinced. All he had to go on was his track record. A part of him was convinced he was just like his mother — sans the alcoholic part. She'd never been able to truly love anyone, either…including him.

At least he was able to love: he loved Julie. He really did. It was the whole romantic love thing he was a lost cause at. And that was something she needed.

If there was even the slightest chance he could hurt Julie because of his shortcomings, then he needed to keep his distance. Better yet, he needed to get the hell out of her place as quickly as he could, before he did something he couldn't take back. Something they'd both regret.

Earlier today, he'd spoken to his insurance agent. They were processing his claim, but it could still take more than a week before he'd see a check. Maybe he'd go ahead and start the search anyway. He hadn't wanted to start looking for a place to live or replacing his furniture until he knew for certain he wasn't going to have any issues with the insurance company. Which was actually pretty damn responsible of him. In the past, he'd just have spent the money. But after the shit had hit the fan, he'd started investing his money, for once thinking of the future.

Either way, he was going to have to find a place to live, and pronto. As for furniture, he'd just get the bare necessities until the check came in. Feeling better with a firm plan, he worked his arms to relieve some of the lingering burn, turned to start the trek to his rental car. And froze.

About fifty feet away, Julie sat beside Brody on a blanket. The two looked so comfy together, their bodies close, her shoulder pressing into his chest, Brody's arm behind her in a possessive way that had Tommy clenching his teeth against a violent surge of jealousy.

The truly fucked-up part was Julie didn't seem to mind being touched at all.

But *he* did. A lot. Seeing her curled up against the other man enraged him in a way that was actually frightening. Unnerved by the foreign emotion, he inhaled deeply. He needed to get the hell out of here before she saw him. The last thing he needed was to have a conversation with her and that man while he was this jacked up inside.

But Julie's gaze snagged his and she didn't seem surprised to see him. Which meant she'd already known he was there.

*All right, dude. This is your best friend. Keep it that way.*

Unable to ignore her direct look, he strolled over to them, keeping his stride relaxed, until he reached the edge of the blanket. "Hey. What are you guys up to?"

Seriously stupid fucking question.

"Enjoying the warm day." Julie smiled up at him. "Seems you and Mac were getting in a really great workout. Looking good out there."

Male satisfaction coursed through him knowing she liked what she saw, and he cast Brody a smug look. The man held his gaze and didn't look the least bit bothered by his date telling another man he was looking good. Why not? What had she told Brody about him?

Why was *he* bothered by the fact Brody *wasn't* bothered? But he was. Big time. He didn't like the confidence the man was exuding, nor the way his hand had just slipped down to touch Julie's lower back.

He was seriously going to rip the motherfucker's throat out.

"Hey, Jules, tell Tommy about the street performer we saw last night."

Jules? All right, it was official. He really hated this asshole.

Tommy tapped the bill of his cap. "Maybe *Brody* would like to know where you got this hat, Julie? Pretty cool, isn't it? She gave it to me for Valentine's Day."

The man's lips cracked into a huge grin as Julie stared wide-eyed between the two of them. "I actually don't think either one of you is interested."

Brody held his gaze. "Oh, you have no idea how interested I am. In fact, this is about the most interesting conversation I've had in months."

Tommy scowled. What was he talking about? Honestly, he didn't care. He just wanted to get Julie and go home. "Come on. I'll give you a ride home."

She blinked at him. "Uh…I came with Brody. I plan to leave with him."

He stared down at her. He wanted her away from this asshole, and she was *choosing* to stay with him. Mac's warning whispered through his head, and what felt like a hundred-pound dumbbell formed in Tommy's gut. "I don't think Brody will mind."

"Oh, no. Brody definitely minds," came the smug

rejoinder.

He shot a murderous glare at the asshole. Anyone else, and the man would've cowered. But he wasn't anyone else, he was fucking Brody "The Iron" Minton, and he didn't cower. He winked.

Fury encased Tommy and squeezed like a vise. Tommy fervently wished Julie were with a pansy, so he could simply say, "Boo!" and scare him off. But intimidation wasn't going to work. One damn thing was for sure, though. Something wasn't adding up with that man. He was acting just plain weird. And Julie was spending time with him. Way too much time.

Tommy didn't like it. Not one little bit.

So until further notice, his house hunting was on hold. He definitely needed to play chaperone.

# CHAPTER 6

Julie strolled up the path toward her front door. Brody still hadn't kissed her.

Correction—he had, but only on the cheek. A grazing that hadn't even warmed her skin. *Gah*. But she enjoyed the man's presence immensely. There was something comforting about not having one iota of attraction and being able to simply enjoy a friendship with a man.

That was something she'd never had on her side of her friendship with Tommy. The insight gave her a peek into his side of their relationship. She envied it, wished she'd been able to feel as relaxed and unaware of him as he'd always been with her. What would their relationship be like if she had truly thought of him as just a friend?

She couldn't go around thinking about how the past—or present—would've changed. All she really cared about was the future. Was Brody it? She didn't think so. But was it possible he might help direct her to the path that would lead to her future? Quite possibly.

And right now she was okay with continuing to let things play out.

After she opened the front door to her house and her dog didn't come yapping, she called, "Lucy?"

Nothing.

"Warrior?"

Silence.

"Tommy?" she finally said.

Crickets.

What the hell?

She hurried into the kitchen and opened the back door, then stumbled to a stop. Tommy was rolling around on the ground, Warrior and Lucy hopping around him. Paws landed on his stomach, shoulders, and head as he laughed out loud. He jumped to his feet, crouching low. The dogs immediately lowered their front legs, barking, and when they sprang forward, Tommy lunged at them, which sent both dogs sprinting into a circle around the yard.

Tommy stood straight, hands on his hips, a grin making his already handsome face even more attractive. Mischief and humor brightened his green eyes. Head high, gaze meeting the world, he looked invincible. Dominating. And so incredibly sexy her heart crashed against her breast.

So, why did she have a sudden sense of doom?

Because no other man made her feel like this. Because no matter what damn road she took, her heart always led back to a man who called her sister. Because she was seriously beginning to fear that she really would end up a spinster.

No!

Did *she* not get any say in this at all? Why did her heart get all the control?

She didn't *want* Tommy.

When he spotted her, he jogged to her side and kissed her cheek. Unlike the kiss Brody had given her, this light peck scorched her skin. She did everything she could not to flinch away. Thankfully, she succeeded.

"How was your date?" There was an edge to his voice that confused her.

She frowned. "What is your problem with Brody?"

"I don't like him."

"You don't— Jeez, Tommy, you don't even know him. How can you not like him?"

He took another step forward, crowding her personal space. As his body came within inches, where just a slight lean forward and their chests would touch, her throat tightened. The scent of his musky cologne enveloped her, and she inhaled, ensnared by the spell of Tommy Sparks— the spell she'd been under since she was ten.

He brought his face closer. "I know enough that I don't like him with you, and I want you to stay the hell away from him."

A thrill shot through her. Before she could stop herself, she said, "Why? Are you jealous?"

Something flashed in his eyes as a muscle jumped in his jaw. "I don't do jealousy, Julie. You're my best friend. It's my job to look out for you, and that man has ulterior motives. You need to stay away from him."

She jerked back, stung by the insult. "Did you seriously just say the only way Brody would be interested in me is because he has a secret agenda? What the hell, Tommy?"

"Don't make it sound worse than I meant it. That man is up to something, and I don't trust him. I especially don't trust him with you."

Anger buzzed inside her. She was no longer the crying ten-year-old maiden he'd swept in and saved with his wooden sword. She was a grown woman who could take care of herself, and it was about damn time he saw it. "You don't get to make demands on me. If I want to see Brody Minton, I'm going to see Brody Minton." She poked him hard in the chest. "I'm done with your big brother shit. So drop it already."

As she whirled to leave, a feral growl erupted from behind her. Strong fingers latched onto her wrist and spun her back around. His other hand snaked around the back of her head, and then his mouth was on hers. His fury was evident in the biting crush of his lips against hers, and all she could do was stand there, absolutely stunned. He kissed her hard, the taste of him searing through her senses as his tongue sliced between her lips to sweep hotly through her mouth. Once. Then he froze. And it was over.

He stumbled back, staring at her with wide eyes.

"Fuck!" He shoved a hand through his hair, then stormed off toward the house, muttering curses the entire way.

Pressing her fingers against her punished lips, she stared after him, just as horrified as he was about the kiss. Because that hadn't been a kiss from a man who'd *wanted* to kiss her. That had been a branding of ownership.

And Julie Rogers was owned by no man.

• • •

What the hell had he just done?

Tommy slammed the back door behind him as he stalked into the kitchen. Fucking hell. Julie'd said the word "brother" again, and he'd simply lost it.

Next thing he knew he was grinding his mouth against hers. He *never* kissed like that. Out of outright jealousy... out of an anger-induced bitterness. That kiss had been the equivalent of his performance the night he defended his title—mind-numbingly pathetic.

Jealousy was not something he'd ever dealt with, and if it made him do stupid shit like this, then he'd rather do without.

Julie slammed into the house behind him. "What the hell was that, Tommy?"

He scrubbed a hand over his face. "A mistake."

"No freaking joke."

Yeah, she was pissed. She had every right to be, too. For more than two decades he'd done nothing but tell the woman she was his sister, and just when she started getting close to some guy, he pulls a chest-pounding me-Tarzan-you-Jane stunt like that. And for what?

Nothing. There wasn't anything he could offer her instead.

Except, maybe, a damn good time in bed. But as much as his libido was all for that option, his heart wasn't in it. He'd rather have his friendship intact. Which it wouldn't be if he was his mother's son—and so far he was.

Her hands jammed onto her hips. "I'm waiting for an explanation, Tommy."

"I don't have one," he ground out.

"That's it? That's all you have to say?"

He clamped his jaw. What did she want him to say? That he wanted to fuck her? Lay her down right there on the floor and pound into her hard? Have his way with her, as he'd had so many women in the past?

With a growl of anger, she shook her head. "This living situation isn't working. I really think it would be best if you found somewhere else to go."

Stunned, his mouth dropped open. "Julie—"

"I do *not* like being kissed like I am owned, especially by a man who has never once looked at me like I'm a woman. I don't know what it is about Brody that has you all worked up, but you need to get over it. Do you understand?"

Fusing his teeth together, he remained silent. He *had* kissed her like he owned her, and he regretted that. But she was so wrong about the woman part, and for the first time, it bothered him that she had no idea how fucking hot he found her. Okay, maybe he had spent years only seeing her as a sibling, but he didn't anymore. Never would again. That was the damn problem.

"I'll start looking tomorrow," he bit out.

She gave a curt nod. "I don't think we should go to the wedding together, either. In fact, I *want* to go with Brody."

First she refused a ride from him at the park, and now she wanted to go to a fighter's wedding with a fighter who wasn't him? Another wave of jealousy punched him right in the sweet spot, making him see stars. That violent urge to brand her as his almost crippled him.

"You would rather take *him* to the wedding?"

She nodded.

He felt his nostrils flare. "Fine. Go with him. I don't

care."

Oh, he fucking cared. He cared so fucking much that if he didn't leave this room right this second, he was liable to punch a fist through a wall.

He stormed past her down the hallway and slammed his bedroom door.

Inhaling deep breaths, he stalked around the room. The kiss played over and over in his mind. Did Brody kiss her differently? Better than he did?

The question made his body quake with anger. Images of her in Brody's arms tormented him, making Tommy fist his hands and want to pummel something.

No, he did not want her with that man.

He didn't want her with *any* man.

He wanted her for himself.

Considering his certainty that he took after his mother, that had to be the most selfish thing he'd ever wanted. But, God help him, he couldn't sit back and let another man steal her away. He could only hope there was some romantic tenderness inside him somewhere. Julie deserved a man who was insanely attracted to her but who could still sit on the couch with her, hold her, kiss her, *without* pouncing on her in blind lust.

Maybe if he could do that much, the urge to flee from her in the morning wouldn't set in and ruin their friendship completely. Maybe with her, he could stick around.

And he planned to prove he could do just that.

To her…and to himself.

· · ·

Julie slipped into the house, giving the dogs a good ruffling as they trotted up to greet her. She glanced but everything was quite. Tommy's rental car was outside, so he had to be here. Today would be the first time she'd seen him in a week. Somehow she'd been able to avoid him, ever since she told him she wanted to take Brody to the wedding. God knew she'd had to stay away. Once the anger had worn off, the realization had set in.

Tommy Sparks, the man she'd spent more of her life in love with than not, had finally kissed her.

Without one ounce of passion.

On the surface, she'd known that. It was why the kiss had made her so furious. The meaning, however, had taken a little longer to sink in.

Even though he'd kissed her, he still wasn't attracted to her. How could he be, and be so cold as he touched her?

Mortification set in, so ugly its shame had burrowed deep in her chest and, for the second time in a week, she had cried over Tommy. Mostly she'd cried for the teenage girl who'd always believed that one day a wonderful kiss would change the way Tommy looked at her.

Because that girl had just been proven wrong.

It hadn't been wonderful, and it hadn't changed him. If anything, it had made things a whole lot worse.

In her teenage fantasies, some other boy's interest in her would always spark a fit of jealousy that had Tommy yanking her to him and kissing her. But unlike what had happened in reality, in her fantasy as soon as his lips touched her, his jealousy fled. He would groan against her mouth in passionate desire, gather her close to his chest, and thoroughly kiss her in a way that made every fantasy she'd ever had seem like child's play to the real thing.

It was supposed to be awe-inspiring, mind-blowing… life-altering.

Okay, yeah. It *had* been life-altering—just not in the way she'd fantasized. She'd had to face the fact that Tommy had finally kissed her…and hadn't felt anything. That had been a hard truth to swallow, and she'd spent the entire week coping with her turbulent feelings. She'd slip out of the house before he got up, remaining at the clinic for lunch, then staying out with Brody or Melody until late. When she got home for the night, she'd pass Tommy with a quick good night and go straight to her room. One thing was clear, though—he hadn't found a place to live yet. And she couldn't continue avoiding him in her own home.

It was time to let it go and move on.

The kiss had been a mistake. Nothing had changed between them. Their relationship was the same as it ever was.

So tonight, instead of going out, she'd decided to stay and face the music. Just her luck he wasn't anywhere in sight. She went into the kitchen and poured herself a glass of Merlot. Now she just wanted to slip into a pair of yoga pants and a T-shirt and enjoy a glass of wine before she took a long bath and enjoyed a second glass of wine. God, that sounded heavenly. She really missed her quiet evenings at home.

After she changed, she wandered into the living room. Still no Tommy. She went to the back door and opened it. Grunts and *oof*s immediately assailed her.

What in the world?

Tommy and Mac were wrestling on a blue mat

they'd laid down on the grass. All kinds of equipment was scattered around, as well. Grappling dummies, pads, gloves, even a freestanding bag with one of those sand-filled bases. So Tommy *was* trying to get back in the cage.

Good for him.

She stepped out on the patio and waited until they broke apart. "How's it going?"

Tommy's head snapped over in her direction, and the smile that came to his lips made her heart stutter.

"Hey, stranger," he said. "Good to see you."

"Seems you've got quite the operation going on."

Chuckling, he jogged over and dropped a kiss on her cheek, as he always had, as if they hadn't had a huge argument a few days before. "Yeah, been doing this every day since the park."

"Here?"

"Yep."

Wow. She really had been MIA.

Mac walked over with a duffel bag full of gear and slapped hands with Tommy. "Okay, I'm out of here."

"All right man, see ya tomorrow."

Mac disappeared through the back door.

"Can I get you to help me with something?" he asked her as he used a towel to wipe the sweat off his face and neck. "I'm rusty on some of the grappling moves and could use the practice."

She hesitated. Not that she hadn't done this in the past. But she wasn't sure if she wanted Tommy to touch her, not after what had happened.

Didn't she want it all to go back to normal?

Yeah, she did.

"Sure. What do you want me to do?"

He motioned for her to follow him on the mat. After he lay down on his back, he beckoned her closer with his fingers and gave her a cocky smile. "Climb on."

"W-What?"

"I'm having a problem with full mounts. So I need for you to mount me."

He said it like it was everyday business for him, which, okay, it was, but straddling that man's hips was an erotic escapade for her.

*You can do this.*

Taking a deep breath, she stepped over him with one foot, then lowered to her knees until her very feminine center met his very manly front. Air whooshed from Tommy, and with almost lightning speed, he yanked her up by the ass to the middle of his torso.

"I thought I needed to be lower than this."

"No. You're shorter. Got to be here." The strain in his voice was evident.

Had she hurt him when she sat on him? Judging by his clenched jaw, she must have.

"What do I do now?" she asked.

"Brace your hands on either side of my head."

As she leaned forward to do as he instructed, he scooted his body farther underneath her. "What are you doing?"

Green eyes jumped to hers. "What?"

"All this shifting?" At least his moving was keeping her from focusing on the fact she had his body between her legs.

"I'm trying to compensate for the fact you're not a six-foot dude, okay?"

She scowled. "You don't have to get all snippy. Jeez."

Two large hands grabbed two handfuls of butt cheek and hauled her even farther up his chest. If he brought her much higher, she'd be sitting on his face.

*Ah, hell.*

Tingles erupted low in her belly. Why, oh, why had she gone and thought *that*?

He whacked down one of the arms she had braced beside his head, and she squealed in surprise. Next thing she knew, she'd been rolled onto her back and was looking up at the darkening sky instead of Tommy. Why? Because his face was lower. So much lower. *Belly button* lower. She was having a very difficult time catching her breath because the weight of his upper chest was pressing very intimately against her, between her legs. And he wasn't moving.

Why wasn't he moving?

Oh, wait. Now he was. Scrambling, actually. As though he couldn't get off her fast enough.

Once he'd turned his back to her, he said, "Thanks. That helped," as he yanked on a pair of gloves, then went to town on the bag.

Sadness lay heavy in her chest. She was watching, helpless, as he slipped away from her.

And it was all because of that damn kiss that never should have happened.

# CHAPTER 7

Julie twisted to look at herself from every angle in the mirror. The coral handkerchief dress she'd put on fit her perfectly. Trimmed with faux diamond rhinestones, the strapless bodice hugged her breasts, while the empire waistline made the fabric drape loosely around her waist and thighs. She'd twisted her hair up in a loose updo, leaving a few strands to curl around her face.

Everything was perfect. Down to the silver-studded peep-toe pumps she'd bought specifically for the wedding.

She could hear Tommy moving around. Pacing. Muttering. A curse here, a curse there. She didn't go investigate. He'd been on edge all morning. After she'd asked him about it, he'd barked out that he wasn't looking forward to the wedding. Then she understood. It would be the first time he'd been around most of the guys, including Mike, in months. After that realization, she'd given him space to deal with the stress of it.

She glanced at the clock. The wedding started in less than an hour. Brody should arrive at any minute to pick her up. When she went into the living room, she froze. Tommy stood in front of the window with his back toward her, wearing a black suit.

As he turned to face her, her stomach twisted. The blazer hugged broad shoulders and was unbuttoned to reveal the tight button-down black shirt underneath. His red tie lay flat against his chest, and it made her gaze zero in on the way the fabric hugged his torso and trim waist.

"Wow," he said.

She searched for a word to describe how he looked. She found many: sinful, delicious, forbidden…a walking wet dream. But she couldn't use those, so she decided against returning the sentiment and instead fanned out her dress and went with, "Not too shabby, huh?"

"God, Julie, you're breathtaking."

A pleased flush warmed her skin. Tommy had complimented her many times over the years, but breathtaking was a new one, and she loved hearing it come out of his mouth.

As he walked toward her, his hand outstretched, time slowed. The sexy lift of one corner of his lips and the appreciative shine in his eyes as he took her hand held her captivated.

She couldn't breathe. Couldn't turn away. Couldn't stop her body from willingly going forward as he tugged her against his chest, his other arm slipping around her waist to hold her close.

As he swayed them, he whispered, "Save a dance for me?"

Words refused to squeeze past her tight throat, so she simply nodded. Then he lowered his head and she thought her lungs would explode from the air trapped inside them. When his lips brushed her cheek, scorching her skin, she closed her eyes, a stuttered exhale finally shooting past her lips.

She instinctively rubbed her face against his as he drew her closer, his cheek resting against hers. The heat of his skin felt so good. She absorbed the feeling, wanting to press her body closer to his. Without thought, she slipped her fingers from his and slid both hands up his arms to wind around his neck.

He skimmed his palm over her waist, then her hip, to join his other hand resting above the curve of her butt. He'd never held her like this before, like a lover, hands touching areas never touched before. It was enthralling. Enticing. And, heaven help her, she couldn't get enough.

When he pulled his head back, she tilted hers up to look at him. Their eyes locked, mouths slightly parted, mere inches apart. Her breath hitched, her body frozen, waiting for him to close the distance between their lips—to really kiss her.

But he never moved, just gazed down at her.

The doorbell rang.

He blinked, cursing under his breath as his arms tightened around her waist for a brief moment before he stepped back. "Your date is here."

She stared at him. Seriously? She was so ready to forget Brody was standing right outside the door, ready to forget the wedding altogether. So how could Tommy simply step away and let her leave? With another man?

Oh God, he *hadn't* felt it. The sizzle. The connection. The rightness of them in each other's arms.

It had all been a figment of her vivid imagination. While she'd formed an elaborate romantic scenario that fed her forbidden desires, he'd simply been dancing with his best friend, completely oblivious to her as a woman. He hadn't closed the distance because it hadn't occurred to him to do so. And it never would.

At what point would that sink into her thick skull? What more did he have to do to prove he didn't see her that way? If giving her a passionless kiss wouldn't do it, shouldn't the horror on his face when he'd seen her naked have done it?

It was as if she was desperate to find something… *anything*…that belied his words, because it was simply pathetic for her to be so deeply in love with someone who couldn't even see her as a desirable woman. The truth of that thought hit her like a hundred pound Great Dane.

In one fell swoop, Tommy had blinked away all the years she'd spent accepting her platonic role in his life. The years he'd always treated her as just his best friend. He had *never* tried anything intimate with her. But with one horrible, lackluster kiss, she was back to being that lovesick teenage girl, wanting desperately to be wrong about his feelings for her.

And it made her so furious she wanted to cry.

When the doorbell rang again, she spun and answered the door.

Brody stood there looking devastatingly handsome in a charcoal suit, but nothing could compare to the devastating sight of Tommy his.

"Wow."

He repeated Tommy's words with the same appreciative tone, but she didn't get the same warm flush, and right now she needed that reaction more than anything. Needed *any* kind of reaction from any man other than Tommy. She forced a smile. "Wow yourself."

"You ready?"

As she grabbed her purse off the table by the door, she glanced toward Tommy standing in the living room. Their eyes connected, and she was stunned by the anger she saw simmering in them.

Had he realized how much she'd wanted him to kiss her—really kiss her? Was he angry at her for making things awkward between them? Was he finally putting together how she felt about him?

God, she didn't need that humiliation on top of everything else. Not because *he'd* changed the rules and kissed her. She'd been fine. They'd been fine. And then *she'd* gone and messed it up.

"Have fun," he said, his voice clipped.

Julie lowered her lashes, pursing her lips in a seductive manner. "Oh, I plan to." As she slipped the palm of one hand through Brody's elbow, she waggled her fingers on the other at Tommy and forced a giggle. "Good-bye, Tommy."

And somehow she had to find a way to make that farewell stick. For good.

• • •

Julie sat beside Brody on a white folding chair inside the Great Hall of the Callenwolde Fine Arts Center.

Candlelight flickered around the inside of the Gothic-Tudor-style mansion, creating the ideal romantic ambiance for a wedding.

When the bridal march pealed into the room, Julie stood and pivoted toward the grand staircase at the back of the room. Cait came into view at the top of the landing in front of the wall-length stained-glass window, dressed in a strapless, sweetheart, pick-up white ball gown, her veil covering her face and red hair. As she took her father's elbow and slowly descended the staircase, the bride looked elegant and completely in love.

Envy shot through Julie and her gaze locked on the man standing three rows behind her, also on his feet, his blond head turned toward the back like everyone else's. She forced her attention back to the bride. Tears stung Julie's eyes as Cait made her way down the rose-petal-strewn white runner toward the man she loved.

As the bride stopped in front of the groom, Julie took Brody's hand and squeezed as she watched Dante's reaction. He looked handsome as always, his black tuxedo encasing his powerful body. His brown hair was freshly trimmed and his cheeks cleanly shaven. But it was his blue eyes, rimmed with tears, locked on Cait as she took her place by his side, that made Julie's chest hurt.

What would it be like to be loved like that?

To feel complete confidence that the man beside you loved you as much as you loved him?

She wanted that so badly. Not a one-sided love, but a complete love. A true partner in life.

She glanced at Brody. If she gave him half a chance, could it be him?

Possibly. But like it or not, Tommy stood in her way. He'd seemed always to stand in her way when it came to finding that type of love.

So as Dante and Cait vowed to love each other until death do they part, Julie made a vow to herself.

She would have a wonderful loving husband who cherished her and amazing children to warm her heart.

And Tommy Sparks would be the one who gave her away on her wedding day, and the man her children called uncle. Just the way it was always supposed to be.

From this moment on, she would put away her foolish notions and accept that he didn't love her, and that he never would.

• • •

Tommy sipped a glass of wine as he scanned the enclosed courtyard. The dim lighting made the bright blue holograph that read DANTE AND CAITLYN stand out on the herringbone-patterned brick dance floor, where round tables covered in white tablecloths and simple daisy centerpieces surrounded the perimeter.

Dinner was over. Though Tommy couldn't have told anyone what he'd eaten, having been too busy scowling at Julie, who had clung to Brody through the entire meal, laughing at his stupid jokes, smiling up at the man like he hung the moon.

Tommy should have kissed her when he had the chance. But he'd known Brody would show at any moment. When he kissed Julie again, he was really going to kiss her—a deep, thorough kiss of discovery that he could lose himself in. Not one that would have been interrupted by that asshole ringing the goddamn doorbell.

After tonight, Brody wouldn't be interrupting anything ever again. She wouldn't be seeing him again.

It'd taken a damn week for Julie to finally come to him—one of the more frustrating decisions he'd made, trying to prove to himself that he wouldn't treat her like other women. He wanted to let her take the lead, do things at her own speed, and if she wanted some space, then he was going to give it to her, whether he liked it or not. He'd also thought some time apart would help him get better control over his raging lust for her. Yeah. *Wrong.* As soon as she'd come out of the house last night, he'd wanted to pounce. Which had presented the perfect opportunity for him to prove once again that he could control himself around her.

Which he had. Barely. But the important point was he *had.* If he could practically have his face planted between her beautiful thighs and *not* ravish her, he was pretty damn sure he could kiss her without turning into a sex-crazed fiend. The last thing he wanted was to be that man with her—the man only seeking physical pleasure for him and his partner. The *physical.* No feeling, no emotion, just raw lust.

He was capable of more than merely fucking. He had to be. For Julie, he had to be able to make love.

Especially after watching her dance with the asshole. Closely. Thighs touching. The man's arms wrapped around her waist, his hands resting exactly where Tommy's had been a few hours before. He wanted her back in his embrace, with her arms wrapped tightly around his neck, her body pressed to his, just as she was holding Brody now.

And why shouldn't he? She had promised him a dance.

After placing his wineglass on a nearby table, he strode across the dance floor and tapped Brody on the shoulder. The other man glanced back. When his eyes connected with Tommy's, amusement immediately brightened the man's gaze. God, Tommy seriously loathed this asshole.

"Hey, man. What brings you by?" Brody said, tugging Julie to his side and under his arm.

The show of possessiveness boiled Tommy's blood, and he curled his fingers into fists.

"Julie promised me a dance," he said, relieved that his voice sounded normal and not coated in hostility. He glanced past Brody to his best friend. Wide eyes gazed up at him and she stole his breath for the second time today. "Isn't that right, Julie?" This time there was a huskiness to his tone he couldn't hide.

Her brows lifted, but he held out his hand. When she sent Brody a questioning glance, as if asking permission, Tommy clenched his teeth. *Patience.* The asshole wouldn't be around much longer. Not if he had anything to say about it. Which he did.

"Go dance with your friend." The other man kissed her on the cheek and Tommy about cold-cocked him. "I'll grab us some drinks while I wait for you." Then he sauntered off, like he didn't have a goddamn care in the world. Like another man wasn't trying to swoop in and take his girl.

Confident fucker, wasn't he?

They'd see how long *that* lasted.

As another slow song started to play, Julie slipped her hand in his and Tommy tugged her close, wrapping one arm around her waist until he had her pressed against the full length of his body. Unlike before, when she'd relaxed into him, she seemed to strain away from him now.

Leaning back, he frowned down at her. "What's the matter with you?"

The smile she gave him was also strained—like, bared-teeth strained. "Nothing. I'm fine."

Earlier at the house, she'd seemed happy to be in his arms, might have even accepted his kiss. Now it was as if, were he to release her, she would bolt in the opposite direction. What the hell had happened?

The rest of the dance didn't go any better. She refused to look at him, her attention on anything and everything but him. When he'd ask her a question, all she gave him was a short answer, an "Uh huh" or "Mmm." When the song was over, she patted him on the biceps and with that same strained smile, said, "Thanks for that dance, Tommy. I'm going to find Brody now."

And she strutted away, those hips swaying side to side, in search of another man.

Jealous fury made Tommy suck a breath through his teeth. That had been a disaster. What was up with her 180-degree switcheroo? Was it because Brody was here? That seemed logical…

But it didn't matter, he told himself. She may be out with the asshole right now, but she'd end the night with Tommy.

…

A bald head grabbed his attention. Nerves hit his stomach as he spotted his former coach grabbing a drink from the bar. He'd been keeping his eye out for Mike all afternoon, but he hadn't been at the ceremony. Tommy had worried that maybe he wouldn't be here at all. Now that he'd spotted Mike, he made a beeline over to him.

Still a towering combination of muscle and intimidation, the other man had on a pair of khaki slacks and a white button-down shirt he'd left unfastened around the wide expanse of his neck. Tommy guessed this was as dressed up as Mike was willing to get. His old coach's eyes narrowed when he saw Tommy approach.

That wasn't a good sign.

"Mike." Tommy held out his hand, which the other man took.

"Tommy. Good to see you."

"Listen, I'm going to cut to the chase here and not waste your time. I'd like to apologize for my shitty behavior after I won the title."

"And the night you lost the title?" Mike asked, his expression unreadable.

Rage immediately erupted within Tommy as the punk kid's jeering circled in his head. Threatening to get Julie alone…to hurt her. "Sorry. I *won't* apologize for that."

A grim smile curved one corner of Mike's mouth and he nodded. "That's what I thought. And just for the record? Nobody expects you to apologize for that. In fact, most of us were stunned he didn't end up hospitalized when we found out what he'd said."

"He's just lucky he crumbled after the first punch and his friends decided to jump in to keep me busy."

"I owe you an apology, too, Tommy. Had I known that the brawl was over what that asshole said about Julie, my reaction would've been different. But you never said anything, so I just assumed it was another one of your out-of-control moments."

"Which is why I didn't defend my actions. If it hadn't been over that, it would've been over something else, Mike. We both know that. Something needed to happen to knock me back on track."

Eyes narrowed, Mike rubbed the top of his bald head. "Mac told me you've been training with him. He also mentioned you might be interested in returning to the cage."

"Interested? Definitely. Is it a possibility? That depends on you and Ethan."

Mike sucked on his teeth while he studied him. "I know I have a rep for being hot-headed and just reacting. I did it to Dante, and I did it to you." He pointed his finger at Tommy. "But in my defense, you both had been screwing up and my patience was gone. Before I even think about venturing down this road with you again, I need to know you are one hundred percent committed to your career. No more of the crap you pulled."

A flare of hope sparked in Tommy's chest. "Mike, there is no one more painfully aware of their part in fucking up their career. Trust me, it's not happening again."

"That's good to know. So you want to come back?"

"Of course I do, but you remember I'm barred from the cage, right? You have a training facility full of high-caliber fighters who are all slotted for matches. The chances of my getting back in are almost nil."

"I won't lie. It won't be easy. We all know why you punched Ethan's son, but your reputation was in the shitter even before that. You're going to have to prove yourself. Show everyone this is what you want. It's as simple as that."

"Do you think Ethan can overlook that last fight?"

"One thing I know about that man." Mike lowered his voice and took a step closer. "Money talks. And you had a lot of fans. Even before you won the championship, you sold out arenas. Ethan isn't going to forget that. He banned you in the heat of the moment. If we can show him you've changed, I think you have a pretty good chance of getting back in." Mike clapped him on the shoulder. "I've always known you had the potential to be one of the greats in MMA, Tommy. One of the guys who still has loyal fans even after retirement. You screwed up, but I think you've learned your lesson. So what do you say we start kicking your ass again on Monday?"

Tommy smiled. "Sounds fucking fantastic."

"Glad to have you back, man."

Hell, yeah. A huge weight lifted from his shoulders. His career was back on track.

Now to get things on the right track with Julie.

. . .

Julie smiled up at Brody, who'd pulled her to a quiet alcove away from the group surrounding Dante and Cait to watch the bride and groom cut the cake. The reception was winding down. After tossing the garter and bouquet, the happy couple would leave to catch a late flight to Aruba, which Dante joked Caitlyn would not see hide nor hair of once they landed. Cait blushed, but Julie noticed she didn't contradict her new husband's prediction.

Another wave of envy hit Julie right where it hurt. The

entire night had been a roller coaster of emotions, starting with her encounter with Tommy at the house. That had pushed her to devote all her attention to Brody, which hadn't been difficult, since he hadn't left her side, not even to hang with the many other fighters in the building, who were grouped together talking shop as usual.

Unfortunately, the more time she spent with him, dancing and touching, the more she realized they would never be more than friends. No matter how much she wanted to feel a spark with the man, she didn't. And she needed to let him know right away, before she ended up hurting him. She'd never forgive herself if she did that, especially since she was allowing Tommy to believe there was more between her and Brody than there really was. Which meant she was using Brody, and honestly, that made her feel sick.

"Cait's about to throw the bouquet," Brody said, nudging her forward. "Go out there and show those women how it's done."

As she watched the single ladies gather on the dance floor, she bit her bottom lip. Should she? She'd never participated in the tradition at other weddings. But just a little while ago, hadn't she made a determined vow to herself that she would marry and have a family? What better way to start looking toward that future than by catching the symbol that said she'd be the next to do just that?

So she took her place beside a giggling woman who had to be in her very early twenties and most definitely did not need to marry.

She caught Cait's gaze, and Cait smiled and pointed at her before she turned around.

"One. Two. Three," Cait counted excitedly.

The bouquet arched up. The young woman launched into the air, aiming for it like a heat-seeking missile. Just as her hands closed around the handle of the daisy-laden bouquet, Julie nudged her with her hip so she lost her grip. When the flowers tumbled from her fingertips, Julie grabbed a fistful of petals and yanked them to her chest, holding them close as she bent over to protect them from the giggling horde who tried to wrestle them away. Hands tugged at the bouquet, but Julie held on until everyone had given up.

She'd done it! She'd caught the bouquet!

Grinning, she glanced up, and her euphoria vanished in an instant.

Tommy was staring at her, frowning furiously.

Crap. Why did *he* have to be the first one she looked at? Why?

And why was he scowling at her like that?

She forced her gaze away and searched out Brody, who stood exactly where she'd left him, a triumphant gleam in his eyes as he gazed back at her. Stunned by the softly possessive look, she swallowed. Slowly she made her way to his side, letting out a little squeak when one of his arms shot forward, yanked her to him, and gave her a tight hug. "Now that's how a woman should catch the bouquet. In true MMA style."

As guilt flooded her chest, she stared up at him. She might as well come clean now rather than later. "Brody, listen—"

"My turn," he interrupted, releasing her and strutting out to the dance floor as Dante led Cait to a chair, where she sat down. Dante slid his hands under Cait's dress and waggled his brows, which made her throw her head back and laugh, then he slowly slid the garter down her leg. After he'd balled it in his fist, lingering long enough to give Cait a sweet kiss, he rose and twirled the garter above his head.

Her gaze slid to Tommy, who hadn't moved to join the single men in the center of the dance floor. Thank God. She really didn't need him to be the one who caught the garter. Not that he appeared eager to win the opportunity to slide the garter up her leg.

Brody, on the other hand, looked more than willing to catch the garter. She didn't want him to, which said a lot. They had to talk. Soon.

Dante used his fingers to slingshot the garter into the air. Julie followed the high upward arc and its fall back down, directly in Brody's direction. Breath held, she prayed for someone else to grab it. *Please, please, for the love of God, please.*

Brody reached up. *No!* Right before his fingers closed around it, another hand shot up past his and snatched it from the air.

Air whooshed out of her lungs and she froze to the spot as she realized, in consternation, who stood there with a look of pure satisfaction on his face, the delicate piece of lace dangling from his finger.

*Tommy.*

The worse of two evils.

Oh, God. What the hell had just happened?

Dismay flooded over her. *Be careful what you wish for.*

Cait hurried over, grabbed her hands, and tugged her forward. The pull toward the empty chair knocked her right out of her daze. "W-What are you doing?"

"It's your turn."

"My turn for what?" She hated the high-pitched squeak that had entered her voice, but she knew exactly what was about to happen…and it scared the hell out of her. "We don't have to do this, Cait! Seriously."

"Oh, yes we do."

When the bride pushed Julie into the chair, all she could do was sit there stiffly, hands gripping the satin fabric covering the chair, and stare wide-eyed at Tommy as he sauntered toward her, twirling that damn piece of lace-covered elastic on his damn finger.

*This cannot be happening.*

He dropped to one knee before her, his blond head bending too close to a part of her anatomy that had started throbbing with unbidden desire. She bunched her fingers into the satin, taking a short, sharp gasp of air. He slipped off one of her heels and inched the garter over her foot, up her calf, over her knee, and then beyond, until his hands were hidden beneath her skirt, heading straight for the stocking tops and garter belt she suddenly fervently wished she hadn't worn on a whim.

Oh. My. God. This really *was* happening.

The tips of his fingers caressed her skin as he slid the garter into place in the middle of her thigh. Between her legs, the throb intensified, and she bit her lip to keep a groan from emerging.

*No*, she told herself firmly. *I feel nothing.* She didn't feel a damn thing. Tommy did *not* make her feel like this anymore. *Damn it, girl. Get it together!*

*Snap.* A slight sting hit her upper thigh.

Had he just plucked one of her garter belt ribbons?

She swallowed. No way. He wouldn't.

*Think of something else. Anything else.*

Oh God, she couldn't. He was consuming her whole being. His touch was burning her alive. When he lifted his head and she saw a cocky, knowing half smile on his face, she was certain she'd incinerate right on the spot.

Or drop straight through the floor in mortification.

He placed her heel back on, stood, and offered his hand. She did *not* want to touch him. All she wanted was to escape. To flee from that smug look on his face and the crowd grinning like a bunch of clowns. But she had no choice. She reluctantly slid her fingers into his hand, and he helped her up. But he didn't let go. She tugged. He held on. With an iron grip. They stared at each other.

Her face heated. "I need to get back to Brody."

When she pulled at her hand again, his grip tightened even more. "But you're coming home to *me*."

Only then did he release her and saunter off the dance floor, leaving her staring after him, completely breathless.

Shaking herself out of her stupor, she went on shaking legs to stand beside Brody.

*But you're coming home to me.*

What on earth had gotten into the man? And why had that comment made her knees weak and shivers *zing* down her spine?

"Do you want to see Dante and Cait off on their honeymoon?"

At the deep, intrusive voice of the man who did nothing to help her forget her unwanted obsession, she jumped. Exhaustion suddenly had her wilting. "Yeah, let's go watch them start their future together. Then I think I'd like to go home."

He nodded and led them outside.

When Dante and Cait appeared at the top of the steps, looking like the perfect wax couple atop a wedding cake, their joy shining like beacons of love as they held hands and ran toward the waiting white limo, Julie could have broken down and cried. From the happiness for her friends, from the longing in her heart…from the fear that she would never find that kind of love.

As they reached the limo, Dante grabbed Cait around the waist and kissed his blushing bride. She gazed adoringly up at her new husband. Julie read the whispered, "I love you, Caitlyn," from Dante's lips before they disappeared inside the car and the driver closed the door.

With the tumult of emotions from the wedding bombarding her, Julie's heart squeezed tightly in her chest. She just wanted to go home, crawl into bed, curl up into a ball, and forget this whole awful night. She turned to Brody, startled by the intense way he was studying her. "What?"

"What are you thinking right now?"

She swallowed. "Why?"

"The expression on your face when you watched Dante and Cait, it was so sad, almost…envious." He gently touched her cheek. "It makes me want to do whatever is in my power to erase it."

Her heart melted a little. But she knew it was time to end this. Brody was a wonderful, thoughtful, attentive man. He'd make someone an amazing husband one day.

But it wouldn't be her.

"Brody, I don't think… I'm so sorry, but this thing between us… It's not going to work."

His eyes softened. "Don't you think I know that?"

She stepped back, completely unprepared for that.

"I see the way you look at him," he added.

He didn't say Tommy's name, but there was no one else

Brody could mean.

Crap. And here she'd always thought she'd hidden her feelings so well.

Apparently not.

How many other people saw the truth?

As if reading her thoughts, he said, "There's always been speculation about you two in the locker room."

Oh. God. She squeezed her eyes shut briefly. "Speculation about the two of us, or speculation about me?"

Brody shifted his weight and grimaced. Terrific. Well, she had her answer.

Her heart fell to her stomach. "So everyone knows I have a thing for Tommy?" she asked, feeling slightly ill.

"Most of us have wondered. Figured." He pushed out a breath. "Okay, fine. Most of us knew."

*Please. Just kill me now.*

"Why'd you ask me out, then?"

He shrugged. "Same reason you accepted."

She blinked. They gazed at each other for a long moment, and suddenly a lightbulb went off. Her jaw dropped. "My God. *You* have feelings for someone *you* don't want to have feelings for?"

"Yep. My best friend's wife."

Wow. And Julie'd thought *she* had a dilemma. "Damn, that sucks. I'm so sorry."

He gave her a wry, humorless smile. "Can't control who we fall in love with, can we?"

She let out a sympathetic breath.

So Tommy had been right. Brody really *did* have a hidden agenda when he'd asked her out. But she totally understood, and she was okay with it. Brody completely got her, because he was living the agony himself. He didn't want to be in love with his best friend's wife any more than she wanted to be in love with Tommy. Damn, it was nice to have someone who was facing the same battle.

"Yeah. Life would be a lot easier if we could control our hearts."

"Julie." Brody hesitated for a moment then asked, "If you had a chance, a real, honest-to-goodness chance, to be with Tommy, would you?"

That was the question of her life, wasn't it?

She pushed out a sigh. "He kissed me that night after he saw us at the park. The first time he'd ever kissed me. Oh, Brody, it was awful. That kiss wasn't a man opening his eyes and suddenly seeing his childhood friend as a woman he can't keep his hands off of." She grimaced, embarrassed to admit it, but saying it aloud somehow helped the pain. "There was no passion in the kiss. Not even a hint."

Brody's head tilted and he looked skeptical. "Are you saying he actually killed your attraction to him?"

She gave a short bark of laughter. "I'd *love* for it to be that easy, but, sadly, no. He still can flip my switch with one stupid look. No, I meant it was obvious *he* felt no passion."

"Okay. More suckage. But you didn't answer my question. Would you be with him if you could?"

"It's hard to imagine being with a man whose only reaction to kissing you was abject horror while professing adamantly that it was a mistake."

"Damn, Jules. What the hell is *wrong* with the man?" Scowling, Brody worked his jaw as he glared into the street.

She sighed. "Hey, don't get mad on my behalf, okay? Tommy has always been honest with me. He's never led me on. Never pretended for a second there was anything more between us than friendship. The kiss happened in a moment of confused emotion." She banded her arms across her middle and studied her feet. "Did it end the way I've always dreamed about? No. Did it confirm some hard truths I didn't want to face? Yeah. It did."

Brody's empathetic eyes drilled into her. "He's a damn fool, you know that?"

She smiled weakly. "I like to tell myself that from time to time."

He offered his elbow. "Shall we call it a night?"

Julie threaded her arm through his and, as they started to walk, her high heel landed on a loose rock. It rolled, and she lost her balance. To keep from falling, she twisted, trying to grab onto Brody. The quick movement seized the muscles in her lower back and she froze in place. After a second, she tried to straighten, but her muscles screamed in pain, keeping her hunched over.

"Oh, shit," she whispered.

"Jules, are you okay?"

"Damn it. I just pulled a muscle in my back."

# CHAPTER 8

The persistent thumping on the front door had Tommy racing the dogs to open it. The sight of Julie cradled in Brody's arms with pain etched in her pale face made his blood run cold.

"Julie? Wh— How—" Words failed Tommy as he tried to make sense of what he was seeing.

Julie lifted her head off Brody's shoulder and looked directly at him. "T-Tommy."

He automatically reached for her, needing to have her in his arms, needing to protect her, but Brody pushed by him into the house.

"Where's her room?" Brody asked.

"I'll take her." Tommy reached for her again, but the other man tightened his grip, turning away.

"Never mind. I'll find it myself."

Rage filling him, Tommy rounded on him, blocking his path, and stared him in the eyes. With deadly calm, he said, "Give her to me. Now."

Brody brows inched up, but he gingerly handed over Julie, who immediately laid her head on Tommy's shoulder. He kissed her forehead and whispered, "I've got you, baby."

Without thought, he turned and strode right to his room. Warrior and Lucy barked, padding after them, their heads both tilted up, as though they knew something was wrong with their mistress.

"Now, what *happened*?" he asked as his shoulder bumped his bedroom door open and stepped inside.

"She twisted her back," Brody said. "Or pulled something."

After Tommy gently placed her on the bed, he tucked pillows under and around her head. Then he gingerly sat on the mattress and braced one arm on the other side of her body, leaning so he hovered over her, blocking Brody's view of her. "Julie." He brushed her hair back. "How are you feeling?"

"Fan-flipping-tastic." She winced as she slowly eased onto her back to look up at him.

A small smile came to his lips, but when Brody inched in, Tommy sent him a scathing look. "I think you've done enough. You can leave now."

Julie shook her head. "This isn't Brody's fault. It's called four-inch heels meets random stone. I threw out my back. You know it's happened before. It's been worse, actually."

"I tried to get her to go to the emergency room, but—"

She waved him off. "Heck, no. A few muscles relaxers, pain relievers, and I'll be good as new."

Brody leaned in, trying to nudge Tommy out of the way. At the intrusion, he stiffened and kept himself firmly in place. Turning nose to nose, he glared at Brody, daring him to come any closer. The other man quirked a brow and his lips twitched.

What did he find so goddamn funny?

Either way, the guy finally took the hint and straightened, running a hand through his hair. "Do you want me to stay, Jules?"

"No, she doesn't want you to stay," Tommy said through clenched teeth.

"Tommy, please," she admonished. Slowly, she turned toward Brody and reached out her hand, which he took.

Jealousy flared white hot through Tommy when she squeezed the other guy's hand and gave him an affectionate smile. He wanted to break their connection and toss Brody out of the house, but he forced himself not to react, waiting to see what Julie would say.

"No, it's okay. Tommy's here. I'm just going to rest anyway. Go on home. But thanks."

Tommy couldn't help sending a satisfied smirk at Brody, and he was rewarded with another amused twitch of the lips. What the hell was this guy's deal?

"I'll stop by tomorrow, then, okay?"

"Okay," she said, and sent him a soft smile.

He paused, shifting his weight as his gaze bounced between Tommy and her, as if expecting him to lean back so they could have a proper good-bye. Not fucking likely. Instead, Tommy nodded toward the door. "You know the way out."

The man sucked through his teeth before nodding and leaving. As he watched his retreat, again Tommy was struck with the sense that Brody was laughing at him. It was really starting to piss him off.

When the front door shut, Julie chided, "You didn't have to be so darn rude."

"He doesn't have to be such a jackass." He didn't want Brody to be a topic of conversation, either. He wanted the man completely gone, now that he'd left. "How bad is it?" he asked.

"*Meh*. It's not that bad, really. Been worse. I just need a muscle relaxer, some anti-inflammatories, and some rest."

He kissed her forehead and scooted back off the bed. "I'll get the meds." He looked at the dogs. "Come on, guys, let her rest."

"No. Let them stay."

He wouldn't argue. Neither Lucy nor Warrior had jumped up on her as they usually did when she came home. They just sat at the side of the bed, peering silently up at her. Protecting her. Exactly like he wanted to.

After he went to the kitchen and grabbed two pills and a bottle of water, he returned to the bedroom. She started to push herself back up, but he placed a hand on her shoulder, stilling her.

"What do you think you're doing?"

"I'd like to go to my own room, if you don't mind."

Actually, he did mind. He didn't know what possessed him to bring her straight in here instead of into her own room, but he liked seeing her laid out on his bed.

"Besides," she continued. "Wouldn't you like to change, too?"

Before she'd arrived, he'd been in the process of doing just that. He'd gotten as far as sliding off his jacket and tie and unbuttoning the first three buttons of his shirt before the banging on the door had interrupted him. Getting comfortable now was the last of his worries. "I'm fine. Let's get you into something more comfortable first."

Alarm dashed across her face. "Uh. I don't need help with my clothes, Tommy."

Didn't stop him from wanting to help, though. "At least

let me help you to your room and get the clothes out for you."

He went to help her sit up, and she smacked him away. "No. I've got this."

And there was that vicious independent streak coming through. He held up his hands, fully aware that fighting her would make her even more irritated. She'd made it halfway into a sitting position when she gasped sharply and her entire body froze.

"Yeah, okay," she gritted out. "Not happening."

No, he didn't see this move happening at all. Until those relaxers kicked in, her muscles were going to seize every time she tried to sit up. He helped her lie back down.

"I'll run to your room and grab you a change of clothing."

He took his time choosing a set of casual fleece PJs, giving her ten minutes before he returned, only to come to an abrupt halt in the doorway.

She had inched herself up so she reclined on the pillows and had unzipped the side of her dress, which had peeled back to reveal one black-lace-covered breast. Why he was surprised she'd taken the initiative to start the changing process, he didn't know. She was always firmly determined to do things herself.

Wracked by pain, she appeared to be even more stubbornly resolute. A trait that both awed and frustrated the hell out of him.

He swallowed, as he couldn't help noticing that the lace gave an enticing peek at the pert nipple beneath. Shaking himself, he hurried to the other side of the bed, as Julie used her foot to kick off her shoes. "Do"—he cleared his throat— "you need any help?"

"No." She planted both feet on the mattress, bending her

knees. The skirt rode all the way up to her hips. His gaze zeroed in on the pale skin above the thigh-high stockings and the silky black ribbons that kept them in place.

He'd known she had on a garter belt. He'd played with the satin ties as he slid the wedding garter over her thigh, and just as before, pure possessiveness sliced through him at the thought she'd worn it for Brody and not for him.

A pained grunt broke into his thoughts as she tried to push the dress down her hips. Her toned, flat stomach drew his gaze and he bit back a curse.

"I can't lift my butt. Can you pull the dress the rest of the way off?"

He swallowed. *All the way off?*

So she'd be lying there, on *his* bed, wearing nothing but a bra, panties, and enticing garter? He didn't know if he could do it. Already his pants were tightening, and he felt like a total ass for it. He glanced at her. The trust in her eyes made him feel like an even bigger ass.

*You are not proving yourself worthy, Sparks.*

If anything, he was disproving everything he'd convinced himself of at the wedding—that he would be able to make love to Julie. Real love.

How? Because he was getting a fucking hard-on even though she was lying there in pain. He could feel the lust building—while she was hurt. What would happen when she was healthy?

*No.* He was better than just his dick. He could do this.

He squared his shoulders and gingerly tugged the dress over her hips and down her legs.

*Fuck me.*

"Help— Help me with the garter belt," she said with a

grimace.

Using an incredible amount of restraint *not* to glide his hand up the inside of her thigh first, he reached around to her lower back and fumbled with the tiny clasp, fingers trembling, until he was able to release it from around her waist.

*She's hurt, she's hurt, she's hurt.*

He repeated the words as, one by one, he unhooked the four satin-covered fasteners that held the hose to the beribboned lace. Then, with his heart in his throat—and his cock making a frantic bid to break through his zipper—he slowly rolled the first stocking down over her knee, down her calf, and over her foot. The chant didn't help. If anything, it made him even more aware of what he was doing.

*Undressing Julie.*

As he removed the other stocking, he couldn't stop the vision of what he would've done next if he'd been stripping Julie in the way he suddenly wanted to, for a whole different reason than he was.

Hell, who was he kidding? They wouldn't even have gotten this far. The stockings would've stayed on, and he'd either have his head or cock thrust firmly between her legs.

He leaned over her and slid off the clingy lace belt that still encased the beautiful swell of her hips. After he tugged it off, he stared at the minuscule piece of material in his hand, swallowed heavily, and slowly lifted his head.

Their eyes connected.

He couldn't look away. He could feel the heat in his own eyes as he communicated exactly what he was feeling with his gaze and not his mouth—and God how he wanted to communicate with his mouth, right between those beautiful thighs. *Jesus.* He tore his gaze away and mentally cursed himself.

This was not a thought he approved of when it came to Julie. This was how he thought about the women he took to his bed who didn't mean anything to him, no more than he'd meant to them. Their focus had been on the sex, the pleasure… the physical gratification. Julie *meant* something to him. With her it *had* to be different. Long kisses. Holding her damn hand. Treating her sweetly. Any other behavior was unacceptable.

Maybe her getting hurt had been some kind of omen. A way for him to see that he was incapable of change. That he would always be the male version of his mom. It was all he knew. All he'd seen. The endless parade of men.. And as soon as he'd started dating, he'd followed the exact same pattern. The older he got, the more he realized he was cut from the same cloth as his mother—because no woman interested him for longer than a really good night in bed. By morning, he was gone, and on to the next.

What if he did that to Julie?

He needed to reassess his plan. Staying away from her was the better option, after all.

"You can give me the outfit now," she said. "I'll get it on."

"I'll help." When he stepped forward, she started shaking her head.

"Uh. No. I've got it." When he hesitated, she said, "Seriously. I've. Got. It. Why don't you, uh, go do something else?"

As he turned to leave, tension knotted his shoulders. There had been no way she hadn't seen his blatant desire for her. And her response had been to tell him to leave. Because of fucking Brody Minton?

Tommy didn't give a rat's ass what the universe was trying

to tell him. Julie would *not* be with that man. And if that meant Tommy had to keep his cock in his pants for the next fucking year, he'd keep his damn cock in his pants, and like it.

Julie deserved better than *both* of them.

. . .

Julie really hated being in Tommy's bed. The pillows smelled like him. His scent surrounded her. Suffocated her. She'd go back to her own bed in a hot minute if she could, but with her muscles all tensed up, she was pretty much stationary. And there was no way she was asking him to carry her again.

*Hell*, no.

Not after what she'd imagined she'd seen in his eyes as he'd looked at her almost naked body. Had the desire really been there, or had it been her own desperation rearing up again?

If it had been any other man, there wouldn't have been a second of doubt in her mind. But he wasn't any other man. He was Tommy. And Tommy came with a long history that directly contradicted anything she thought she might have seen. But…

*No*. She gave herself a mental shake. It *hadn't* been there. He did not want her. Not that way.

When he walked into the bedroom carrying some muscle ointment and an ice pack, she focused on petting the top of Lucy's head.

The pup whined but pushed her head up into Julie's palm.

"Come on," he said. "Let's get you under the covers. That muscle relaxer should start kicking in soon."

After he pulled the covers back, he helped her under them—thank God she'd been able to pull on the fleece sweats by herself—and tucked the blankets around her, then he leaned down and kissed her cheek. The heat of his lips seared her skin. He lifted slightly to gaze down at her. As she met his green eyes, her breath hitched hard in her lungs. Had they just dropped to her lips?

*Don't do that!*

"I'm going to take good care of you," he murmured. "Now I think we need to get some sleep. It's been a long day."

He straightened and grabbed some clothes out of the dresser. Over the course of the last hour, his black shirt had come untucked and he'd rolled the sleeves up to his elbows. His blond hair, perfectly styled hours ago, now stuck up in odd directions, as though he'd continuously run his hand through it.

Guilt swamped over her. Here she was picking apart every one of his actions, while he was simply worried about her pain level.

He dropped his clothes on the end of the bed and unbuttoned his shirt, paying no mind to the fact that she lay mere feet away, acting as if she found herself in his bed every day, watching him get undressed.

When he finished with the buttons and peeled his shirt back over his shoulders, revealing his chiseled six-pack, she bit the inside of her bottom lip. His muscles moved, holding her captivated. A wave of lust pooled low in her stomach. Her mouth went dry, and she had to force a swallow.

She knew he didn't think it was a big deal, since he walked around here shirtless all the time. But it was a big deal to her. It had always been.

Pain or no pain, Tommy's actions still made forbidden thoughts fly through her head.

God, she was pathetic.

Closing her eyes, she turned her head into the pillows, blocking out the image of him. She carefully shifted onto her side, turning her body away from the empty side of the bed, needing to avoid looking at him.

When the mattress dipped, her eyes sprang open. "What are you doing?"

"Getting into bed. What do you think?"

Gingerly she rolled over to look at him, then immediately wished she hadn't, since the jerk didn't have a damn shirt on and his well-defined pecs dusted with blond hair filled her vision, tormenting her. She pointed to the door. "I think you need to get your ass down the hall into *my* bed?"

Oh man, she'd liked giving him that order way too much. He needed to go. Now.

"You're kidding, right?" The hurt confusion on his face irked her even more. The man had no clue why she didn't want him in the same bed as her.

"Uh, no? What the hell, Tommy?"

"No way am I leaving you on your own, hurt like this. You couldn't even get up to go to your own room a minute ago. Besides, it's not like I haven't done this before."

"That was years ago, when I was home from college. I've pulled my back since then, and I've done just fine on my own."

"I. Don't. Care." He slid into bed, obviously intending to completely ignore her wishes. "It's what best friends do."

*Best friends*, she reminded herself sternly as her heart sank ten different ways. *That's all this is.*

She clenched her eyes closed, her entire body stiffening as the blankets shifted, and his naked leg brushed against hers. He spooned up next to her, wrapping his arm around her waist and perching his chin on her shoulder. A half-naked Tommy all cuddled up behind her—*holy Mother of God.*

"How you feeling?"

How the hell did he *think*? Like she was jumping out of her damn skin. "Fine," she managed to croak.

"Come on, I'm serious. Does it still hurt as much?"

Oh. My. God. He wanted to *talk*? All she could think about was the feel of his freaking *naked* body pressed behind hers, him holding her tight.

Okay. *Deep breath.* At least he was trying to give her something to do other than wanting to wiggle her body backward, closer to his. "No, I'm b-better."

"Meds working?"

"Moving…a little easier. Making me sleepy, too."

"Good. Slide your top off."

Her eyes popped open again. "W-What?"

"I'll massage your shoulders. You're so rigid. I also want to put some muscle cream on your back. Trust me, this stuff works great."

"I'm fine." There was no possible way she was allowing him to touch her like that.

He scooted backward then rose to kneel beside her. "Come on, Julie. I feel terrible you're hurting, and it's something I can do. Let me help. Please."

The pleading in his voice made her waver. "Fine. But I'll keep my shirt on, thank you."

"You know as well as I do that you can't get a proper massage with a shirt on. It's not a big deal. Take it off."

*Not a big deal*, she mimicked in her mind. Of course it wasn't. For *him.*

God. How many more reminders would she need before it

finally sank in?

Sighing, she tugged on the sleeves and pulled the top over her head. Thank God she still had her bra on. Easing onto her stomach, she balled the shirt under her chin. As the sharp smell of mint hit her nose, his warm hands rubbed into the sore muscles across her lower back first. The medicated rub heated her skin, penetrating deep. But the heat was nothing in comparison to the way his palms scorched her flesh as he moved to knead her shoulders. She kept focus on the way the massage made her feel and not on who was doing it. The more he manipulated the stiff muscles of her shoulders, the more she felt the tension leave her body.

Until he unclasped the back of her bra—then all the tension poured back in. She gasped. "Tommy! What are you doing?"

His hands hesitated for a moment. "Rubbing your back."

His tone made her annoyed at herself. He was just trying to make her feel better. It wasn't his fault that unclasping her bra made *her* immediately think of sex.

She scrunched farther down onto the mattress, trying again to focus only on the massage and not the towering, dominating man who had his hands roaming over her naked back. It didn't work quite as well this time. She could feel his warm breath on her neck as he bent over her and the gentle way he handled her, as if she were made of precious glass.

She inhaled, and her eyes drooped. She blinked a few times, astonished at her sudden sleepiness, thankful that the muscles relaxers had finally worked their way into her system. She gave a drowsy smile. Well, if she couldn't ignore him, at least she'd pass out.

His hands worked their way down the middle of her spine, then spread out to her sides. Again he kneaded every bit of tension out of her muscles, the mixture of meds and his lulling massage making her feel like a puddle of honey. She sighed, sinking deeper and deeper into the fuzzy shirt under her chin.

She needed some good, solid rest, so she could beat this thing and get back on her feet. Fast.

She couldn't let him take care of her.

If she did, she might never recover from the damage he'd do to her heart.

# CHAPTER 9

The soft, even breathing coming from beside him slowly penetrated Tommy's dreamless sleep. He blinked open his eyes, immediately aware of the feminine body curled under the blankets next to him.

*Julie.*

He studied the ceiling before turning his head on the pillow to stare at the naked shoulder peeking out from under the covers, tempting him. On the rare occasion he woke up next to a woman, his immediate instinct was to get her out of his bed—out of his house. Or vice versa. He didn't feel that need right now. Not at all. It was quite the opposite, actually. He wanted to roll over to her side and wake her with deliberate touches. Kiss the beautiful skin of her shoulder.

Was that only because he hadn't slept with her yet? Would that change the moment he did? If his past was any indication, the answer was yes. Then he'd lose her. If he did nothing, he would eventually lose her to someone else.

God, both outcomes scared the hell out of him. *She* scared the hell out of him.

As he glanced at her bare back again, he smothered a groan. He should've made her put her top back on last night. Thank God he'd had the foresight to re-hook her bra. After he'd massaged her shoulders for a few minutes, he'd glanced up to see she'd passed out. He hadn't had the heart to wake her.

And he still didn't. So he needed to get the hell out of this room. Before he did something he'd regret.

Or worse, that he *didn't* regret…

He slid out of bed and glanced at the clock.

Eight thirty a.m.

Mac would be here in thirty minutes. He had called his friend last night while waiting for Julie to change into her fleece PJs. He wanted to do something special for her so she didn't have to lift a finger today. Cooking was not his specialty. Luckily, he happened to know a Michelin-star chef who loved to cook for others.

He gathered some clothes from the closet, then quietly called the dogs off the end of the bed and headed out of the room, closing the door behind them. After unlocking the doggie door and filling their bowls, he went into the bathroom and showered.

Just as he stepped into the living room, a soft knock came from the front door. Tommy cringed, waiting for the animals to start barking and wake Julie, but they didn't utter a peep. As he made his way to let Mac in, he peered into the kitchen to see their bowls empty and not one dog in sight. God, he loved that doggie door.

Tommy ushered Mac in, who had two bags of groceries in his arms.

"How much do I owe you?" he asked, knowing nothing in those bags had been cheap. Not if Mac was making it.

Shaking his head, his friend set the bags on the counter. "My treat." When Tommy immediately opened his mouth to object, his friend held up his hand. "No. Seriously. The last meal I made for someone else was Dante and Cait. I miss cooking for other people, so I really want to do this."

"If you're sure, but I owe you, okay? Anything. All you have to do is ask."

Mac smiled. "I'll keep that in mind. You never know when you need to cash in a favor."

"You know, if you miss cooking so much, you should get your ass back in a swanky restaurant." Tommy rounded the counter and came to stand beside his friend in front of the stove.

The easy smile on Mac's lips vanished as a haunted look darkened the man's eyes and his jaw tensed. "That's not an option."

Then he turned away, opening cabinets. Noting the tension radiating from his friend, Tommy dropped the subject. "Whatchya looking for?"

"Pots and pans."

He pointed to the cabinet two doors down.

"Ah. Thanks." Mac grabbed a pot, filled it with water, and set it on the stove.

"So what are we making for breakfast?" Tommy asked.

"A classic. Eggs Benedict with a side of sliced fresh fruit." Mac started pulling items from the grocery bag—eggs, English muffins, strawberries, pineapple. And the ingredients kept coming.

"Jeez. And for lunch and dinner, too, I take it?"

Mac made a face at him. "Lunch is a nice lobster bisque and mixed green salad with a red-wine vinaigrette. And for dinner, we're going all out. Dover sole with crabmeat and seafood stuffing."

Most of this sounded Greek to Tommy. He sighed. "You do realize Julie will know I didn't make this alone, right?"

Mac chuckled. "Sorry about that. When I got to shopping, I got a little carried away."

The statement made Tommy wonder even more why Mac refused to be a chef again. He obviously loved to cook. Had been—still was—damn good at it. What could have happened that made his friend stop doing something he loved so much?

Mac unwrapped the fresh English muffins and thrust them at Tommy, breaking into his thoughts. "Throw these in the oven. Then we'll start on the hollandaise sauce."

Mac took the lead on poaching the eggs, which was fine with Tommy. If they weren't scrambled he had no idea how to fix them. He watched Mac slide the eggs into simmering water while Tommy sautéed the Canadian bacon.

"How is Julie, anyway?" Mac asked, breaking the companionable silence.

"She was hurting pretty badly last night. I'm hoping the muscle cream and relaxers have worked some their magic today."

Mac removed the eggs from the water with a slotted spoon and placed them on a paper towel, dabbing off the excess water. "Glad it wasn't worse." He paused a moment before saying, "Mike let the guys know you're coming back tomorrow. Thought I'd give you a heads up that some of the guys aren't too thrilled."

Tommy had expected that. Right before it all imploded

around him, several of the guys didn't even want to be in the gym while he was there. Damn, he must have been a real douche. "Mike said I had a lot to prove, and I know I do. Not just to him and Ethan, either. To everyone. I wronged a lot of people there at the end, so I get that it's going to take time for people to trust me again."

"I won't sugarcoat it. The guys were glad to see you go back then." His friend looked over at him as Tommy winced. "There were a couple of times I wanted to punch you in the face myself. Especially when you'd show up an hour late for practice, then be a complete dickhead to everyone around you."

He shook his head. "I don't have any excuses, Mac. Something happened to me after I won that belt. I changed, and not for the better. Priorities got skewed." He slashed a hand through his hair. "Some people handle fame with grace. I was not one of them. If I get a second chance, believe me, the outcome won't be the same. I realize I have way more to lose now."

"Unfortunately, it takes losing everything you have to realize what meant the most." Mac squinted for a second, then gave his head a shake.

Tommy wanted to offer his friend support, but Mac was a very private person and wouldn't appreciate the gesture, so he said, "Anyway, the guys may get a bit of a reprieve. I'm going to postpone my return until Julie is up and moving around on her own."

"I figured that would be the case." Mac stepped back from the stove and clapped his hands. "Okay. Sauce is done. All we've got to do is set the plate. You want to do that?"

"Yeah, sure."

Mac instructed Tommy on how to layer the English muffin just right. "Now drizzle the sauce on top."

After he'd done so, and added a serving of grapes, pineapples, and strawberries, he placed the plate on a tray with a tall glass of orange juice.

Mac frowned.

"What?" Tommy asked.

"It needs something. Hold on." He sliced another ring from the pineapple, then cut away the hard exterior and carved out chunks until it had six pointed sides like a star. Grabbing a toothpick, he stabbed it through one of the smaller strawberries and threaded it through the middle of the pineapple so the red fruit sat on top. Then he placed it on the corner of the plate.

"Damn, man. Really?" It looked like a tasty flower, making the entire plate come to life.

Mac shrugged. "It's all about presentation."

"Well, you got that down, dude. Julie will know for *damn* sure I had nothing to do with this."

Mac clapped him on the shoulder. "It's the thought that counts. Go feed your woman."

*His woman.* Damn, but he liked the sound of that.

"I'll be back to help with lunch," he said.

Tommy paused with the tray. "You don't have to do that."

Mac lifted a brow. "So, you're going to make the lobster bisque yourself?"

Tommy puffed out a breath. "Good point. Okay, I'll see you in a few hours."

Chuckling, his friend started to leave.

"Hey, Mac?"

He stopped and looked back at him.

"Thanks. Seriously."

Mac nodded before leaving.

Tommy made his way to his bedroom. Julie was still curled up under the covers, asleep. Those pills had really knocked her out. He placed the tray on the nightstand and whispered her name.

A light groan was his answer, then her eyes slowly opened.

He smiled at her. "Morning."

She blinked a couple of times, lifting her head to look around the room. "Oh, yeah." She sighed. "Damn, it wasn't a bad dream." She squinted at the clock. "Is it really almost ten?"

"Yep. You needed the sleep."

"And what else am I going to do when I can barely move?" She slowly rolled onto her back. The blanket slipped, giving him an enticing view of her cleavage. She inhaled sharply, grabbing onto the material and clutching it to her chest. "Where's my shirt?"

He snatched it up off the floor. "It must've fallen last night while you were sleeping."

As she took it from him, she motioned with her finger for him to turn around. Reluctantly, he did. He could hear the swish of the fabric and knew she was in the process of pulling the shirt over her head. Possibly with her breasts jutted forward, nipples erect, as she arched to tug it down. He breathed out, running a hand over his eyes. God, he needed to get a grip.

"What smells so good?" she asked, and Tommy was thankful to think of something other than her naked breasts.

Turning around, he pointed to the nightstand. "Breakfast."

She tilted her head up and her eyes grew wide. "You made that?"

"Yeah. Well, no. Mac did. But I put it on the plate." He

gave her a boyish smile.

"Mac was here? Wow. Those pills really did knock me out." She eased up to recline against the pillows.

"How are you feeling?"

"Actually, not bad. Between all the meds and that cream, the muscles are just a bit sore. Probably should do some stretches later to work out the rest."

Inhaling, she pushed the covers back.

Alarm shot through him. "What are you doing?"

She quirked a brow. "I have to pee. Is that okay?"

He bit back a smile and was relieved to see that she was able to get out of the bed on her own. Though her posture was a bit stiff and she was a little on the slow side, she was moving around easily. When she returned, she climbed back into bed. He sat on the edge of the mattress, picked up the tray, and placed it over her lap. Before she could grasp the silverware, he lifted the fork and knife, cut up the food, then offered her the fork. He didn't even try to give her a bite of it.

Amusement pursed her lips as she studied the food. "You know me so well, don't you?"

"That one of your turnoffs is a man trying to feed you? Yes. I know this. Which is why I'm not placing that fork anywhere near your mouth."

His comment hung in the air, and he watched for her reaction, which was immediate. As her entire body stiffened, her gaze shot up from the plate to his, a confused expression twisting her lovely face. He thought the meaning was pretty clear—he had no intentions of turning her off. He wanted to turn her *on*. But apparently she still had no clue how hot he found her and wasn't connecting his intentions.

It was high time to change that. If he was really going to

prove that he could be with Julie, then he had to *be* with Julie. Which meant he had to start touching her, kissing her—and hopefully more. The prospect both excited and terrified him at the same time. The whole leaving thing still worried him. A lot. But nothing ventured, nothing gained.

"Tommy—"

The doorbell rang, making Julie blink and lightly shake her head. Tommy let out a silent curse before striding from the room to answer it. Whoever it was better have a fucking *damn* good reason for being here. He flung open the door.

Brody stood on the other side, a white paper bag that smelled of fresh bagels and two coffees cradled in the crook of his other arm. "I brought Jules breakfast."

"I've already cooked her breakfast."

"You cooked?"

He didn't like the surprise in the other man's voice. "Yeah, I did. And I also have lunch and dinner covered, so you can forget about stopping by with those, too."

Brody studied him for a moment, then walked past him into the house.

What the fuck!

"Hey. I didn't invite you in."

The man didn't even pause. "Not your house. Don't need your permission."

Tommy latched a hand on Brody's shoulder and yanked him around. Brody's eyes flashed as his jaw tightened.

"You're really pissing me off, and we need to set some boundaries," Tommy said.

"You're right, we do." He held up fingers as he counted. "One: You don't get to set those boundaries. Two: Jules does. Three: Unless she tells me I can't come in, I'm coming in.

Four: Got it?"

Tommy stared at the bastard in outrage. "You've been around for, what? A couple of fucking weeks?" He leaned into his face. "You don't get to come in here and start making demands."

And there it was again—that amusement in the slight twitch of his lips. Tommy fisted his hands tightly, the need to knock him into next Sunday so strong he could barely contain it.

"Oh, so it's a time deal now? You think because you've known her longer, another man can't come along and take your place?" Brody chuckled. He actually *chuckled*. "Here's the thing. I don't want to be her best friend. She already has one of those." He poked his finger at Tommy's chest. "You." He shifted closer, nose-to-nose. "*I* want to be everything you're *not* to her, and I'm pretty damn certain there are a few important things she's not getting from you—which she can most definitely get from me. Trust me, I am more than willing to volunteer for the job."

Fury had Tommy stepping right into Brody, pushing him backward despite the other man's greater bulk. He poked his own finger into the jerk's chest. "You so much as lay a hand on that woman and I'll make sure you *never* step foot in the cage again. Julie is *mine*. So, back. The fuck. *Off*."

The hardness eased from the man's eyes before a cocky tilt curved his lips. "Game on, bro. You want her? Then you need to truly make her yours. Before I make her *mine*."

"Dude," he ground out, "you are walking a very fine line."

"I'm not afraid of you, Tommy." And in truth, Brody really didn't look the least bit daunted. "I think that's why you're so pissed off, because you're used to intimidating Julie's dates and scaring them off so easily. But I'm warning you, until you actually claim that woman, *publically*, I'm not going anywhere."

Stunned at the man's audacity—and at that last accusation—Tommy could only watch him turn and stroll into her room.

*Had* he unknowingly used intimidation to get rid of any man who ventured too near Julie? Yeah, okay, he'd warned a few of them off while she'd been in the restroom at the clubs over the years. Mostly because he'd sensed a bad vibe about the guy and wanted to keep her safe. That had been his job—that would *always* be his job. One he didn't plan to relinquish any time soon.

But…there was a ring of truth to Brody's words. Before the other fighter had started sniffing around Julie, Tommy had never once been jealous. And now he realized there'd never been an opportunity to be. It'd been too damn easy to get rid of any possible competition for Julie's affections. But with Brody, Tommy's jealousy had roared to life in full force… because the man had never flinched. He wasn't afraid of him. And that had made Tommy see red.

Jesus H. Christ. Was *he* the reason Julie had been alone all this years? Had he unconsciously kept her all to himself, and unattached, while he continued to have a grand ole time with any woman he met?

If that were true, he was an even bigger bastard than he'd realized. And holy hell, he had a shit-ton of crap to make up to her for.

. . .

Julie sneaked a surreptitious peek at Tommy. He was still scowling. An hour ago, she'd been so happy to see Brody when he'd walked into the room...but Tommy had stormed in right after him and taken up residence in a corner chair, bringing along a frosty tension that had sucked the air right from the room.

He hadn't moved since.

She tried again to budge him. "Tommy, Brody is here if I need anything. Please, go and take some time for yourself. You've waited on me hand and foot since last night."

A muscle jumped in his jaw. "I'm fine where I am."

Brody leaned forward with a knowing half smile. "I'd take her up on her offer, man. From what I've heard, Mike's planning a major ass-whooping for you tomorrow."

She whipped her head around to stare at Brody. "What are you talking about?" Then she whipped her head around to Tommy. "What's he talking about?"

The glare he sent Brody could have frozen hell. "How about keeping your fucking mouth shut?" He then looked at her. "It's nothing."

Yeah. She believed that.

She glanced at Brody, who was staring at Tommy with a mixture of disbelief and dawning respect. The disbelief she'd seen before, but the respect was new. Something wasn't adding up. "Spill, Tommy."

Tommy stiffened his jaw, refusing to answer.

She pinned Brody with a stare. "How do you know about this ass-whooping?"

His hand froze on the back of his neck. "Huh?"

"How do *you* know about it?"

He shot a glance at Tommy, an apologetic grimace on his face as he shrugged. "Word spreads, Jules. You know how it is."

The muscles in Tommy's cheeks twisted. "Jesus Christ, Mike's letting me back in the gym. Okay?" he ground out. "I was supposed to start training tomorrow, but I'm going to wait until you're at least moving around again."

Stunned, she stared at him. "Do you think that's a good idea…postponing going back on your first day?" She bit her lip. "You know, with the way you…" She gave up and exhaled.

"Decided to show up whenever I damn well felt like it before?" he helpfully supplied. "I really don't give two flying fucks what anyone down there thinks, Julie. You are my priority. You always have been. Those who know me know that, and those who want to make an issue of it can take it up with me." He gave Brody a pointed stare.

Warmth spread across her chest at the conviction in his words. "Why didn't you tell me?"

"We've been a little busy with back rubs and breakfast in bed."

How had he managed to make that sound way more sensual than it really had been?

But, Lord, he had. The low, husky voice he'd used painted an erotic picture that spread a current of desire throughout her body. Was this about Brody being here? Tommy had said he didn't like the man. Was this some kind of weird attempt to get him to go away?

She wasn't sure. Tommy was confusing the hell out of her, especially with the insinuation he'd made about wanting to make sure he didn't turn her off. That *was* the only way to take the statement, right? She couldn't think of any other, best-friend way to spin those words.

A defiant part of her made her smile and tell him, "Go train at the gym, Tommy. Brody can take care of me here."

Eyes narrowing, his gaze held hers, heated. "Over my dead body."

Raw possessiveness sharpened every word. A claiming. Just as before, with the kiss.

But this time it snared her ability to breathe. Before this very minute, Tommy had never looked at her like a man hell-bent on claiming her for himself.

But he sure as hell did now.

. . .

Julie wanted out of this bed, but Tommy wouldn't let her. Other than to do some stretches that had felt freaking awesome, he'd kept her confined to the bed. And she was bored…so bored.

She hadn't pulled her back muscles as badly as she'd initially thought, thank God. Or maybe it had been that rub Tommy had used last night and this morning. Some kind of MMA super muscle rub. Whatever it was, she was feeling pretty good—physically.

Mentally—well, that was a different matter.

Brody had left a few hours ago. Mac had returned to make a delicious lunch. And Tommy had been at her beck and call… all calm and relaxed. Like he hadn't stared at her with a need so fierce it had made her belly tremble. In fact, as soon as Brody had left, Tommy'd become the same old Tommy again. Had all that intensity just been a show for the other man?

While that thought should have made her angry, she was surprised to feel something akin to relief.

Considering she'd been stone cold in love with Tommy Sparks since she was ten years old, that seemed kind of an odd reaction. But since she had nothing to do but lay in the bed and think about it, she realized it really wasn't that odd. As things stood between them now, they had their friendship. A really good friendship.

But as well as they got along as friends, it didn't mean that would carry over into a more intimate relationship. The idea of losing Tommy completely scared the absolute crap out of her.

"I ran you a bath."

She glanced up to find Tommy standing in the doorway. She let her gaze travel over the tight shirt encasing the breadth of his chest and down to the jeans riding low on his hips. When her eyes slid to his bare feet, a small smile tilted her lips. "That sounds great."

As she pushed the blanket aside, he came over to help her, but she didn't need his help. Other than some lingering soreness, which she blamed more on lack of movement than she did the injury, she was better. She wouldn't even hesitate to take on one of the bigger animals at the clinic right now. At least she wouldn't miss any work over this.

She made it down the hall to the bathroom, opened the door, and halted in surprise. It took a moment for her to realize what she was seeing.

"Oh. Tommy."

"You like?"

"I love."

A pleased smile quirked his lips as she stepped inside. He hadn't just run her a bath; he'd orchestrated a whole relaxing atmosphere. All the overhead lights had been turned off. In their place was the soft, orangey glow from a dozen votive candles he'd placed around the room. A wicker stool had been pulled up next to the deep Jacuzzi tub she'd splurged on a year ago, the jets set on low and peacefully rippling the water. On the stool was a folded towel, a glass of iced sweet tea, and her favorite book. She spotted a neat pile of clothes sitting on the counter.

"It's wonderful, thank you."

"I'll leave you to it, then," he said as he gently closed the door.

After she stripped off her PJs, she sank into the tub, letting the jets soothe the remaining soreness from her muscles.

She groaned softly. What she really could go for was another of his massages, but this time for her arms and legs.

She could ask for one… Tommy would give her another massage in a heartbeat.

But no. As tempting as it was, the torture of having his hands on her again wouldn't be worth it.

Better, instead, to let the jets dissolve as much of the tension as they could. She reached for her book to read while they worked their magic. She'd gotten about twenty minutes in when the bathroom door opened. She froze as Tommy stepped in without a second's hesitation, crowding the small area with his massive body, overwhelming the space with his mere presence.

And making her extremely aware that she was naked under the rippling water and bubbles. "Hey! W-What are you doing in here?" She floated her arms to strategic positions over herself.

He held up a pink bucket—the bucket from the bathroom cabinet, full of her pedicure stuff. "Thought your feet would like to be pampered, too."

A sweet thought, but probably still a bit much for her to try and do right now—she'd have to bend over to reach her toes.

"Oh. Sure. Thanks." After a brief hesitation, she lifted a hand from the water, expecting him to pass the bucket to her.

He hiked a brow, cocking his head to the side. "You don't think I'm letting you do it yourself, do you?"

She dropped her hand while his meaning sank in. "What?"

He perched on the side of the tub and casually dipped his hand into the water, as if testing the temperature. His palm slipped between her legs, high on her inner thigh.

Jerking away, she let out a shuddered gasp. "Hey!"

"Oops. Sorry about that."

Her mouth parted.

He didn't look the least bit sorry! If anything, he seemed to be enjoying the hell out of himself. What in the world was he doing?

All her thoughts scattered as his hand slid down her thigh, past her knee, over her calf to encircle her ankle, leaving a blazing trail from his touch.

Pivoting his body around to face her feet, he lifted one out of the water and cradled it in both hands, massaging his thumbs across the top, then kneading deep into her arch with his fingers. Closing her eyes, she relaxed a little, and softly moaned. God, it felt good.

"That's right. Enjoy my touch."

Her eyes opened and she stared at the white cotton T-shirt straining against the muscles of his back. Had he really said that? The words had been whispered, barely audible, but she swore that was what he'd said.

He rubbed deep again, pulling another appreciative moan from her. This time, she definitely did hear a growled, *"Fuck,"* under his breath.

A raging ache formed between her legs at the graphic word as her nipples instantly hardened into tight peaks. A very naughty side reared up. Watching him closely, she deliberately moaned this time, making the sound more breathless...and sexual. All massaging stopped on her foot as his spine stiffened. Then he worked his head back and forth, rolled his shoulders, and continued kneading into her arch.

He *was* trying to turn her on.

And there wasn't another man in sight. No one he needed to put on a fake show for. The same desire she'd seen in him this morning had been as ripe in that growled "Fuck" as it had been in his eyes earlier today. Desire for *her*.

He *did* want her.

She didn't need any damn kiss to confirm that. Didn't need a moment of jealousy that pushed him to take her into his arms. There was absolutely no doubt that all she had to do was give him the go-ahead and Tommy would ravish her body the way she had dreamed about.

With the confirmation, emotions bombarded her from every direction. Fear, excitement...rampant uncertainty. But the one that stood out the most was how incredibly much she wanted this man. No matter what the consequences would be.

And that terrified her more than anything.

He switched to the other foot, giving that one the same treatment, coaxing more sounds from her—genuine sounds—as easily as he coaxed the tension from her muscles. And coaxed her to surrender to him and forget everything else.

Didn't he always say she didn't play enough? That she needed to let go?

Well, here was her big chance.

No other man had ever made her body come alive the way Tommy did without even touching her. What if no other man ever did?

She studied her best friend, the tremors now quaking his

shoulders. And she knew he was fighting himself, struggling not to ravish *her*.

No matter how hard either of them fought this attraction, and even if they succeeded, their relationship had changed forever.

The only question was…would they still be together in the end? Or would they both spend forever apart…and alone?

• • •

She was fucking killing him.

Tommy scrubbed pumice stone over the bottom of Julie's foot. His cock was hard as steel and wedged at an awkward angle in his jeans. Highly uncomfortable. But other than standing and grabbing the front of his pants to reposition himself, thus bringing Julie's focus to that very stiff part of him, he was just going to have to deal.

He was almost done with the pedi, and then he was getting the ever-loving hell out of here.

This had been a superbly dumb idea. Her first soft moan should have been a clue. Her second, a red flag waving in his face. He'd never wanted to be on top of a woman faster, or more urgently. Inhaling deeply, he finally lowered her foot into the water. "All right. You're done. Get dressed and meet me in the living room."

Where he had another colossal mistake waiting.

As he left, he didn't look at her. Once he had the door closed, he reached down and rearranged his aching cock, groaning. God, he was so turned on. The little mewls she'd made from him touching her were some insanely dangerous shit. And he found himself teetering on the brink of blind lust—just from the noises she made. And he hadn't even been doing anything erotic to her, just rubbing her damn feet.

What the hell would happen when he started rubbing other places—his favorite places? What kind of noises would she make then? Could he make the soft moans louder? The languid moans more frantic? The contented moans more desperate? Lust shot through him at the mere thought of trying.

*Shit!* He needed to calm down or he was going to do something he regretted. Fucking Julie Rogers was *not* an option. He refused to let the friendship he treasured with that woman be ruined by treating her like every other meaningless encounter he'd had.

If he were going to be with her, it *would* be special. He would be slow and thorough…a true lover. He would *not* fuck her brains out and leave.

*Not, not, not.*

Calmed by the inner pep talk, he went to his room to change into a pair of black silk pajama bottoms, needing to get out the restrictive jeans or he risked permanent damage. As tempted as he was to go shirtless, that was begging for disaster, so he tossed on a black wife-beater, then went back into the kitchen. When she walked into the living room wearing one of his oversized amateur MMA shirts from years ago, his gut twisted. There was something massively arousing about her wearing his shirt, and as far as he was concerned, that could be all she wore for the rest of her life and he'd never tire of seeing it.

As he'd been sifting through her drawer earlier and found it, male satisfaction had gripped him, and he wondered how many nights she'd slept in it, and if she thought of him every time she put it on. After that, his search for the perfect outfit had been over. He had to have her in it…see her in it.

The hem reached mid-thigh, making him think of the bright
pink satin panties he'd chosen to go with it. Going through her
underwear drawer had been an eye-opening experience. He'd
never considered what she wore under her clothes, but the
drawer full of colorful lace, satin, and silk had both shocked
and pleased him. Picking out the one he wanted her to wear, to
know she it on right now, was so damn hot. Everything about
that woman made him hot.

It was like his body had stored up twenty-three years of
lust and was bombarding him with it all at the same time.

"How are you feeling?" he asked to distract himself.

"Fantastic. That bath worked out the rest of the soreness."

"To be on the safe side, lie down on the couch, and I'll rub
more ointment on your back."

He was surprised when she didn't argue. When she pretty
much flopped belly-first onto the couch without hesitation, he
knew she wasn't lying about feeling better. After he raised her
top, he exhaled slowly at the smooth skin he'd give anything
to place his lips against right now. Instead, he squirted a liberal
amount of the medicated gel into his palm, then rubbed it onto
her lower back. His gaze kept drifting down to the swell of her
ass.

Oh, God, he needed to touch her there. *Had* to touch her
there.

Being just a *little* bad wouldn't hurt.

Right?

Slipping his hand under the waistband of her PJ bottoms,
he massaged low onto one round cheek, biting back a groan as
the flesh filled his palm perfectly, as he'd known it would. One
day he had to have his hands on both of these luscious cheeks
while she rode him.

Realizing his mind was going into dangerous territory, and fast, he jerked his hand out. "Okay, you're good."

She rolled over onto her back, and he helped her sit so she was propped against the arms of the couch.

"That okay?" he asked.

"I told you, I'm feeling fine."

"Can I sit with you?"

When she nodded, he lifted her legs and slid in beside her, pulled her thighs across his lap, then slung his arms across the back of the sofa. It was intimate. A couple's position.

He liked it.

Picking up a strand of her hair, he ran it absently through his fingers, enjoying the scent of the lavender bath oil lingering on her skin. "The night is yours. What would you like to do?"

When a moment passed and she hadn't said anything, he glanced up from the lock of dark hair and met her eyes. A wallop hit him hard in the chest and he couldn't drag his gaze away. He hadn't wanted to kiss her tonight, had just wanted to spend time with her, pamper her, make her feel special—let her know his intentions, get used to seeing him this way. Prove to himself he was capable of taking pleasure from simply holding a woman instead of from how many times he'd made her come.

But this was *the* moment—he felt it to his very core.

Their faces were inches apart. Tension crackled in the air. As he gave in, leaning toward her to close the distance, he knew this kiss would be different from any he'd ever given in the past. Gently pressing his lips to hers, he kept the kiss soft and coaxing, sweet and lingering, as their lips became acquainted. Needing more, he shifted his body toward hers and angled his head as he cupped her face between his hands.

The silkiness of her mouth was intoxicating, keeping him coming back for more. He yearned to take her mouth the way he wanted to take her body—hard and fast and screamingly thorough—but he forced himself to keep it slow and easy. When he flicked his tongue across the seam of her lips and she parted for him, he delved inside and discovered the sweet, addicting taste of Julie.

And all rational thought fled.

Raking one hand into her hair, he knotted his fingers at her nape and tugged her head back as he shifted onto his knees. He moved his body between her legs, grunting his approval against her lips when she spread them without coaxing. As he devoured her mouth, his hand tightening farther in her hair, holding her immobile, his to do with as he pleased. He loved that fucking thought. Encouraged by her mewls of pleasure, he shifted closer, pressing her into the couch cushions. His cock stood proudly forward against the silk of his bottoms, making contact with her belly.

She gasped into his mouth as she slid her palms around his waist to grip his ass, drawing him closer into her. The feel of his cock flattening onto her stomach made him groan with desire.

He wanted her under him. *Now.*

Blind with need, he ripped his mouth from hers and shifted backward. Grasping her behind the calves, he dragged her down until she was flat on her back, hair fanned out around her face. Lips swollen from his kisses. Desire for him burning in her eyes. *Breathtaking.*

As he positioned her gorgeous thighs on either side of his hips, he scooted closer on his knees, easing her legs wider apart. But not enough for him. Nowhere near enough.

He growled his disapproval. "I want you open, like this." Pulling her knees up and out, he moved forward until his pelvis was pressed right against her center.

Her gasped "Yes!" drove him wild. He pushed her thighs wider still, showing her what he wanted—her completely revealed to him. Nothing hidden. The pink satin–covered mound beneath him made his mouth water. "Yeah. Like that. I want to see. Everything."

He rubbed his palms up and down the insides of her thighs. Her lips parted on a moan as she arched up. Watching her respond to him shoved him into oblivion.

"You like that? What about this?"

He slid his rigid cock against the place he wanted so badly to invade, grinding his teeth at the friction. When she shuddered and moved helplessly against him, he could almost feel himself pounding into her. He wanted it. Her. He ground harder against her, right into that blissful valley between her legs. *Fuck. Yes.*

Running his hand up her stomach, he engulfed one breast in his palm, pinching the erect nipple between his fingers. She cried out, loudly this time.

The sound snapped him out of his sexual stupor.

He froze, staring down at her, horrified at what he'd done.

She blinked up at him. "W-Why did you stop?"

He jerked up off the couch, backing away.

Damn! Damn, damn, *damn*.

"Tommy. What's wrong?"

He was treating her like all the rest. Damn it! He didn't know *how* to make love. He didn't know how to love at all. All he knew how to do was fuck.

Forget the leaving her afterward fear. They would never

get to that point. He'd make damn sure of it. Julie deserved better than him.

She deserved a man who truly knew how to love her.

# CHAPTER 10

The next morning, Julie cracked open her bedroom door and sneaked into the living room, trying not to wake Tommy. She'd gone ahead and taken a sick day.

She and Tommy needed to have a long talk, and she wasn't giving him the chance to escape her.

After his freak-out last night, he had locked himself in his bedroom, leaving her to go back to hers, where she'd proceeded to lay awake mulling over what had happened between them, wavering dangerously between hurt and puzzlement.

Wondering why he'd looked so horrified before he'd run off.

He'd been totally into what was happening, of that she was certain. Heck, he'd been more than into it. The man who'd tugged her on her back then compelled her legs apart when she hadn't parted them wide enough for him had been overwrought with lust. Tense lines had grooved his face as he'd rubbed himself against her over and over. And his cock—how big and hard could a man get? The thought of it thrusting inside her made her shiver with wicked desire.

Just the small sample of him she'd had last night convinced her that sex with Tommy would be dirty-good, raw, and totally exposed. And it would be like nothing she'd ever experienced before.

Dear God, she had never been more turned on in her life. She'd almost found release from the sheer intensity of him.

That thrilled her as much as it frightened her.

The fear was coming from a place of self-preservation. She'd already lost her heart to the man, but what if she lost her body, too? She may not have found anyone to replace Tommy in her heart, but she did have physical needs she succumbed to from time to time. And her encounters had been…satisfying. At least she'd thought they'd been.

Funny, until last night, she had always believed she'd had pretty good sex. Apparently not. Tommy had made her realize how very wrong she was, and he'd only just begun to demonstrate what he was capable of. Once she'd had him inside her, she had no doubt her definition of good sex would be permanently altered, and anything else would pale in comparison.

What was worse? Winding up alone and remaining ignorant of absolutely amazing sex, so that mediocre sex would still be good enough? Or winding up alone, knowing how mind-blowing sex could be…and never finding it again?

Jeez, talk about a crap choice.

As much as she would love to think of her and Tommy having something more than they'd always had, it was hard to envision it actually happening. She'd spent so long seeing their relationship for what it really was, not how she *wanted* it to be, that she wasn't blinded by the romantic notion that just because this unexpected mutual attraction had blossomed, they'd find a happily-ever-after.

She wished it would be that easy. But she'd seen too much, experienced too much with the man to be so naive. They lived two very different lives, and she really couldn't see him being happy settling down. Maybe he'd prove her wrong…but it was hard to overlook the glaring evidence of the past fifteen years since he started dating.

Sighing, she fed the dogs, then made herself a bowl of oatmeal and eased down on the couch to eat. A few minutes later, she heard the click of Tommy's door opening, then the pad of his feet on the hardwood. Her stomach fluttered in both excitement and anxiety. How was he going to act toward her now? She would just die if he looked at her with disdain.

When he stepped into the living room, he froze, and she saw him swallow. Not the best reaction, but at least he didn't do an about-face and go back to his room.

"Morning," she said.

"Morning," he mumbled, then hurried toward the kitchen.

She let out a frustrated breath. "Tommy?"

He stopped but didn't turn to look at her, and her frustration grew. She didn't know how to handle this Tommy—how to talk to him, or even begin to. It was like she was dealing with an entirely different man than the one she'd known most of her life.

And she was, wasn't she? The man in the room with her now *wasn't* her friend. He was a stranger, and she hated the distance between them.

"I think we should talk," she said.

A long moment of silence followed before he asked, "Are

you feeling better?"

"Why?" she hedged.

"Thought I'd look at a couple of rentals today. My insurance check arrived. Think it's time to move on."

Okay. Wow.

So now he was in a rush to move out? "Y-You're not going to stay home with me?"

"Looks like you're moving around fine." He still wasn't looking at her.

Without another word, he disappeared into the kitchen.

Julie chewed on her lip. Maybe she should just let him go. Obviously he was still freaked out about last night and wasn't looking to repeat it. Maybe if he moved out and they got back to their normal routines, their friendship could come out of this unscathed. But as she listened to him rummage through the refrigerator, she realized she wasn't ready for him to go. Not yet. She still had too many questions left unanswered, and she needed him *here* to get those answers.

Unfortunately, he seemed hell-bent on getting out of the house today. How could she get him to stay?

An idea formed, one so manipulative it made her feel totally guilty for even thinking it. She never stooped to such tactics. But he wasn't going to stay willingly.

Feeling like a heel, but backed into a corner, she waited until she heard his footsteps approach the living room again, then she started to stand. Making it halfway up, she let out a pained, "Oh!" and grabbed her lower back.

A crash sounded behind her, then Tommy was at her side, his hands on her arms. As he helped her sit back down, he crouched by her knees, his worried gaze scanning over her. "Are you okay? Shit. Did I hurt you last night?"

*Only my feelings…*

The concern pinching his face made guilt slam hard into her, but she shook her head. "Things didn't get far enough to hurt," she said drily. She didn't have to feign a grimace when he ignored her pointed remark. "No, I just tried to do too much this morning. Help me put my feet up before you go."

Eyes jerking up to hers, he stared at her like she was nuts. "I'm not going anywhere now."

"Tommy. It was only a little pinch. I'm okay. I just tried to get up too fast. Please don't let me stop you from—"

"I *said* I'm not going anywhere. Let me grab the back ointment and some meds. I'll be right back."

As he left the room, she couldn't stop a small smile. She didn't normally get that devious, but for a novice, she'd handled that one perfectly. And she'd gotten exactly what she wanted. Tommy was staying. Even better, he seemed to be somewhat back to his old self.

Maybe now he'd chill out and explain to her what had happened last night. There was no denying he'd wanted her, but she couldn't come up with an explanation for why he had stopped.

After he returned, he placed the tube on the coffee table and helped her turn over. A shiver went through her as she remembered this was just how it had all started last night. When Tommy had slipped his hand over her butt cheek, she'd been lost.

The repeat performance she was secretly hoping for, however, did not happen. He had that lotion on her and her shirt pulled back down within five seconds. She frowned into the pillow.

She rolled back over and he tried to push a muscle relaxer

into her hand. Waving him off, she shook her head. "No. Just the anti-inflammatory."

He nudged both pills at her. "You need this, too."

Did he want her knocked out? "I'm fine. I don't want it," she said more forcibly.

That muscle went to town in his cheek and she realized he *was* trying to knock her out. Probably cursing his decision to stay, if she were going to be awake. He really didn't want to talk.

Ignoring the muscle relaxer, she took the anti-inflammatory, popped it in her mouth, and washed it down with some water. Then an awkward silence fell over the room.

"Would you please sit down?" she said.

He glared at her. Then went and sat on the other end of the couch, his entire body rigid.

Well, the old Tommy had been here all of thirty seconds before the insufferable new one decided to return. She suppressed an exasperated groan. How could a man she'd known for so damn long have this annoying, obstinate... *male*...inside him and she not be aware of it?

*Don't be stupid, girl.*

Fine, she *was* aware that Tommy could be like this. Just not with her. Not until sex had reared its ugly head between them. And she hated every damn second he shut her out.

When she couldn't handle any more of his unyielding silence, she ground out, "Are we ever going to talk about last night?"

That's all it took. He shot off the couch and headed toward the hall.

"Tommy Sparks!" she yelled, furious at his refusal to communicate. "You better stop right where you are if you know what's good for you."

His back to her, he halted.

"I'm *not* someone you can ignore! I'm your best friend. I deserve better than this kind of treatment!"

There was a long pause. "You're right. You do. I *know* this, and yet I still treated you just like I do everyone else. Which is exactly why I'm leaving."

Stunned by his statement, she stared after him as he disappeared into the hallway. What the hell did he mean by that? He *didn't* treat her like everyone else. She was different. Always had been. Just as he'd always been different for her. Their relationship was special. And it really irked her that he'd just lumped her in with every other person in his life.

Ten minutes later, he stalked back into the room, dressed in jeans and a long-sleeved T-shirt, a duffel bag slung over his shoulder.

"Where are you going?"

"I've got stuff to do," he said, without even glancing at her. As the front door closed behind him, he said, "Don't worry. I called Brody. He'll help you today. He's better for you, anyway."

Then the door closed.

Shocked, her mouth dropped open. He'd *called* Brody? The same man Tommy had told her in no uncertain terms he wanted her to stay away from? The same one he'd said he didn't trust with her?

Tommy was now giving her to Brody because he was *better* for her?

For a man she thought she knew inside and out, she was learning she didn't know her best friend at all.

• • •

Tommy had spent the day looking at different rental houses and apartments, finding nothing he wanted to put down a deposit on. Finding a place shouldn't be this hard. For the most part, all he really did was sleep and eat there, spending most of his time out.

Hell, he'd found his other place within a couple of hours. It had met his needs, and he had put down the deposit and started moving in that same day. The search today had been the complete opposite. Each of the places he looked at had been missing something. What that was, he had no fucking clue. But as he'd looked around at each new rental, he just wasn't feeling the walls around him. So he'd gone on to the next. And then felt the same.

Twelve places, and not a damn one of them suited him.

As he walked down the sidewalk to Mike's gym, he shook his head in disgust. Maybe he'd been too distracted because he'd known Julie was with Brody all day. He'd called the man in the heat of anger—at himself. Having Julie say she wasn't like everyone else and she deserved better had just reminded him that he had once again failed her. And he would continue to do so if he didn't find some way to get their relationship back to where it used to be. So he'd pushed Brody back at her.

At least *he* would know how to treat her right. If Tommy really cared for Julie, he'd want that for her. So he *was* being the bigger man. He sure as fuck didn't feel like it, though. Jealousy had churned in his gut all day as he thought about what they could be doing. And it had taken a massive amount of willpower to not go back to her place and kick the ass out. Somehow, he'd managed not to make a total fool of himself and actually do it.

Now, for the next three hours, Mike would kick *his* ass,

and then hopefully he'd be too exhausted to give a shit.

He yanked open the door, immensely thankful that the first face he saw was Mac's. As he stepped inside, the rest of the place seemed to slow, then stilled altogether. God, where were his spurs when he needed them? It was just like a showdown in some old Western movie. His peers stared at him. Some openly scowled. Others watched curiously. Tommy had known his first day back wasn't going to be a piece of cake, but this was bordering on worse than he'd thought.

Inhaling, he forced a collective smile. "Don't let me stop you."

Everyone continued to stare. A muttered, "This is bullshit," rang loud inside the quieted room.

All righty, then. *Here goes nothing.* Dropping his bag to the floor, he stepped farther inside. "You're right. It is bullshit. If I were one of you guys, I'd think the exact same thing. I fucked up. I let everyone in this building down, including myself. I don't expect anyone to accept me back with pats on the back and hearty welcomes. I don't deserve it. Not after the way I acted, not after many of the choices I made. But I have changed. I'm going to prove that to each one of you. I'm going to *earn* your respect back. Are we clear?"

A few mumbles echoed around as the men nodded, and everyone went back to what they'd been doing. That was as good an agreement as he was going to get, and he'd take it.

As Mac passed behind him, he squeezed his shoulder. Mike strode up to him. "I hope you mean everything you just said."

"I do."

"Then get your butt into that locker room and change. We've got a lot of work to do."

. . .

On edge, Julie stalked around the living room, then climbed up on the end of the couch, bringing her knees to her chest, and gnawed her thumbnail.

Brody gave an exasperated curse. "Are you going to at least tell me why I'm here, since it looks like you're moving around just fine on your own?"

She stopped chewing on her nail and shot a glance at him. He sat on the edge of the cushion with his elbows braced on his jean-clad knees, studying her. God, she kept forgetting he was here.

"I'm sorry," she said. "I'm not being much company, am I?"

"Yeah. Try *no* company."

Puffing out a breath, she lowered her legs and sat on the couch like a civilized person and not one completely agitated by a pain-in-the-ass jerk who'd just handed her over to another man. "I did try to tell you not to come by."

"I also didn't believe you when you said you were fine, since it was *Tommy* who called me."

The rat bastard. "That one shocked me, too," she admitted.

When she'd called Brody back after Tommy left this morning, she'd known he wasn't buying any of her reassurances. And she couldn't bring herself to admit what had motivated him to call Brody. That he just wanted to get away from her.

She had finally convinced Brody she wanted to take a nap because she really wasn't in the mood for company. But all it had done was buy her a few hours. Brody had knocked on her front door about an hour ago, and had pretty much watched her stalk around the house ever since.

"Going to tell me what happened?" he pressed.

Should she? She scrunched her nose, studying him. "We're friends, right?"

"I'd like to think so."

All right. Going over this repeatedly in her head all day hadn't gotten her anywhere. She needed some outside perspective. And he *had* helped her last time they'd talked.

She shifted toward him on the couch. "Okay. I've got a problem."

"Obviously."

"Tommy kissed me. And things got…heated." Her skin warmed as she remembered exactly how heated. "Then he totally freaked out, and now I'm not sure if I'm regretting what happened and want to leave well enough alone, or if I want to push him to see what might happen next."

His head tilted slightly to the side. "Why would you regret it, Jules? Haven't you been in love with the man most of your life?"

"Yes. But I've also been very rational when it comes to him. And that rational part is blaring an air raid siren, telling me to leave it alone."

"Why?"

"If we do this, everything changes, and there is no going back."

"Isn't that the way it already is?"

"I thought so when I believed the attraction was mutual. Then he kissed me, and…and everything else happened… and I realized I must be wrong. He ran practically screaming from the room, Brody. So I'm pretty sure I can still escape this intact, if I do it now. But if we go any further and we really can't make it work…I lose him. If that happens, it may destroy me." She held up her hands. "I'm worried about *me*. Is that selfish?"

He was silent for a moment. "No. It's not selfish. You and Tommy have been a part of each other's lives for a very long time. I think it's natural for both of you to be scared to change that. But there's a problem with your rational thinking."

"What's that?"

"You're in *love* with him. And no matter what, or how rational you believe you are, there will always be what-ifs. And *this* what-if will eventually eat you alive. If you don't see this through, you're going to look back on this moment and always wander how it would have been different, if you'd just taken the chance."

Lord, she had never thought of it like that. She'd thought only of *losing* Tommy, and had never looked at the possible consequences from the other side of the coin. To be honest, it was still hard to let go of that thinking.

"What if we do go ahead, and it ends up being something I look back on and regret? He's my best friend, Brody. I can't see my life without him in it."

"All right, the counterargument to that is, what if you and Tommy are *supposed* to be together as a couple? What if this is the *start* of your relationship together? What if you don't try, and the two of you never find anyone else?" When she opened her mouth to voice a rebuttal, he held up his hand. "I'm not making light of your worries. They are real, and could very well be the outcome. But there *is* another side of this scenario. And that side could possibly bring a lifetime of happiness."

She peered at him, letting his words sink in for a long moment.

He was right. She didn't necessarily like it, but he was right. "And if it doesn't work out, I'll at least finally know for sure, right?"

"Right."

She let out a breath. This was a terrifying road she was about to venture down. She could very well end up with her heart shattered in a million pieces. Even worse, she could lose her best friend forever. But she had to stop thinking that way, stop looking at only the negative. Because if this went in the opposite direction from her worries, a whole lot of positive would happen.

"So you think I should just go for it?"

"I would. But you said Tommy freaked out. Did he say anything?"

"No. He honestly just jerked away from me as though he suddenly realized who I was, and then bolted from the room. Didn't really say anything to me this morning, either, other than he called you to help me and that you would be better for me anyway."

"Did he?" There was a slow, interested edge to Brody's tone. "Hmm."

"What?"

"Just seems Tommy is going to need a little more prodding than I realized."

She leaned closer. "Any ideas?"

Amusement lit his eyes as he laughed softly. "Give me a little time, but I'm sure I can come up with something before he gets back."

Julie nodded. Nervous energy gripped her. While part of her was ready to go for broke, she wasn't sure what would happen when she came face-to-face with Tommy. A part of

her was worried she'd chicken out in fear of him storming off
again. She didn't know if she could handle him winding her
up so tight, and then just leaving. As secure as she was with
herself and her body, having a man jump off her and bolt from
the room in horror was a blow to the self-confidence.

"I'm getting thirsty. You mind if I grab a drink?" Brody
asked.

"Oh my God. I'm being a terrible hostess. What would
you like?"

When she started to rise, he shook his head and stood. "No.
I'll get it. Want anything while I'm up?"

"Water would be nice. Thank you."

He smiled and went into the kitchen.

She sat back against the cushions. If she wanted to push
Tommy, what would be the best way to go about it? He seemed
freaked out about touching her, or even being near her at this
point. How would she be able to start anything if he refused
to get close? She'd just have to play it by ear. Not her usual
method of doing things, and definitely outside her comfort
zone, but she did need to learn to relax and go with the flow.

Brody returned, carrying two glasses of Merlot. As he
handed her one, he said, "For some liquid courage."

Chuckling, she smiled. "Good idea."

As Julie took a long swallow of the drink, Brody sat next
to her on the couch and placed his glass on the coffee table.
"How's the back feeling?"

"Much better. A little sore, but I can feel like this from
raking leaves."

"So you're moving okay now? No catches or anything?"

"Nope."

"Absolutely sure?"

"Yeah. Why—"

A key jingled in the door.

Brody met her gaze with a wink. "Okay, now don't get pissed."

She frowned. "What are you—"

As the door opened, Brody lunged on top of her, pushing her back against the cushions, his chest pressed against hers, lips latched onto hers. She was so stunned she froze, hands on his shoulder, vaguely aware of the roar that came from the background. One moment Brody was laying on top of her, the next Tommy had hurled him across the room by the back of the shirt. He advanced on the man, all raged out, hands clenched at his sides.

"I told you if you laid another fucking hand on her, I'd make sure you'd never enter the cage again."

Brody pushed to his feet. "And I said you'd better claim her quick, then, didn't I? Since *you* called *me*, I figured that was you telling me she was free for the taking."

Julie gaped. When had *this* conversation happened? Really, she should get up and stop this nonsense, but she was completely captivated by what was unfolding in front of her. No man had ever been this furious over another man touching her—especially not Tommy—and it was…okay, it was absolutely thrilling to watch.

"Julie is not an object you can just take, asshole."

A smug smile came to Brody's face. "No. But she's a *woman* I can take—over and over again, and she'll enjoy every fucking second of it."

The punch snapped Brody's head to the side. So much for thrilling. Julie shot to her feet, clapping her hands over her mouth. "Tommy! *No*!"

Brody slowly brought his head back around, used his thumb to wipe away the blood on his bottom lip as he regarded Tommy, who was so enraged the cords in his throat strained against the tension encasing his entire body. She'd seen him like this once before. The night he punched Ethan's son. That had been over her, too—she just hadn't known it at the time.

"Get the *fuck* out of this house."

Brody glanced over at her. "Jules?"

When Tommy shifted forward like he was going to attack again, Julie quickly said, "I think you'd better go, Brody."

Scowling, he glared between her and Tommy. "Fine."

All tense, he spun toward the door, but before he stalked forward, he sent her a conspiratorial wink, and then left. *Crazy man*.

"Tom—"

Before she had time to get out his entire name, he was across the room with his mouth crushed to hers. Fire swept through her instantly, pooling low in her gut. Any lingering worries about them, the consequences, him bolting, vanished. Only one thing was clear.

She had to have him.

His tongue sailed into her mouth, his fingers biting into her hips as he forced her to walk backward. Where he was taking her, she didn't care, just as long as he didn't stop kissing her. The backs of her knees hit the couch, but he continued to push her. Losing her balance, she tumbled against the cushions. Tommy immediately dropped to his knees before her and yanked her hips to the edge of the couch.

Within seconds, he had her pajama bottoms and panties off and her thighs shoved open wide, and his mouth was buried between her legs, devouring her. The mere speed of it almost made her come, and she released slow, rough breaths, trying to control the tightening in her lower body.

If she didn't move away from that exquisite mouth, she'd orgasm and become too sensitive for more. She wanted it to last. Shifting her hips to the left, she freed her clit from his wicked tongue, relieved to feel the pressure ebb.

A growl came from his mouth, vibrating against her, as his hand clamped onto her hip and moved her right back where she'd been. His mouth pressing into her, his tongue circled her, then flicked. The pressure sprang back. Threatened to explode. She tried to shift away again, but his fingers bit into her skin, keeping her immobile, refusing her any control. The longer he continued his unrelenting pursuit for her orgasm, the more the intense pleasure took away her ability to think. She was numb to everything but what he was doing to her and how it made her feel. Surrendering to him, she moaned, and grabbed his hair in one hand and the back of the couch in the other. "Oh, God!" she cried out.

Tommy held nothing back. There wasn't any tenderness, no apology for his aggressiveness. He took, just as she'd known he would. And it was so much more than she could've imagined. He focused on her, finding that nub and not giving it a second to relax. There wasn't teasing or a slow building. He licked and sucked with the same intensity that he'd started this with. This wasn't foreplay. He wanted her orgasm, and he wanted it fast. By the greedy noises he made, this was a man completely lost in the moment, who got just as turned on by pleasuring a woman like this as he did by being inside her.

He sucked her clit deep into his mouth one last time, and her body shattered. Arching her back, she gave a long moan of ecstasy as her climax ripped through her. His hands on her hips kept her lower body on lockdown, and he held her clit prisoner against his mouth, never releasing the pressure of his lips as she rode the intensity of her release. As she reached the most sensitive peak, she tried to jerk away. He denied her escape, his tongue as aggressive as ever.

"Too much," she cried.

A noise she could only decipher as "No" came from him as he licked her again.

She grabbed his hair and pulled, but he stayed exactly where he was.

"I—I can't. Too—"

He sucked her deep into his mouth again and the explosion was instant. Her body went rigid and she screamed as a second release barreled through her, more intense than the first. She bucked against his mouth as he made it go on and on, until she collapsed against the cushions.

"Holy shit," she whispered over and over. Multiples. The man had just given her multiples.

After he finally lifted his head, he flipped her onto her stomach, her knees on the ground, her torso bent over the cushion. Anticipation shivered through her. He was going to take her. Two warm hands kneaded her bottom as a low growl echoed through the room. "Such a perfect ass."

His words sent new waves of lust through her, and all she wanted was to have him inside her. Have him thrust into her with the same intensity as he just had with his mouth. She heard the low rasp of his zipper. Felt the head of his cock probe her center. And she knew she was moments from having him inside her.

"Please, Tommy." She wiggled backward. "Now!"

He made a strangled noise.

*"Jesus."* The warmth of his body leaving hers was shocking. She pushed up slightly to look over her shoulder. He was pacing the room, thrusting his hand through his hair.

"Tommy?"

His gaze flashed to hers, lowered to her ass, and his jaw clenched. "Jesus Christ, Julie, stand up and put your clothes on."

He had to be kidding. He was doing this *again*? "But—"

"Now!" he roared, then turned his back on her.

She reluctantly pulled her pajama pants back on. When she stood, he finally faced her. "This can't happen again, Julie. I don't *want* it to happen again."

Hurt and confusion flooded through her in equal measure. "I don't understand. Why do you keep stopping?"

"*Why*? I just punched Brody for saying he was going to take you. I *said* you weren't a fucking object, and not five minutes later I'm treating you like one. Just having my goddamn way with you with no regard for your feelings."

"I don't mind. I—"

Anger flashed in his eyes. "*I* mind. You deserve better than that. You deserve someone who is going to treat you better. And someone who's going to stick around afterward. What was I *thinking*?"

She gasped as his words from this morning came back tenfold. Stepping forward, she reached for him.

He flinched backward, shaking his head. "Stay away from me," he hissed, then whirled around and slammed out of the house.

And finally she understood. Tommy *wanted* to fuck her. He wanted to fuck her just as badly as he *didn't* want to fuck her. She really wasn't sure why that was. But she had a feeling it had to do with that protective instinct he'd always felt toward her. Except this time he was protecting her from himself.

Too bad for him she'd decided she didn't need protecting. Especially from Tommy Sparks.

She had to have him.

And she intended to do just that.

# CHAPTER 11

Tommy stood outside the house with his keys in his hand. It was a little after midnight, and he'd expected the house to be dark when he got home—the way it had been all week. But the living room light was shining brightly, letting him know Julie was waiting for him inside. He turned back to his car, moved toward the vehicle, then stopped, glanced back at the house, scrubbed his hand on the top of his head, and groaned. He couldn't keep avoiding her. Hell, he missed her. *Really* missed her.

Which, it seemed, was why he had yet to find a place to live. Not from lack of searching, though. Any time he was shown a new rental, a rock formed in his gut and all he could think about was Julie and the mess of things he'd made with her. He desperately wanted to fix it. Couldn't seem to be able to move on until he did.

Unfortunately, he was terrified to be around her. He couldn't seem to be able to keep his hands to himself when he was alone with her. So he found himself in the frustrating situation of not being able to move out until he mended things with Julie but unable to do so because if he was around her, he'd just make everything worse.

When he was home, he kept himself locked in his room until she'd left for work each morning, and he'd stayed out past her bedtime each night for the past week. Some nights he stayed at the gym longer, some he drove around aimlessly, and others he went out with one of the guys and had a couple of drinks—as he had tonight.

Training had gone really well all week, and one by one the guys had started to come around. Not all of them, but most. And tonight he'd been invited to join them for a drink after practice. It'd been nice to hang out with the guys again, talk shop, bullshit.

But through it all, he missed Julie.

And now she was still awake, no doubt waiting up for him.

Inhaling a steadying breath, he strode up the walkway. *You're a man. So be a man.*

When he opened the front door, he found her sitting on the couch. Lucy was curled up on her lap, while Warrior was nestled against her hip. It was a beautiful sight to come home to. He stepped inside and closed the door behind him, then went farther into the living room. A bottle of wine sat on the coffee table and she held a glass in her hand. Seeing him, she brought it to her lips and drained it.

"Rough day?" he asked.

"You can say that."

"Want to talk about it?"

"Sure. Where've you been all week?"

He noticed the slight wobble to her head as she turned

to look at him. She wasn't drunk yet, but she was past tipsy. Her buzz gave him a security blanket, and he relaxed. Drunk women did nothing for him. When he took a woman to bed, he didn't want anything dulling her senses. He wanted her completely aware of every decision she made, and everything he did to her.

"I've been out."

"Obviously." She lifted Lucy off her lap and rose. "With who?"

"The guys."

"Uh huh." Swaying, she crossed her arms across her chest. "To the bars?"

"Yes."

"How many women did you fuck?"

Hearing that word uttered by the only woman he wanted to do it with was a very dangerous turn of events, flashing images through his mind that would ensure he'd only make things worse between them. He needed to take control. Immediately.

He started toward her. "I think it's time to go to bed."

Her brows rose in challenge.

*"Alone."*

She snorted. "I thought so." She swayed again. "How *many*, Tommy?"

"Julie, don't be—"

She slashed a hand toward him. "You won't fuck me, so I know you have to be fucking someone else."

*Stop saying that word!*

"I'm not fucking *anyone*," he gritted out.

"Really?" She made her way to him, tripping over her feet. "So you're just plain mean, then. Is that it?"

He jerked back. "What the hell are you talking about?"

When she stopped in front of him, she placed a finger on his lips, and the sultry awe on her face as she gazed at them made his cock instantly harden. "This mouth did wicked things to me, Tommy. *Wicked* things. I came so hard. Twice. I never came twice like that before."

A gust of air whooshed out of him, and he was damn close to giving her another taste of his wicked mouth if she didn't stop. *She's been drinking.* The reminder helped…a little.

She ran her finger from his lips down his chin, between his pecs, over his abs, and then cupped a whole handful of *him* and rubbed. A groan slipped out, long and low, as his body stiffened right along with his cock. *Fuck. Me.* He couldn't have moved away from her kneading fingers even if he'd wanted to. Which he didn't.

One minute. He'd enjoy the feel of her hands on him for one more minute, then he'd stop her.

"Yeah, you were hard just like this, too," she said as she pressed into the length of him, ripping another groan from him. He tried to smother it and failed miserably.

Latching on to her wrist, he started to tug her hand away, but froze when her other hand slipped between her own legs, stealing his ability to move. He watched, spellbound, as she began to rub herself. He'd give anything to replace her hand with his right now. Make her scream again. Taste her again.

*So, why don't you?*

Because she deserved better than him.

"Then I felt you here, Tommy. Probing. Getting ready to thrust into me. I was so *fucking* wet and ready for you. And then you left me. *You left me.* "

She dropped both of her hands and Tommy released a stuttered breath as she put some space between them.

"Do you want to know what *I've* been doing all week?"

No, he didn't think he did. In the mood she was in right now, God only knew what might come out of that tempting mouth of hers.

"I've been fucking my vibrator. And guess what? It's pissing me off. Why? Because I have a perfectly good *real* cock right there"—she pointed to the bulge in his pants—"that promises to seriously rock my world, but *you* won't let me have it. I'd say that's the definition of mean, wouldn't you?"

He swallowed. It should be illegal for Julie to say the words "cock" and "fuck," because watching her lips form around those dirty words made *him* want to get dirty. Goddamn it, he should have left while he had the chance. Or even better, should never have come inside.

He didn't need to hear all this. Doing right by her was hard enough without hearing her say how much she wanted him. He stepped forward, taking her arm. "Julie, you need to go to bed. You've had too much to drink and have no idea what you're saying."

She yanked her arm away and scowled at him. "To *hell* with you. I am perfectly aware of what I'm saying, Tommy Sparks. You left me all alone and whimpering for more. You just walked away while I had my naked ass up in the air, begging for it. What the *hell*, Tommy?"

There was a world of hurt in that last question that punched him right in the heart. He really hadn't thought about how his actions might have felt to her. He'd just been thinking about doing the right thing. Not wanting to hurt her had been the reason he'd stopped. But he'd hurt her anyway, and that killed him inside.

So it was time to be honest.

"Julie, I love you. You are my best friend. I can't treat you the same way I've treated every other woman in my life. I won't. Do you understand that?"

"Treat me like what? Like you want me so badly you're almost out of control? *Every* woman wants to make a man feel like that. Jesus, Tommy, it's *hot* watching you get that turned on."

He shook his head. "You don't get it. You deserve a man who can take his time, caress you, just simply love on you for hours and hours. I'm not that man. It's just sex to me. There are no emotions involved. It's all about the physical, the pleasure. I won't do that to you."

She studied him for a long time. "Are you actually telling me that anything between us would only be physical, nothing more?"

"Considering the way I've been with you so far, the way my baser side just takes over… Yeah, it's going to be physical. If I can't slow down with you—someone who means the world to me, someone I *want* to treat special, and tried damn hard to treat special, but failed—then, yeah. I really don't think I'm capable of anything else. I'm just like my mom, Julie. You know how she was. I'm the same way."

She appeared appalled. "You are *not* your mother."

"Aren't I? I've never had a relationship. Never *wanted* a relationship. I go through women the same way she went through men. I seem to be just as incapable of feelings as she was."

Julie's jaw worked. "Your mother was a heartless bitch, Tommy." He didn't even flinch at her sharp tone. She'd said those exact words many times in the past. "You *do* love," she insisted. "Don't you *ever* compare yourself to that woman again." Eyes narrowed with unreadable emotions, she studied him again, then nodded once. "Okay, fine. We keep it physical. And we both go into it knowing that physical is all it is."

Was she *insane*? Bringing sex into their relationship would mean the end of them. Of their valued friendship.

He waved a hand back and forth. "No way. I can't take that risk with you. You mean too much to me. I can't lose you. I won't."

"Too late. The moment you buried your head between my legs, you crossed that line. You are *way* past the point of no return, my friend."

He dropped his jaw.

She shrugged, no apology in her expression. "I *want* you to fuck me, any way you want to, and I'm giving you permission." She walked down the hallway toward her room. "If you continue to be a pain in the ass about it, I'm going to make damn sure you get the worst case of blue balls you've ever experienced. But I'll give you some time to think about it. Since I've been drinking, and you have that stupid no-drunk rule, I know tonight is off the table. But this is fair warning. Tomorrow? I'm coming for you, Tommy Sparks."

. . .

She'd scared off the jerk.

Julie didn't know whether to laugh or cry.

Tommy was gone before she got up Saturday morning, and she had no idea when he'd returned that night. At some point he must have, though, because there were dishes in the empty dishwasher when she'd gotten up this morning, Sunday. She'd tried calling him, but he'd refused to pick up his damn phone. And now he was nowhere to be found.

Again.

Damn wine, letting her mouth get away from her. All she had done was warn him. Big mistake. Tommy clearly didn't need a warning—he needed to be taken by surprise. Especially if he'd resorted to thinking he was anything like his mother. Yeah, the bitch had gone through men a bit like Tommy went through women. But that was where the similarities stopped. That woman hadn't cared for anyone but her damn self. She'd left Tommy to fend for himself on more than a few occasions. Just disappeared for days on end, with no food in the house and no money left behind for him.

But Tommy never missed a day of school, always had a smile on his face, and, considering where he'd come from, had risen above the odds to be a damn good man. He wouldn't be so worried about hurting her if he wasn't such a good man.

But now that man was on the run.

Groaning in frustration, she flopped down on the couch. Lucy immediately jumped up on her lap and she scratched the top of the dog's head.

While she found Tommy's reasoning admirable in theory—refusing to touch her because he believed she deserved better—in practice it annoyed the piss out of her. She was a grown woman. It wasn't his place to decide what was best for her. That was up to her.

Though she did get his fear about losing her. Hadn't she worried about exactly the same thing? However, his declaration last night that the physical was all he *could* give her had made her realize that the only thing Tommy was feeling for her was desire. Nothing more. Part of her was crushed about that. But the rest of her had to be realistic about the situation.

And reality was, the only way she'd ever get Tommy

completely out of her system was if there was nothing left to wonder about.

She knew now what an amazing kisser he was. He was also masterful with his mouth in other ways. But ever since he'd knelt between her legs and slid his cock over her mound, she'd been tortured by the question of what he would be like in bed.

And until she found out the answer firsthand, Tommy Sparks would always consume her thoughts.

She refused to let that happen. Somehow, she had to get him to stop doing the disappearing act so she could proceed with some hands-on research. Maybe she needed to take Warrior hostage. Tommy might actually show his face then.

Speaking of the Labradoodle…

She glanced around. "Where's Warrior?"

Normally he was with Lucy at all times. If they weren't in the house, they were outside curled up under the tree together. But Lucy was right here. And Warrior was nowhere to be seen. She sat up as she looked by the front door.

His leash was missing from the hook.

Sudden panic clawed at her chest as she jumped off the couch and raced back to Tommy's room. He wouldn't just pack up and leave.

He *wouldn't*.

Would he?

She yanked open a dresser drawer. Neatly folded clothes appeared inside. *Oh, thank God*. Her heart rate returning to normal, she straightened with her hands on her hips. Okay. If Warrior was with him, that meant he wasn't at the gym.

Had he taken his car? She hurried back into the living room and pulled down one of the blinds. His rental sat by the curb.

*Ah-ha.* He was out running. Which meant he'd be back soon.

She had to act fast.

After rushing to her room, she went through her workout clothes drawer, tossing things willy-nilly until she found her yoga bra and shorts. A year ago she'd tried practicing yoga at home. It had lasted about a month. While it had been a great muscle-lengthening workout, she had a hard time with the calm, composed part of it and decided she preferred running and kickboxing to get rid of her tension.

However, she'd kept the outfit. The sports bra was pale yellow and bordered with a wide black hem. The matching cotton shorts were form-fitting and stopped right at the top of her thighs. She would never go out in public wearing shorts these short, but for home they had been perfect. And were *beyond* perfect for this moment.

She quickly changed, dug out her mat and blocks from the back of the closet, and hurried into the living room. She'd barely had time to get the mat spread out before she heard him run up onto the front porch.

Angling her body toward the front door, she bent in a downward dog pose, making sure her butt was the first thing he'd see. As the door opened, she glanced upside down behind her. Tommy had frozen right inside the doorway, his gaze glued exactly where she'd known it would go. Pretending she was unaware he was there, she lifted her right leg in the air, bent her knee, and caught the top of her foot in her right hand, opening herself up for him to see.

A strangled male groan was her reward, and she fought back a smile. She held the pose for a second, then released it. Lowering onto all fours, she went into a cat pose and arched her back. And then the grand finale—the dog tilt. She dropped the center of her spine toward the floor at the same time she tilted her tailbone to the ceiling. The movement made her ass jut pertly in the air.

A vehement curse rent the air, and she waited for his hands to grab her hips, his pelvis to grind behind her. What she got was the slamming of the door.

Sitting back on her haunches, she blew the hair out of her eyes.

*Well, damn.*

Okay. Round one to Tommy.

Warrior trotted over and licked her face. She ruffled the sides of his face but froze when an engine cranked in the background, followed by squealing tires. She grimaced.

And once more he was gone.

Fine.

Desperate times called for desperate measures. If seduction wasn't going to work, she'd just have to outright lie.

If she could get him to lose control, keep him in a place where he didn't think, just acted, she'd have him. Once it was over, done was done. It couldn't be taken back. Then maybe he'd stop being so damn jumpy and become the man who'd held her so mesmerized as he'd rubbed himself against her and devoured her with his mouth.

What would it be like to be around *that* man all the time?

She shivered. Definitely an intense ride. One she may never want to get off of.

Shaking her head, she pushed those thoughts aside. She'd decided that she had to be with Tommy. Whatever else happened, she'd face it when she crossed that bridge.

She grabbed her phone off her coffee table and opened a text message.

*TRUCE? PLEASE. I MISS YOU.*

Twenty minutes passed before he responded, and she'd almost burned a hole in the carpet from her pacing.

*MISS YOU, TOO.*

Was she doing the right thing by pushing him? She bit her lip, wavering. Yes, she was. This attraction was here between them, and it wasn't going away no matter how much he tried to run from it or tried to protect her from himself. If their relationship was going to be damaged, it wasn't going to be over him fighting his desires for her. It would be from the consequences of it.

*MOVIE TONIGHT? SPEND SOME TIME TOGETHER?* she sent.

Another ten full minutes passed before she received: *SURE.*

Not the most encouraging response, but his guard was still up.

Tonight, however, she was determined to break down every one of those frustrating barriers.

He didn't stand a chance.

. . .

Tommy sat down on one of the benches in the locker room, lowered his elbows to his knees, and cupped his head in his hands. He'd been here at the gym all afternoon lifting weights, sparring, running…anything not to go back home.

Unfortunately, Mike would be locking up soon, which meant unless he wanted to head to a bar or drive around, neither of which appealed to him, he had to face Julie.

*Watch a movie.* Right.

Unless it entailed a pizza boy showing up at some scantily clad woman's home, a *movie* was not what Julie had in mind. No matter how much she was trying to convince him otherwise. The image of her ass up in the air swept through his mind. He shifted on the bench. It had taken everything in him not to grab her hips and yank her backside against his crotch. She'd wanted that, had been egging him on. Hell, she'd actually *told* him to fuck her. Had given him goddamn permission.

Even if her wiggling ass had been a clear come-and-get-it invitation this morning, she hadn't been thinking clearly when she'd said it. Probably didn't even remember the very valid reasons he'd given as to why he couldn't do it.

She deserved more than being used and then abandoned.

And if *he* had to be the voice of fucking reason, so be it. Unfortunately, he hadn't been able to get the taste or smell of her out of his senses, or the sound of her coming out of his mind since Friday night. His resistance was waning. That spelled trouble.

And trouble was exactly what was waiting for him at home.

Tonight.

A slap to his shoulder made him jump. "That was a hell of a sparring session, Tommy."

He glanced up at Mac. "Thanks."

His friend's brows drew together. "Everything okay?"

"Yeah." Tommy sighed, leaning back as he scrubbed his hands down his face. "Fine."

"You sure?"

What could he say? He was scared of a tiny woman and her not-so-subtle messages? That for the first time in his entire damn life, he was terrified of having sex? "Yep. Just been a long week."

"How's Julie doing?"

The very subject he wanted to avoid. "Much better. Seems to be back to normal."

If trying to get him to bend her over and have his way with her constituted being normal. In his mind, it did not.

"Well, good. I'm glad that back thing didn't keep her down for long."

Mac didn't know the half of it. *Nothing* kept her down, not even him saying no—*twice*—when she had her mind set.

And what she had her mind set on right now could not happen.

Somehow he'd have to derail her. Blow her plans straight out of the water.

The question was: how?

• • •

Julie parked in front of The Carnal Cat and stared at the scantily clad mannequins in the display window. All three pieces of lingerie were gorgeous, but two of them had a sweet, innocent vibe with their pastel colors and baby-doll style. The last thing she needed to do was wear something that would make Tommy think he had to handle her with care. *That* was the whole problem.

Which the third one definitely didn't inspire. It screamed naughty. Seductress. A woman who wasn't looking for caresses and lingering kisses but wanted to get straight to the nit and the grit.

A sheer ribbed black corset with satin red trimming

hugged the mannequin's torso. The top ended at the midriff, leaving the stomach bare. A wispy, see-through skirt hung low on the mannequin's hips and barely covered the tops of its thighs. Two red bows were sewn above each of the satin-ribboned garters and held up black silk stockings.

It. Was. Perfect.

She checked the time. A little after six now. Only a couple of hours to prepare. She needed to bust some ass. When she entered the shop, a woman with light brown hair turned and smiled. "Can I help you?"

"I'd like to try on the black corset in the window."

The woman's smile grew. "Gorgeous, isn't it?"

"Oh, yeah."

"I have one. My husband loves it. Can't keep his hands off me."

Julie hoped Tommy reacted the same way, and didn't completely shut down the moment he saw her in it. She was prepared for that reaction, but everything would go much more smoothly if he'd just play along.

The woman went to a rack and sifted through, finally pulling one off the hanger. "This is a small. It should work."

After Julie closed herself inside a dressing room and stripped down to her panties, she quickly put the corset and skirt on. As she examined herself in the three-way mirror, her eyes kept going back to how the sheer skirt hit directly below her butt cheeks and showed off the silhouette of her red panties. The lingerie came with a matching black thong, which she had no intentions of wearing. As far as she was concerned, the less she had on between him and his goal, the less chance he'd have a moment to stop and think. The whisper-thin skirt would bring his eyes directly to the naked skin beneath.

She smiled. Tommy was such an ass man; he wouldn't know what hit him. Excited anticipation shivered through her. He'd be stunned the moment he walked through the door, taken completely off-guard. She'd have the advantage.

*Round two goes to me.*

Feeling confident, she purchased the outfit and left. By the time she got home, some of her triumph had faded. Traffic had been horrible and the food she'd ordered had taken too long to be prepared. Tommy would be here in less than an hour, and she still hadn't showered.

She popped the food in the oven, then hurried to the bathroom. As she bathed, primping for a night she'd only dreamed about, the reality of what was about to happen crept in. Butterfly flutters swarmed her chest, momentarily stealing her breath away.

Pushing aside her anxiety, she blow-dried her hair and styled it so it fluffed around her head, then she quickly dressed, choosing a pair of black, four-inch spiky heels she rarely wore to top off the outfit. She applied her eye makeup darker than normal for a sultrier look. As she gazed in the mirror when she was ready, she barely recognized herself. The woman staring back at her appeared confident, knowledgeable in the ways of a bedroom, didn't shy away from a little kink. She loved it.

Now she just had to get the living room ready. There was still a chance that Tommy would bolt the moment he walked in the house. What would she do if that happened?

There was always *his* room. She could wait for him to return—in his bed.

She went to the kitchen and plated the food on her best dishes. After she poured two glasses of wine, she set the dining room table. As she flicked the lighter to the tapered candles, she heard the sound of a key being inserted into the door.

Shit. Shit. Shit.

She tossed the lighter on the sideboard and did a little don't-know-which-way-to-go dance before her eyes locked onto the couch. She rushed across the room and threw her body on the cushions. She'd propped up on her elbow, her chest pushed forward, bottom lip jutted out, just as Tommy walked into the room.

With Mac following right behind him.

Horror rounding her eyes, she scrambled for a pillow. Tommy let out a stream of curses as he did an about-face and shoved Mac outside.

When she heard Mac's "Sorry, dude," her skin scorched with embarrassment. She pushed into the corner of the couch, drew her knees to her chest, and buried her face in her hands.

How utterly mortifying.

*Round three to Tommy.*

She didn't need to question why he'd brought Mac home. It was painfully obvious. A buffer. With his friend here, no hanky-panky would happen. Oh God, how would she ever face Mac again?

A few seconds later, Tommy slammed back into the house, murder on his face.

She hurried to her feet, feeling very stupid. "Tommy, I'm so sorry. I had no idea—"

"Shut up, Julie," he said as he stormed toward her,

lifted the Braves hat off his head, and tossed it on the coffee table. When he reached her, he curled his hand around the back of her neck and yanked her forward. His mouth crushed to hers.

Wetness gushed between her legs as desire shot through her. She moaned against his mouth. His tongue sailed past her lips and his other hand shot around her waist, pulling her to his chest. After he had her kissed stupid, he ripped his mouth from hers. He walked her backward until her back met the wall. Tangling his hand in her hair, he tugged her head back. Her nipples tightened into painful peaks. She loved it every time he did that, loved the dominance and possessiveness of the action.

Anger tightened the muscles in his face as he slipped his other hand between their bodies. Fingers probed between her legs. "Widen them," he demanded. "Now."

She nearly melted. And did as she was told. One finger circled her clit before he inserted two fingers deep inside her. The pads of his fingers pressed forward. As his palm rubbed her clit, he pumped his hand, causing those fingers to grind against that sensitive spot deep within her.

Pleasure shot through her whole body and she gasped, latching her hand onto his wrist. "T-Tommy."

His grip in her hair tightened. "This is what you want, isn't it? What you've been pushing for."

The sound of his harsh breathing filled her ears, intoxicated her. The sensations he created in her as he zealously rubbed his fingers inside her made her legs weak. Staring up at him, gaze locked with his, she could do nothing but feel what he was doing to her. The pressure he built, the pleasure he gave. She panted out a cry from between parted lips. Then another. She couldn't stay quiet. There was no way. Only moan, whimper, and hold the gaze of the man who was doing such wonderful things to her body.

As his jaw clenched, his pupils dilated. "Oh. Fuck. Yes," he bit out. "That's it, baby."

He pumped harder. Every muscle in her body seemed to tighten and shake. An unfamiliar sensation built deep inside her. Different from any pending release she'd ever had. "T-Tommy?"

"Don't fight it," he grunted. "You're almost there."

A powerful orgasm erupted over her, rolling pleasure through every inch of her flesh. Unable to make a sound, she rode the intense wave, jerking as her entire body was consumed by it. Never had she felt anything like this climax. Legs mush, she started to crumble. Fingers still thrusting deep inside, he pressed her into the wall with his shoulder, keeping her from falling. As the intensity slackened, she sucked in a deep breath, then released a long, agonized moan.

"So goddamn beautiful," he murmured as he removed his hand and placed his lips against her ear. "You're going to get what you asked for, Julie. I'm going to fuck you. Hard."

Then his mouth was on hers. She fisted her hands in his shirt, both to stay standing and to bring him closer, and met each fierce swipe of his tongue with hers. He groaned into her mouth, his fingers releasing her to grab the backs of her knees and haul her up around his waist.

The man had already turned every muscle in her body to liquid. And now he was devouring her, all his control gone, just as she'd planned.

He might have won the battles, but she had won the war.

And now he was going to do amazing things to her.

He set her on the arm of the couch, moved his hands to cup her face, and assaulted her mouth with deep, hungry kisses. Then he ripped his mouth from hers and buried his head in her neck, biting the skin. She arched against him, gasping.

When he ended the kiss, she was shocked to still see anger on his face. "You know I'm going to have to kill Mac for seeing you like that. But for now, I'll exact punishment from you." His gaze lowered to her breasts. "Take that thing off."

The authority in his voice, the determined glint in his eyes, made her body throb with need.

Reaching behind her, she started popping the hooks free. His hands settled on her hips and tugged her closer. The feel of his cock pressing against her center almost undid her. When the corset fell from her body, he caught it and flung it across the room. Then his mouth was on her nipple, sucking deeply. No gentleness or subtlety. Just pure taking.

She gasped, thrusting her chest up as she wove her fingers into his thick hair. As he drew deeply on one tip, he tweaked the other between his fingers, sending a flood of desire rippling through her. Without lifting his head from her breast, he made some movements, and she heard the sounds of his zipper and ripping foil. Then he yanked her forward by the knees and thrust inside her.

Just like that.

She cried out. "Oh, God!"

Not from pain, but from the intense feeling of being so empty one second and then so incredibly full the next. As he thrust deep and fast, their moist skin slapping at his frantic pace, he nipped her earlobe and whispered gruffly, "Julie, you feel so fucking good." He plunged deep, then ground hard against her. His groan warmed her neck. "Never felt this fucking good."

His words sent her arousal into hyperspace. "Oh, God. Tommy."

His hands roamed over her hips and slid to cup the naked mounds of her butt. Muttering a curse, he pulled out of her. She started to protest, but the words were lost when he tugged her off the arm of the couch and spun her around.

A whistling inhale came from him. "Bend over," he commanded gruffly.

She smiled through her aching desire. So damn predictable. *Thank God.*

Slowly, she bent over the arm, feeling the sheer fabric of the skirt rise over her butt. To tease him, she wiggled her backside.

A snap on her cheek as he plucked her garter made her squeak, then moan as he rubbed the area with his palm.

"Don't tease me, Julie," he ground out.

She was so tempted. She loved the feel of his hand on her ass.

"Damn, you're so beautiful."

His palms glided over the swell of her cheeks, and low around to the front of her thighs. He nudged her backward.

His cock probed her center, then scythed deep into her. A sharp breath flew from her lungs. And then there was no thought. Just Tommy, his fingers biting into her hips as he thrust into her from behind.

Over and over.

Faster and faster.

Harder and harder.

Until he had drilled himself into every fiber of her being.

When she came for the second time, he quickly followed. And she knew she would never, ever be the same again.

•••

Hell. He hadn't even taken his damn pants off.

Tommy shoved himself back into his jeans and zipped up as Julie straightened. Turning away from her, he scrubbed his hands across his face. God, how could he have done that? He knew he'd wanted Julie…horribly. But to the point he hadn't even taken off his pants, his shoes… not even his damn shirt? While all she'd had on was that flimsy skirt that hid nothing, a garter belt, stockings, and those fuck-me-hard heels.

God, he hadn't even undressed her completely. Just bent her over and took her.

He was such a bastard.

Making himself face her, he noticed she was grimacing as she tried to move.

Skin going cold, he rushed over to her. "Jesus. Did I hurt you?"

A soft laugh was his answer. "The *last* thing you did

was hurt me, Tommy. I think you've removed every muscle I have in my body. I don't think I've ever felt this unhurt in my life."

An insane amount of male satisfaction shot through him and he couldn't help a smile. "No complaints, then?"

"Not a damn one." She gave him a sleepy smile, her eyelids at half masts.

So she wasn't *bothered* by the way he'd taken her? The roughness? The lack of caressing? Holding? Finesse...?

He helped her onto the couch and she leaned back against the cushions, closing her eyes, a light, contented hum seeping from her mouth. He raked his gaze over her. Her nipples were still pebbled from her orgasm. Red marks marred her thighs from his fingers gripping her. Her skin glowed with a pink flush. She looked completely sated...in such peace.

She was the most breathtaking woman he'd ever laid eyes on.

And he had not the slightest desire to leave.

"Need anything?" he asked, and had to clear the gruffness from his voice. "A drink. Something to eat?"

"Glass of water would be nice," she said without opening her eyes.

He walked toward the kitchen but stumbled to a halt when he saw the dining room table. Food sat out on plates, and glasses of wine sparkled in the light of candles burning in the middle. A lead weight formed in his stomach. She'd been planning a night of romance, and what had he done?

Ravished her like a wild animal. She might say that she was fine with it, but this, right here, proved she wanted more. That she wanted the kissing, the slow dancing, the hand holding. The cuddling in the morning.

Panic squeezed his throat. He couldn't give her that, and she needed it…deserved it all.

So he had to walk away.

And wasn't *that* the ultimate irony? The one time in his fucking life he desperately wanted to stay, he was forced to leave.

For her sake.

He compelled himself into the kitchen, grabbed a bottle of water from the refrigerator, and strode back to her. She didn't stir.

"Julie?" he whispered.

She made a soft noise and turned her head, whispering his name. Desire burned red hot through him. His heart clutched in agony.

*No.* He couldn't walk away. *Not yet.* He still wanted her…had to have her. Just once more. He had a whole damn list of different ways he wanted to take her. Pleasurable things he wanted to show her.

Maybe he couldn't give her true intimacy, or forever, but he could take her body places it had never been. For right now.

After setting the water on the coffee table, he lifted her into his arms and walked down the hall. He stopped outside her room and hesitated. Frowning, he stared at her sweet face, then at the knob. Panic trickled through him. This was when he always left.

He had a serious, unbreakable, no-sleepover rule.

But the idea of leaving Julie on her bed and going to his own room…

*Hell*, no. So not happening.

Smothering a frustrated groan, he continued on to his room, tugged back the covers, and gently laid Julie under them. She'd slept here just over a week ago. He'd liked her in his bed then, and he liked it even more now. Loved the fact that he could reach over at any given moment and coax her awake with small, deliberate touches. And the thought of morning sex when she was still sleepy-eyed and disheveled from a full night's rest? Oh, yeah. He wasn't going anywhere, and neither was she.

He stripped off his clothes, then crawled in beside her, propped up on his elbow, and just watched her sleep. He'd taken his best friend. Hard and fast and unrelenting. No undoing that now. All he could hope for was that one day she didn't look back and regret it.

And he prayed to God he didn't lose her completely when she realized what he already knew. That although the sex was amazing, that's all there would ever be.

Because that's all he was capable of.

# CHAPTER 12

This morning had been *so* goddamn awkward.

Pulling in controlled breaths, Tommy lowered his body toward the floor as he completed one last set of triceps dips off the side of a workout bench. Then he shoved up and off, and jogged to the next circuit. After straddling the next bench, he gripped the hanging bar apparatus and pulled it to his chest.

Because of the late night, they'd gone to bed without setting the alarm. Julie's frantic cursing had woken him up, and he'd realized she was already thirty minutes late for work. *Whoops.*

After a quick shower, she'd hastily dressed. That's when it had gotten weird. Did he kiss her good-bye? On the lips? Cheek?

She hadn't seemed to know the answer, either. Finally, she'd just given him a wave and a high-pitched, "See ya later," and was out the door.

He jogged over to the rowing machine. How was he

supposed to treat her now? She wasn't his girlfriend, but they were *sleeping* together while living under the same roof. Man, he sure as hell hadn't thought of that problem, had he? Talk about awkward.

Affection made him very uncomfortable. Which was odd, considering he'd never hesitated to wrap an arm around Julie or kiss her hair or cheek before. But this was a different type of affection—*relationship* affection. And *that* he was so not comfortable with.

God, he couldn't keep thinking about this. It had driven him crazy all damn morning. How hard would it be to hold her hand? Give her a little more than just a rough tumble?

Finishing up the rowing, he jogged over to the weights, putting his focus back on his training as he did his squat reps.

Training had been going phenomenally and had given him some hope that maybe, sometime in the future, he'd get a chance to prove himself—where it really mattered.

In the cage.

A hand landed on his shoulder, and he glanced up to see Mike. "Let's talk."

Tommy set the bar back on the stand, then twisted to face his coach as he wiped sweat off his face with a towel. "What's up?"

"I'm holding a really important sparring match on Saturday. Some extra training for Tate. I need you to be his partner."

Tommy blinked. Next to Dante, Tate Donovan was Mike's biggest name in the gym—an honor Tommy used to hold before everything went south. Tate was only one win away from being a contender for the Middleweight belt. Tommy didn't know how he felt about being the practice dummy for a man who wanted to claim his former title.

"Can't Dante fill in?"

"He's welterweight."

"He's a title holder, Mike," he shot back. "He'd be just as good, if not better, than me, even with the weight difference." Mike was already shaking his head. Tommy persisted, "Okay, if not Dante, there are other middleweight guys in the gym. Why not one of them?"

"They don't have the experience you do. I want this match to be as close to the real thing as possible. This is a very important training session, okay? It has to be you."

Tommy studied his coach, noted the shifting of feet and tension coming off him. "You're not telling me something."

"I've told you everything you need to know. You'd better be in here training your ass off this week. Got it?"

One thing Tommy had learned long ago was when his coach started throwing "Got it?" around, he was dead serious and wouldn't take any more arguing. Tommy held up his hands in surrender. "All right. I'll spar with Tate on Saturday."

· · ·

With a huge sigh of relief, Tommy opened the front door to the house, totally exhausted. Mike had made him stay for some extra training and had run him through the ringer. He dropped his duffel bag on the floor, then flopped backward on the couch and tugged the baseball cap over his eyes.

"Rough day?"

Julie's voice came from beside him. Without thought, he reached out his free hand, blindly searching for her. When she placed her hand in his, he yanked her down on top of him and rolled them to their sides, knocking the hat onto the floor. He inserted one of his legs between hers, put his hand on her hip, and snuggled deeper into the cushion. The sweet lavender scent that was Julie soothed him as nothing else could.

"Tommy," she whispered.

"Hmm?"

"Why don't you take a shower?"

He cracked one eye. "Are you telling me I stink?" Not possible. He'd actually taken a shower before he left the gym.

She chuckled. "You *are* a little ripe."

A slow grin came to his face as he caught the teasing tone of her voice. Someone wanted to play. He was completely game. "Holy shit. You *are* telling me I stink."

"Yeah, and you're getting it all over me."

"Oh. I can make sure it gets all over you." He rolled her under him.

Her squeal of laughter bounced around the room as she squirmed. "Tommy! No!" She gasped and he attacked her side. "That tickles."

"Seems to me you're the one getting it all over you now." Grinning, he released her and gazed down at her, her face bright with laughter, eyes shining. *So beautiful.* Slowly, he felt his smile fade.

Dipping his head, he captured her lips and brought his hand up to cup her cheek, rubbing his thumb over her soft skin as he caressed the inside of her mouth with his tongue. He ran his palm down her throat, and lower, kneading her breast and tweaking the erect nipple that greeted his palm. She sucked in a breath, shifting beneath him so he fit between her legs.

Lust flared through him, hot and potent. He rubbed

against her, pinching the tip a little harder. She whimpered his name and grabbed his ass, pressing him fully into her, and suddenly he had to be inside her. This time, however, he was going to get his damn clothes off first.

He shoved to his feet and held out his hand.

As she slipped her hand in it, she asked, "Where are we going?"

"I think you said I need a shower."

A slow smile curved her lips. "I do believe I did."

He yanked her up and tossed her over his shoulder. Her delighted squeal made something light and warm bloom in his chest, and he popped her on her ass, chuckling as she squealed again. He didn't put her back on her feet until they were in the bathroom. After placing a condom within reach, he turned on the water then tugged his shirt over his head.

"Touch me," he said.

Desperate to have her hands on him for a change, he squared his shoulders, bringing his chest forward. When she pressed her palms against it, he closed his eyes and stifled a groan. God, it felt so fucking good to have her hands skate over his skin. Her lips closed over his nipple as her fingers wandered lower and grazed the front of his pants.

If that was the way she wanted it…

He yanked her T-shirt over her head, and seconds later had both their pants off. Spinning her around so her back was against his chest, he slid one of his arms around between her breasts, clamped onto her shoulder, and slid his other hand down over her belly until he cupped between her legs.

With his mouth to her ear, he walked them into the spray of the shower and murmured, "Watching you come yesterday was so fucking hot. I want to see it again."

Inserting two fingers deep inside her, he pressed the heel of his palm against her intimately. She clutched his wrist and moaned, her head falling back against his shoulder. He nipped the side of her neck as he started moving his fingers inside her.

"I'm the first man to give you one of those, aren't I?"

Panting, she nodded. He'd known by the shock on her face as the orgasm had taken her, but a fierce possessiveness stormed through him at her acknowledgment, and his arm tightened around her.

"I'll be the *only* man to give you one."

Curving his fingers just right as he thrust, he pulled that intense release out of her again. Wetness saturated his hand as her entire body stiffened against his, and he took in the beauty of her in the throes of release.

She'd stolen his ability to breathe yesterday, and she did so again now as she finally found her voice and screamed, her muscles convulsing around him. When he'd pulled the last quake from her body, he removed his hand. One night he was going to give those to her over and over again, and take his pleasure simply by watching her.

She slowly turned in his arms, her head lolling on his chest. Then she dropped to her knees before him and looked up at him, water cascading over her shoulders and slicking down her body. That unbidden catch happened in his chest again.

The woman was the most breathtaking creature to walk the planet.

"You got to have your fun. Now I want to have mine," she murmured mischievously.

The feel of her slender fingers wrapping around him made him jerk, but he wasn't fool enough to stop her. He wanted to feel her lips around him. Feel the suction.

Then he did. The sweet, wet heat of her mouth encased him. "Julie— Oh, *fuck* me!"

As she bobbed up and down, gently cupping his balls, he was aware of nothing but her.

Closing his eyes, he groaned, knotting his fingers in the back of her hair. Nothing compared to the pull of her mouth. The vibration of her moans. He'd never get enough of this. He could live the rest of his life pleasing this woman and her pleasing him.

When he felt his release coming, he lifted her up and pinned her against the wall. Wrapping her legs around his waist, he blindly fumbled for the foil packet, ripped it open, sheathed himself then thrust deep inside her. He kissed her, deep and slow, keeping the same pace with his hips. Even. Steady. He flicked his tongue across hers as he pulled back and rocked forward. The slow rhythm felt amazing. "Oh, shit," he groaned against her lips. "So damn good."

The breathless hitches of her moans as he thrust into her kept him spellbound, and he lifted his head to look at her. Eyes closed, wet hair clinging to her face, she dropped her head back against the tile. He wanted to watch her lips part in the sharp gasps he could elicit.

Beautiful music he could listen to for a lifetime. The sound of Julie being taken—by him.

As he quickened his pace, she gifted him with her desire, pushed him closer to the brink with each sucked inhale, each murmured plea, each heart-tugging moan.

When she shuddered and clamped around him as another orgasm took her, he followed her over the edge.

And for one brief, amazing moment, he actually wanted to believe they could always be like this. Together. That he was somehow capable of being everything she needed—everything she deserved.

That he could be her man.

...

A few days later, Julie walked into the clinic after lunch. Tommy had surprised her at the house, and she'd ended up having to stop at the drive-through on the way back. It had been like that all week. The man was insatiable. Muscles she'd never used before pleasantly ached after he'd introduced her to positions she'd only ever heard about. He had shown her a whole new world of sex. Taught her things about her body she had never known. One being that she was capable of multiple orgasms…not just two, but many. *God*, so many. He'd continued pulling them out of her until she'd had to beg him to stop, not being able to handle another one.

And he'd loved every moment. The man truly believed himself capable of only thinking about the physical, but he was so wrong. That would have meant focusing only on his own pleasure. Since there wasn't a single time he hadn't made her feel like warm jelly, the man was a born lover, not a man who simply fucked.

Melody whistled as she spun her chair and leaned back. "Girl, I'll have what you're having. Damn. Who is he, and does he have a brother?"

Julie chuckled and sat at her desk. "That obvious,

huh?"

"You've had that I've-been-rocked-good look all week. Spill. Is it that handsome fighter?"

She couldn't be referring to Tommy, since Melody would've used his name. What fighter was she—

"Brody? Oh, God no, we're just friends." Over the last few days, they'd talked on the phone a few times. He'd been happy to hear that she hadn't chickened out. She figured there was a little bit of vicarious living involved.

"Then who?"

She bit her lip, not really wanting to say. She hadn't told anyone except Brody about the change in her and Tommy's relationship. Mostly out of fear of how it would end. But she needed a woman's perspective. She took a deep breath and confessed, "Tommy."

Her friend's eyes widened. "No shit? Really?"

"Yeah."

"So are you two...together?"

"No. Yeah. No." Julie slumped her shoulders. "God, I don't know."

And she really didn't. When he was mindless with desire, she knew exactly where they were. But it was when he kissed her super slowly or thrust into her while gazing tenderly down into her eyes...those were the brief moments that confused her—left her wanting to know what it would be like to really make love to Tommy.

At the same time, she wasn't sure if that was a good place to go with him. She was already a changed woman from being with him. If he ever— She shook her head. Not going there.

"Umm...what do you mean you don't know if you're

together?" Melody asked.

Why had she even said that? "It's just physical. No big deal."

Her friend arched an eyebrow. "How could anything be just physical between you and Tommy? You had a relationship before this. For years. Emotions were already there. You guys *love* each other."

"Well...it's complicated."

"Bullshit. That's a Facebook relationship status. This is you and Tommy. So, un-complicate it, for heaven's sake. What do *you* want?"

She didn't know the answer to that one, either. She wanted him in all the exquisite ways he'd shown her and in all the ways he'd yet to show her. That was a definite. Anything more? She just didn't let her mind go there. One: Tommy said himself he wasn't capable of more. Two: She was terrified of what more would mean.

"You know Tommy's reputation, right?" she murmured.

"You mean the confirmed bachelor who loves to party and loves women even more? Yeah, I've heard."

"But that's only part of it, Mel. After Tommy started getting big in MMA, he changed. A lot. There were nights I would stand off to the side after one of his fights while he was literally mobbed by people, and he wouldn't even notice."

"But there's that picture of you in the cage after he won the belt," Melody objected. "Someone who's not important to him wouldn't be given that privilege."

"This is true. And I've never doubted Tommy wanted me there. But he tends to forget me when the spotlight is on him." *God.* She'd never shared this with anyone before. She'd kept the hurt locked away because she'd felt so selfish for feeling it, when he'd worked so hard for years to earn that spotlight fair and square. But the first time he'd excluded her had hurt deeply, and she'd been standing right beside him in the cage. "Do you know he thanked everyone, including this guy from our childhood who dared him to join the wrestling team, in that victory speech? Everyone but me." When Melody's eyes softened in sympathy, Julie continued, "That night at the party, I stood alone by a wall for hours, watching him four-deep in admirers. I ended up leaving without even saying good-bye." As tears pricked her eyes, she blinked them away and glanced at the floor. "He didn't notice. Never even mentioned it. Whenever that spotlight is on him, he forgets all about me."

"Dang, Julie. I had no idea."

She let out a slow breath. "I refused to let his moments of insensitivity ruin our friendship. When it came down to it, those moments were really small in comparison to the other stuff that man does for me. How he *is* there when I need him for other things. I had—have—no right to be upset. Those were *his* moments, and I *wasn't* his girlfriend. I was just his best friend. But it hurt badly enough as that. It would crush me as his girlfriend."

Melody leaned forward. "But it would be different, Julie. You have to realize that. A man really does treat a friend differently than he treats a girlfriend."

"Or it could be more of exactly the same. Who knows? He's never actually *had* a girlfriend."

Melody studied her. "Well. At least he isn't actively

fighting now. He's just training, right?"

"Yeah. He's not sure if Ethan will ever let him in the cage again."

"Then maybe you have nothing to worry about. Here's my suggestion." A wicked grin spread on her friend's lips. "I'd enjoy the hell out of that man every second I had him, because I've never seen you so happy and relaxed. Whatever that man is doing to you beats out a day in the spa anytime, and I gotta say, I'm green with envy."

Julie couldn't help a laugh. What Melody said was true. She'd never felt more blissfully relaxed or so deliciously exhausted. And it was also right that she just needed to enjoy Tommy and what he did to her…and not worry about what the future held.

Live in the moment.

For as long as it lasted.

• • •

All Tommy wanted to do was sink into the woman waiting for him at home.

It'd been like this all week. While he was away from Julie, all he thought about was walking through the door and being with her again. Having her in his arms. Making her come apart. Over and over. When he was with her, it was just more of the same.

He couldn't get enough of the woman. She was an aphrodisiac that had gotten into his bloodstream, spreading quickly all over his body until he was consumed by need every single second.

Leave her? Not in a million years.

He strode through the training facility, intent on

getting out, when Mike stopped him.

"The sparring session will be at eleven in the morning. I need you here by ten thirty. Got it?"

"Got it" again. Coach was dead serious. "Yep. Ten thirty."

Mike came to stand beside him. "I'm extremely pleased with the way training has gone for the last two weeks, Tommy. I know you hadn't been training as usual while you were gone, but you can't tell it. You look just as good, if not better, than you did before you won the title. This is the fighter I believe in. This is the fighter I want to show up tomorrow, okay?"

The praise from his coach made Tommy's chest swell with pride. He'd been determined to come in and prove he'd changed. And Mike had just let him know he'd seen it. "I'm not going to let you down, Mike. You're giving me a second chance and I'm not going to fuck this one up. I'm not going to let *anyone* down ever again. This is where I want to be."

"Hell, yeah." Mike clapped him hard on the back. "Can't wait for tomorrow."

Twenty minutes later, he parked the car, jogged up the walkway, and entered the house.

"I'm home," he called out.

And it felt damn good to be here. Then he realized what he'd said and froze.

*Home.*

When had he started considering Julie's place his home?

Was this unfamiliar feeling of belonging the reason none of the apartments he'd looked at had felt right? Why, whenever he walked through the door for the past week and taken Julie in his arms, it had?

His chest tightened. Yes, this was his home. And he didn't think it had anything to do with the walls that surrounded him. It was simply Julie's presence. She'd *always* been home to him. The only one he could always be himself around.

She walked into the living room from the kitchen and the dogs raced around her toward him. He gave both a quick ruffle on the head, then went to her. As he gathered her in his arms, she looped hers around his neck and smiled up at him.

"Have a good day?" she asked.

His chest tightened again from an emotion he was terrified to name, but he couldn't stop himself from saying, "Yes, and it just got better," and taking her lips in a sweet, lingering kiss.

She stiffened against him for a second, and he didn't blame her. This change in him had to be confusing. All he ever did was jump her bones and ravish her. But this…this tender, loving kiss was how Julie was supposed to be kissed.

Like she was treasured.

And he did treasure her.

Bending, he hoisted her up into his arms, keeping his lips firmly on hers, teasing the inside of her mouth with his tongue. When he reached his bed, he laid her on the mattress, knowing he would take his time exploring every part of her.

Leaning down, he started on the top button of her blouse. With each one he undid, he placed a light kiss on her skin. Her chest jumped on stuttered exhales, but she didn't move away, allowed him to do as he wished. As he parted the shirt, he sat down on the edge of the bed and ran his fingers over her belly, then grazed the tip of one breast until the nipple strained against the pale purple satin of her bra. Then he met her eyes.

At the tender way she gazed down at him, his chest felt like a two-hundred-and-fifty-pound fighter was lying across it. God, he was such a fucking fool. She had everything every other woman he'd been with had lacked—laughter, joy, and home, all wrapped into one.

She was perfect. So fucking perfect.

He palmed the plump flesh of her breast with his hand, running his thumb over the erect nipple. Her sharp inhale made him do it again. When she reached for the clasp in front, he brushed her hands aside, wanting to do it himself. After he flicked it open and peeled the fabric back, her pert nipples jutted forward, asking for his mouth. Ignoring his instant need, he turned his attention to getting her completely undressed. He undid her pants, tugged them and her panties off, and dropping them to the floor. He stood and peeled her blouse and bra over her shoulders, tossed them aside, and removed his own clothing.

As he joined her on the bed, he stretched out beside her, loving the length of her body pressed against his. He leaned down and took the tip of her breast between his lips, flicking his tongue across it. Her fingers dug into his hair, and she pushed herself farther into his waiting mouth.

"I-I want," she gasped as he sucked the nipple into his mouth. "Oh, God, Tommy."

He loved hearing her breathe his name in abject pleasure. Wanted to hear it again and again. He switched to the other nipple. Her mewls of excitement filled his head. She met him each step, pulling him closer. Begging. He got lost in the feel of her, the smell of her. All he was aware of was her and her response to his touch. Returning to her mouth, he saw to her pleasure first, lowering his hands between her thighs. She immediately parted for him. As he used his fingers to love on her body, he used his lips to love on her mouth, feeding on each one of her glorious gasps as she climbed higher and higher. When she climaxed, her body arcing like a bow against his, her long moan wrapping him in shivers of passion, there was no need to take or to devour.

All he wanted was to be inside her. No kinky positions. No fast and hard fucking. Just feeling her body beneath his, joined as one.

Rolling between her legs, his chest met her naked breasts and the air gushed from his lungs at the feel of her tight nipples scraping his skin. He braced his forearms on either side of her and gazed down, watching her wide hazel eyes as he slowly entered her. Her lips parted on a soft sigh. Just to hear that sigh once more, he did it again, closing his eyes as the sounds of her pleasure wrapped around him. He loved listening to her.

He loved *her*.

Not in the way he'd spent the last twenty-three years loving her. Because now she was his. For richer, for poorer, for better, for worse.

And suddenly he knew she always had been.

He *wasn't* his mother's son. He *was* capable of love. Deep, wanting to have a family with the love of his life, lasting-forever love.

*That* was why he'd gone from woman to woman. Not because he had some kind of fucked-up broken gene from his crap mom. He'd *known*, deep down, the women were nothing compared to Julie. She had always had his heart.

It had just taken a bit longer for his head to catch up.

He'd been incapable of making love to anyone but Julie. This slow, even pace was just as thrilling and fulfilling as a hard, fast rhythm because Julie was the one beneath him looking up, eyes glazed with passion, lips swollen from his kisses.

*His*.

Capturing her mouth, he poured every bit of his incredible discovery into that kiss, letting her feel the change, grow accustomed—accept it. Sure, he'd continue to crave this woman with a lust that bordered on insanity, continue to fuck her with a mindlessness he only reached with her, but now he'd learned the true beauty of lovemaking, and he wanted everything that came with it.

He wanted her. And her alone.

When her palm cupped his cheek, he took that as her acceptance.

Their relationship had changed.

They were a couple.

Afterward, he cradled Julie in his arms, kissing the top of her head. A part of him wanted to tell her he loved her, to put words to what he'd just shown her with his body. But they'd said those same words to each other thousands of times in the past. They didn't have the same meaning as they would have if spoken for the first time after making love.

And just because he'd finally *made* love to her, that didn't mean she was willing to accept he was *in* love with her. It went against everything he'd always done. Everything he'd always said, even to her. Hell, especially to her.

He had to show Julie he loved her.

He wanted to be her boyfriend—and to be a great one.

He'd never held that title—not with her, not with any woman. He'd never wanted it, had never even *trained* for it, and he was more than worried he'd somehow screw it up. He hugged her tighter. No, he would be the best damn boyfriend ever, because if he wasn't, he would lose this woman…and that just wasn't an option.

He drew in a deep, steadying breath.

He was about to enter a big fight. The biggest, most important fight of his life.

And he aimed to win by a knockout.

# CHAPTER 13

Tommy walked into the gym just as Mike was closing the door of his office. Tommy kept walking, but his coach quickened his steps toward him, clapped him on the shoulder, and steered him in the opposite direction. "We don't have time for a pre-fight chat," Mike said. "Tate had something come up, so we have to get started now."

"Shouldn't we cancel, then?"

"No. It's got to happen now."

Tommy frowned, not understanding Mike's insistence that the fight happen today. This was just sparring at a gym, not a real fight. They could do it later this week.

He spotted Tate over in the corner getting his hands wrapped with tape, and he dropped the subject. Maybe the guy had something serious going on and wouldn't be able to fight in a sparring session all week.

"All right, let me get geared up," Tommy said, and snatched up his headgear.

"No gear. Get your hands taped, your gloves on, and that's it."

Tommy stared at his coach with a frown. "This is a sparring session, right?"

Mike sucked on his teeth for a second before saying, "No. You're fighting."

Tommy's mouth dropped in surprise. "Mike, what the hell's going on?"

"I need to see what you've got. Tate is a good opponent for you, for me to gauge how far you still have to go."

"So this was never about me being an opponent for him?"

"It's for both of you. Tate needs the practice, too, and you *are* a good match-up for him. I'm killing two birds with one stone. So get out there and give me, and him, everything you've got." Mike looked at Tate, who'd walked up to join the conversation. "That goes for you, too. Don't be easy on him."

Nerves hit Tommy, and he hated the moment of weakness. This was important. He didn't have time for nerves. But he felt them nonetheless. He inhaled deeply, then breathed out, cleansing the anxiety away and focusing on what he had to do.

He didn't want to put on a good show. He didn't want Mike impressed with his progress. He didn't want him coming back with a list of things he needed to work on.

He wanted his coach to be confident that Tommy "Lightning" Sparks was back, and there would be hell to pay.

Which meant he had to beat Tate. And beat him good.

One of the other guys taped Tommy's hands and shoved his gloves on. He warmed up for five minutes, then Mike called him and Tate over. After a quick smear-down of Vaseline over their faces and their mouth guards put into place, they were ready to duck under the ropes.

As Tommy hopped around the middle of the ring, getting his blood flowing even more, he studied his opponent. The auburn-haired man had the same look—firm resolve narrowed his eyes as he studied Tommy.

Tate was just as determined to win as Tommy was. Excitement shivered through him. The thrill of an impending good fight enveloped him, and he smiled, welcoming the sensation.

He was so ready for this.

"All right, we're doing five five-minute rounds," Mike yelled from the side of the ring.

That took Tommy aback, and he shot a glance at his coach. Mike was watching him closely for his reaction, so Tommy sent him a calm nod, as if that information hadn't just shocked the shit out of him. He'd been training for *three* five-minute rounds, a regular bout in the cage.

Not a damn championship fight.

A bell echoed inside the gym, and Tommy had no more time to think. He automatically brought his gloves up to his chin and searched for his opening. It wasn't easy, since Tate was a southpaw.

Being a left-handed fighter, Tate definitely had the advantage. Orthodox fighters like Tommy mostly went up against other orthodox fighters, with a southpaw thrown in only on occasion. Southpaws, however, went up against right-handed fighters all the time, so they didn't need a period of adjustment.

Because Tate's stance mirrored his own, Tommy had to do opposite of what came naturally to him, which was circling right. Every move felt off, even though he'd actually practiced this over the past few days.

He had a couple of options to take the fight onto a more even playing field. Get Tate in a clinch or take him to the ground. Tate was weaker in the clinch, but if things went in Tommy's favor, he wouldn't get a chance to show Mike what he had on the ground.

Crap. Ground it was, then.

Tommy studied Tate. With his right leg forward, his opponent's stance made a double-legged takedown difficult, but he could always go for the single leg.

*Fake it. Open up his stance more.*

Tommy feigned a right hook, which made Tate react with his left side, opening him up. Tommy delved into the pocket, pressing his face against the other man's chest and locked his arms around his opponent's left thigh as he dropped to his knees.

As soon as they hit the mat, Tommy scrambled for the half-guard by sprawling across Tate's upper torso. Both fought for dominance. One second, Tommy had Tate pinned as he tried for a submission hold, the next, Tate had landed a mind-boggling left punch that made Tommy loosen his grip. Tate took the opportunity to worm his way out of the hold and get back on his feet.

They circled each other again. That southpaw left-cross caught Tommy on the side of the head, but he shook off the impact, giving back fist for fist.

Four rounds went by where they beat the bloody hell out of each other. One round Tate would dominate, the next Tommy would. Tommy succeeded in getting the other fighter into a clinch three times, landing damaging body shots. But Tate never wavered. It became clear why he was close to being a contender for the belt.

His opponent landed another left. Blood gushed down Tommy's face into his eyes. He tried to wipe it from his face so he could see Tate, but it was useless. More blood just poured out. Tommy locked his arms around Tate's waist and lifted him high in the air before crashing him against the mat. He'd just landed a jab that opened up a gash under Tate's eye when the bell dinged, signaling the end of the round.

Breathing heavily, he made his way to the corner.

"You're doing great out there, Tommy," Mike said as one of the guys from the team pressed an ice-cold piece of metal against the gash to control the swelling. "One more round. Tate's just as tired as you are right now. Take advantage of that."

Mike slapped him on the shoulder then hurried over to Tate, most likely to tell him the exact same thing. There'd be no special treatment for either of them.

The bell rang for the start of the fifth and last round.

Tommy jumped to his feet and met Tate in the middle of the ring, fist protecting his chin.

He was exhausted, arms heavy, face and body hurting to high hell. But he was satisfied to see fatigue in his opponent's moves, too. The seasoned fighter *was* just as wrung out, just as beat up—and just as determined to finish this before the final bell rang.

A fighter never wanted a decision to go to the judges. Tommy wanted an outright win, which meant he had five more minutes either to knock Tate out or submit him.

He was pretty damn positive Tate was thinking the exact same thing.

They exploded toward each other.

Two minutes in, Tommy's wound reopened in an exchange,

as did Tate's. Blood flowed down both their faces and over their chests as Tommy pushed the other fighter back against the ropes. He grabbed the back of Tate's head and yanked it down as he raised his leg high. Knee connected with nose, and Tate's body slumped to the ground.

Tommy went down to cover him, intending to deliver a few more punches to seal the knockout, as he would in any other fight, but saw that Tate was out cold, and backed off.

Mike hurried into the ring and bent over Tate. His eyes had opened and he was staring straight ahead in an unfocused sort of way. Tommy watched as the team crowded around Tate, remembering the time his team had done the same to him, when he'd lost his belt.

He knew exactly how Tate felt right now: the confusion, trying to make sense of the questions being yelled at him, trying to answer them back as he cleared his rattled head. When Mike and another fighter helped Tate to his feet, Tommy breathed a sigh of relief at the clear eyes that looked back at him.

Tate shook them off. Popping his guard out of his mouth, he stepped up to Tommy and hugged him. When Tate leaned back, he said, "You're going to fuck Ricky Moon up bad."

At the mention of the man who had laid Tommy on the canvas and taken his title, he frowned. "What are you talking about?"

Giving a pained chuckle as he patted Tommy on the shoulder, Tate only shook his head. Mike joined them, pride and excitement in the huge grin on his face. "I think you just earned yourself a fight, son."

What the hell was going on? "What do you mean?"

Mike jerked his head toward the back of the gym. Tommy looked over his shoulder and followed the direction of the nod.

Standing with his arms crossed over his chest, legs spread apart, nary an emotion on his face, was Ethan Porter—the president of CMC.

All Tommy could do was stand and stare at the man. When he finally found his tongue, he asked, "Did you know he was going to be here?"

"Yeah, we had a meeting scheduled for this morning. I convinced him to stay and observe."

"Why didn't you tell me?"

"Because I didn't want you thinking about him. I wanted him to see *you*."

Tommy guessed he could understand that logic. If he'd known he was fighting in front of the man who'd banned him from the cage, his focus would've been shot to hell.

"Go get cleaned up and meet me in the office."

Tommy went to the locker room and cringed at his reflection. His eyebrow was split open. Purple was already staining the skin under the eye, promising a pretty impressive shiner come tomorrow. A bruise was forming on his jaw. He looked as if he'd just come out of the cage. And even though the mesh wiring hadn't been around him, he figured he had.

He'd just fought the most important fight of his career, and hadn't even known it.

An assistant taped up his eye. After a quick shower, he yanked on his clothes and headed for the office. Mike sat behind his desk and Ethan sat in a chair in front of it. Tommy took the other seat. The tension in the room was thick. And only got thicker as Ethan sat there staring at him without saying a word.

Mike cleared his throat. "So, Ethan has a proposition for you."

Tommy lifted a brow. "Okay."

Ethan shifted in his seat. The muscular older man with graying brown hair made a sucking sound with his teeth. "Before we get to that, I guess we need to discuss the most pressing issue."

Tommy swallowed. Was his past going to ruin things for him again? Of all the people who had reason to hate him, this man had the most.

"I owe you an apology."

That was the last thing Tommy had expected. "An apology?"

"On behalf of my son." He leaned back, and Tommy noticed that the man looked ten years older than his fifty-four years. "As a father, you try the best you can to instill morals into your children. I guess I did an okay job with two of mine, since they are functioning adults contributing to society. But my youngest..." He tsked. "I was always making excuses for that boy, since he was the one most affected during the divorce. I let him run wild, feeling like he was entitled to some rebellion, seeing the way his mother and I had fought over him. I didn't know how out of control he'd gotten, though.

"I should have come to you earlier," Ethan continued, "but honestly, I'm still trying to figure out how to handle the situation." He made a noise of self-derision. "I'm the man who brought MMA into the mainstream, made it popular. I'm able to see a potential star in one fight, but I couldn't see that my own son needed help. Did you know he was doing drugs?"

"No. I knew he was drinking a lot. Not drugs, though."

"Heroin. He's in rehab right now." Ethan shook his head. "Still hard to believe. Signs were all there, though. I just refused to see them, even after you hit him. I know I was pissed about the fight before that, but I *am* sorry for how I treated you, especially after I learned he threatened to hurt Julie."

Angry bile rose in Tommy's throat at the remembered threats. "No one threatens to touch her, Ethan."

He raised his hand. "I get it. You've always been protective of that woman. And the connection you two have is special. I would have flipped, too, in your shoes. Can we put this shit behind us and move on?"

A huge weight lifted from Tommy's shoulders. "I'd like nothing more."

Ethan nodded. "All right, then, I have a proposition for you. Chris Dolven is the number one contender for the belt. He was slotted to fight Ricky Moon in four weeks. Unfortunately, he injured his shoulder during training, and the doctors won't give him clearance to fight. So we need a substitute. My intention was to give the fight to Tate, but you can thank your coach here for suggesting I watch you before making the decision—"

"That's not exactly what I said," Mike interrupted. He looked at Tommy. "You know I don't take sides with my guys, Tommy, but when Ethan called last week, I saw an opportunity to get you back in the cage. If Tate would've won, he'd be the one we'd be talking to right now."

Ringing sounded in Tommy's ears as the coach's words slowly sank in. He held up his hands. "Wait. Are you saying you're giving me a chance to win back my *title*?"

"That's exactly what we're saying," Mike confirmed.

He frowned. "You mean I just stole Tate's chance at the title?"

"You didn't steal anything. You won it. Tate knew the score."

*You're going to fuck Ricky Moon up bad.*

Tate must have been aware of what was going on and didn't hold any grudges at the loss.

It still didn't sit well with Tommy. "You should've told me."

"I thought about it, honestly. Tate was the one who suggested I didn't. He wanted a fair fight, and he didn't think it would be if half your concentration was on Ethan. In the end, I agreed with his reasoning. You needed to be completely focused."

"So what do you say?" Ethan asked him. "Can you be ready to fight for the belt in four weeks?"

*Say?* He couldn't even process it. A fight for the belt in four short weeks?

Not that something like this was unheard of. Injuries did happen in training, and fighters were asked to fill in on very short notice. But was he ready for a fight that big? So soon?

"Tommy?"

He ran his hand through his hair. "Sorry. Just trying to wrap my mind around it."

"I know it's short notice," Mike said. "But you'll be ready."

"Yeah, of course, I'd be stupid to pass it up."

And he would be. But this meant his available time was about to tighten up even more. How was he supposed to be good boyfriend material if he was training all day and never around? He'd have to get creative. Make every moment he spent with Julie count.

Make sure she knew she was just as important to him as his career.

. . .

Tommy had made love to her last night. Not sex. Love.

Smiling, Julie opened the front door and stepped inside. As she shut it, she tossed her purse on the couch and went into the kitchen to feed the dogs and pour a glass of wine. He'd also kissed her sweetly this morning and told her to have a good day at work before she'd left.

Was it possible that she and Tommy could actually work as a couple? The idea thrilled her and made all the wants and desires she'd kept padlocked away burst forward. She tamped them back but didn't completely restrain them as she always had in the past, not wanting to totally close herself off from him.

She'd spent so many years protecting herself, believing Tommy could never see her as anything more than a friend, and now when he finally did, she was still pretty convinced he'd never see her as more than a bed partner. Someone to have sex with, nothing more. Tommy had made that crystal clear.

But last night he'd made love to her. Almost certainly for the first time in his life, he'd truly made love. And it had been with her.

That said something. Didn't it?

If he were willing to change, she couldn't let her past hurts and fears keep her from doing the same. At least about that part.

And as for the boyfriend stuff, Melody was right—he was only in training right now. There was no certainty he would ever fight in the cage again. Even if there were, it would be months, maybe a year down the road. And by then they'd either have broken up or would be in a stable relationship, not brand new, still trying to find their footing as they transitioned from best friends, to lovers, to a steady couple.

She filled the dog's bowls with food and a glass with wine, and was walking into the living room just as Tommy came through the front door. Clamping her hands to her mouth in horror, she let go of the glass of wine and it shattered on the floor, sending red liquid all over her slacks. Tommy dropped the bouquet of red roses in his hand and hurried to her side, guiding her around the crimson puddle on the hardwood floor.

She couldn't tear her gaze away from his battered face. His left eye was all but swollen shut, with a dark, purple bruise under it. The skin along his jaw was also discolored. "W-What happened to you? You've never looked like that from a training session. Did you get mugged, or—"

Tommy grabbed the flowers off the floor and handed them to her. "I got these for you."

She blinked and took them, trepidation flowing through her. "Thank you. But...what are they for?"

"Just because."

"Just because?"

Tommy didn't "just because" anything. Good God, had he gotten into a brawl already, and the flowers were a don't-get-pissed bribe?

"I was thinking of you and bought them. Didn't I get it right?" He scratched the back of his head, his face twisting in confusion.

*Oh. My. God.* This wasn't an apology gift; he was trying to be sweet. Gathering the roses in her arms, she stood on tiptoe and kissed his cheek. "They're beautiful. Thank you."

A goofy smile came to his face and his chest puffed up. "What do you say we take the dogs for a walk around the neighborhood before we eat dinner?"

Roses, and now a walk? What had gotten into him?

Normally he rushed in and took her straight to bed.

"All right. A walk sounds nice. You can explain your face on the way."

While she changed clothes and put on tennis shoes, Tommy leashed the dogs.

They stepped outside, and Tommy reached over to entwine his fingers with hers. Biting her bottom lip, she glanced down at their joined hands as they made their way across the yard to the sidewalk. His thumb lazily caressed the inside of her palm, causing tingles to spread low in her belly.

This was why he'd wanted to take a walk. He wanted to hold her hand. The absolute sweetness of his desire made tears sting her eyes. Oh, he was going to make her into such a sap.

They walked in silence for a few minutes. And she realized something. She was still aware of Tommy, overwhelmingly so, but it wasn't uncomfortable like it used to be. It was very comfortable, almost calming. As though taking this leisurely walk, holding this man's hand, was exactly how she was supposed to unwind from her hectic day at the clinic.

He was her peace and her calm.

She laid her head on his biceps and he stopped to kiss the top of her head, as he'd done so many times in the past. But there was a new intimacy to it now. An overwhelming tenderness.

In that one gesture, he toppled twenty-three years of her self-preservation.

And she fell completely, totally, absolutely in love with Tommy Sparks.

Letting the dogs stop to sniff and mark every telephone pole they passed, she'd counted more than a dozen before she finally couldn't stand it any longer. She looked up at him and asked, "So, why do you look like you went five rounds?"

He hesitated a few seconds, then said, "Because I did."

She halted. *Say what?* "Has Mike lost his mind?"

"Surprisingly, I think this was the smartest thing he's done for my career since taking me on in his gym."

She tried to figure out what he was saying but drew a blank. "What do you mean?"

"Ethan offered me a comeback fight ...in four weeks."

Shock slammed into her. A fight? A *real* fight? Not that she should be so surprised; the man was good. But still...

He was going back in the cage. Back where he changed to someone else. Back to where he ignored her.

Panic clawed at the back of her throat, but she shoved it down, forcing herself to concentrate on the conversation. "D-Did you say four weeks?"

"Yeah."

It wasn't enough time. They needed more time. "That's, um...great."

"Guess who I'm fighting?"

"Do I even want to know?"

"Ricky Moon."

Her heart stopped. Then thumped hard with disbelief. It took her a minute to be able to form coherent words. "They're giving you a chance to win your title back?"

"Yep."

She stared up at him, saw the excitement, the pride etched in every line of his face, and felt like a complete bitch for feeling nothing but fear. He loved to fight. This was what he was meant for. Being in that cage made him come to life. She *wanted* that for him so badly it hurt.

But she wanted *him* more...and that was so selfish.

"How do you feel about it?" she asked.

"I feel like things are finally falling back into place," he said. "It feels good."

And that was what scared her most. "What'd they offer you?"

His grin said it all. He was going to be paid, and paid well.

"Eighty-five to just show up."

Eighty-five thousand dollars. Holy crap. She swallowed. It was less than what he'd made when he first fought Ricky Moon but a whole lot more than he earned modeling for catalogs. "Doubled if you win?"

"Yep. Ethan said we'll talk long-term contract after the fight. Even though our conversation went really well, I think he wants to make sure I'm not going to go in there and screw off like I did before."

"Did he give any details?"

Tommy nodded. "Depends on if I win or lose, how I perform, and of course how the fans react to my return. Promotion for my return will start as soon as I sign the contract for this fight."

"You haven't signed yet?"

"Ethan is sending Mike all the paperwork. I'm supposed to sign tomorrow. I was glad about that. It gave me a chance to talk to you first."

"Me?"

He took a step closer. "I wanted to make sure you're okay with it."

She stared up at him. Who was this man? It sure wasn't Tommy "Lightning" Sparks, a man who did exactly what he wanted and only told her about it afterward.

"My opinion shouldn't matter."

"It does matter." His voice was low, almost a whisper, but the words were strong. "My decisions affect you now, too. It's not just about me anymore."

Was it possible he wouldn't revert? He was saying all the right things. Making sure she was included in the decisions he made. He'd never done that before. He hadn't needed to, because they'd only been friends. But now they were a couple. And he'd *included* her. The tension eased out of her shoulders and she smiled, really smiled. "Oh, Tommy. I want you to win your title back."

He smiled, tinged with relief…and happiness. "I won't be home much."

*Home.* He'd started using that word a lot lately. It gave her a warm feeling. Them together. A family. One day maybe making a larger one.

"I'll be waiting. Go train your ass off and beat that Ricky Moon."

He cupped her cheek. "You're wonderful, you know that?"

His lips found hers in a sweet kiss. He pulled back just an inch, his breath warming her face. She slid her palms up his shoulders, behind his neck, and tugged his head down. When his mouth met hers, she angled her head to the side, swiping her tongue across the seam of his lips. He shuddered against her, inhaling a deep breath.

His arms wound around her waist, fingers splaying across her back as he deepened the kiss. When he finally pulled back, desire clouded his green gaze. "Woman, I'm trying to be all sweet and shit, and you're making me hard as a rock."

She chuckled. "While I do like the sweet, I have so much fun when you want to get dirty."

"So you're okay with me putting an end to the wooing,

and just taking you back home and doing nasty things to you?"

Her stomach fluttered. "Do you have something new to show me?"

"Baby, I have all kinds of tricks up my sleeves we haven't tried yet."

A shiver raked over her. "Then you need to get me home. Fast."

As Tommy pretty much dragged her back to the house, she felt light and happy.

They were really going to make this work.

# CHAPTER 14

Tommy straddled the vinyl grappling dummy, pummeling it with quick left-rights and tossing an elbow in here and there. Sweat poured down his face and arms. He'd been grappling for almost an hour, first starting with a live partner to work on his technique, then switching to the dummy so he could strengthen his hits. Satisfaction coursed through him with every loud pop of his fist hitting the torso-shaped bag.

"That's enough for now," Mike called. "Let's take a break."

Tommy rose to his feet, using his forearm to wipe the sweat off his brow. After tugging his gloves off, he grabbed a towel.

Mike motioned him to the office. When he entered, Tommy noticed a TV set up. "What are we doing?"

"Watching your fight against Ricky Moon."

He blew out a breath. "Well, that won't take long."

Mike didn't even try to make him feel better about it. Just sighed and said, "Nope, it won't."

Mike never sugarcoated anything. If a fighter screwed up,

he didn't get a pat on the back and a "we'll get him next time." Nope, his coach let him know exactly how he'd screwed up, then went on to train him to make sure it wouldn't happen again.

Tommy pulled a chair closer and sat down. Mike cued up the fight, fast-forwarding through all the fanfare of the entrances to the actual fight where Tommy and Ricky were circling each other. Tommy frowned at the laziness of his stance. He wasn't braced or even protecting his chin correctly. Hell, he didn't even look like he wanted to be there. Like he was bored. Or so damn cocky that he thought the fight would be easy. Probably the latter.

Ricky took advantage and had him in a clinch within two minutes in the first round. One knee to the face and Tommy was out cold, just as he'd done to Tate the day before. Mike forced him to listen to the announcer declare Ricky the new Middleweight Champion and watch his opponent lift *his* belt over his head.

Mike paused the fight. "What did you see?"

"A fighter not defending his title."

"Damn straight. Do you think Ricky Moon will be like that when you meet this time?"

"Nope."

"No. He won't. He's going in this to win, Tommy. He's not going to give you back your title the same way you let him win it."

*Ouch.* But Mike was spot-on. Tommy hadn't even tried to fight that day. He might as well have handed over the belt to Moon the moment they'd entered the octagon.

Tommy hung his head. How could he ever have stepped foot inside the cage and not given it his all?

But he had. And he'd paid the price.

He lifted his head and looked Mike in the eye. "That won't happen a second time."

Mike smiled. "Am I looking at the fighter who won the title from Pete Griffin?"

"You bet your sweet ass you are."

"Then let's pull up a different fight to study."

Mike traded DVDs again, and Ricky Moon came up fighting against Buddy Triton. He hated the fact that his coach had to show a completely different fight for Tommy to really be able to pick apart his pending opponent. But he understood. If he wanted to see all of Moon's weaknesses and strengths, it wouldn't be in the fight against him. And he was going in completely prepared to win this time.

Tommy pointed to the screen. "Moon is weak on his feet."

Mike nodded his approval. Watching Moon, Tommy couldn't believe the man had won the belt from him by KO. His reach was shorter and any time his opponent went to brawl, Moon tried for a takedown.

"Man, but he's good on the ground."

"Almost as good as Richard Sentori used to be."

Richard Sentori used to be the Welterweight Champion until Dante "Inferno" Jones had won the title from him a year and a half ago. Since then Richard had lost his last two fights, and if his losing streak continued, he would be forced to retire from fighting.

Tommy studied the fight closely, seeing how Moon concentrated on the lower body as he wrapped his body around Triton's left leg and twisted. "Kneebar."

"Moon has won with a variety of leg-locks. He'll win any way he can, but if he's controlling the fight, most of the time he will go for a submission with the leg."

He glanced at his coach and smiled. "I guess I need to make sure he doesn't control the fight then, huh?"

• • •

Julie sighed as a whirring sound penetrated her sleep. Slowly, she opened her eyes, zeroing in on the noise in the kitchen. What times was it?

She looked at the clock on the cable box.

Almost two in the afternoon.

When had she fallen asleep?

It had been a week since Tommy started training for the fight. While she was at the clinic, the workweek had sped by. But today, her day off, had dragged. She'd stretched out on the couch after lunch and must have dozed off from sheer boredom.

As she sat up, Tommy walked out of the kitchen, holding a shake.

Her stomach growled. A smile split his lips when he saw her. "Hey, beautiful. I was about to wake you up."

*Beautiful.* A pleased shiver went through her. "I hope that's for me."

He stopped by the couch and leaned down. She didn't hesitate to tilt her head back to accept his kiss. She'd come to expect them. Tommy might not be around as much, but when he was, he was touching her, kissing her, or holding her.

When he leaned back, he handed her the shake. "Chocolate and peanut butter."

*"Mmm."*

She took a long sip from the straw, very aware of Tommy watching her. Closing her eyes, she made a show of enjoying it with a long, satisfying, yummy sound, then licked her lips.

"You naughty girl," he growled, slipping his hand between her legs and rubbing his knuckle against her. She moaned. Arousal flooded her body, and her nipples tightened. Tommy might be away a lot, but he made sure to take her as often as possible when he was here. In the process, he'd conditioned her body to respond to him in an instant. "But we don't have time for naughty today. I'm planning for sweet."

She opened her eyes and lifted a brow. "I'm listening."

"It's a surprise. I've spent so much time at the gym this week, I just wanted to get home, and I didn't shower. I'm going to take a quick one, and then we'll leave." He pointed at her as he backed out of the room. "Do not follow me. I said quick. And anything I do to you won't be quick."

She shivered.

After he went into the bathroom, she walked to her bedroom. Looking in the oval mirror above her dresser, she cringed at her reflection. Her hair was knotted on one side from her nap. Thanks to Tommy keeping her up late most nights, dark circles stained the skin beneath her eyes. Grabbing a brush, she worked the tangles out of her hair, dabbed a little concealer under her eyes, and added a bit of mascara to her eyelashes and eye shadow to her lids. There was no point bothering with lipstick; he'd have it off before they left the house anyway.

She glanced down at her yoga pants and T-shirt. Nope. If they were going out, she was dressing up. Studying her closet, she pursed her lips. Casual? Sexy?

She went to the bathroom door, opened it, and smiled when he bellowed, "I told you not to follow me!"

"I just wanted to know if you have to go back to the gym today."

"Yeah, practice from six until nine tonight."

She closed the door. Better not wear anything too sexy, then. They wouldn't have time to play. She finally settled on a pair of designer jeans that she knew looked amazing on her and a tight red sweater. After she pulled on her knee-high boots, she walked out into the living room and found Tommy already waiting for her.

Dressed in a pair of dark denim jeans that hugged his butt and a button-down flannel shirt that stretched across his muscular back, he looked rugged and completely edible. The fabric clung to him, teasing her with the body she yearned for.

His gaze raked over her and heated. "I'm one lucky fuck."

He strode over and grabbed her by the waist, then kissed her hard. She leaned into him, opening her mouth without hesitation. God, she loved kissing him. Loved being in his arms. She wrapped her arms around his neck.

Tommy released her and asked, "Ready to go?"

"Yeah."

They went to the car, and soon they were driving down the road.

The mystery of their destination filled her with a buzz of excitement. Half an hour later he pulled into a parking lot and Julie gasped, knowing exactly where they were.

The Georgia Aquarium.

She clapped her hands. "Oh, Tommy, thank you! This is perfect."

After he found a place to park, he opened her door and helped her out. "Do you remember trying to get me to come here with you last year?"

"I do." She chuckled. "You came up with a lame excuse about needing to go through your closet."

He took her head between his hands, running his thumbs over her cheeks. "I regret that now."

"It's not like I hadn't made you come with me before. Besides, we were just friends. You didn't have to go."

"We're not just friends anymore, right?"

She frowned. "I think it's pretty obvious we're not."

"You and me. We're together now. Nothing's going to come between us."

Now she was getting worried. "Tommy, is everything okay?"

There was a distress in his expression she hadn't seen before. Tommy was always so damn confident, so it took her aback.

"I just need to know that my absence hasn't messed anything up. That you and I are still good."

She eased out a breath. "We're more than good."

He smiled, and the tension released from his shoulders as he threaded his fingers through hers and started walking toward the aquarium. "Okay."

After he paid for their tickets, they walked inside.

"I'm yours to lead," he said, and opened the door.

Smiling, she walked farther into the foyer, realizing this was actually the first time she was out in public with Tommy as his girlfriend. The thought was thrilling.

"Where do you want to go first?" he asked.

"The penguins," she said without hesitation.

"How did I know you'd say that?"

She stuck out her tongue at him, making him laugh. She'd only dragged Tommy to the penguin exhibit about a thousand times since it opened. "Know-it-all."

As she headed for the Coldwater Quest exhibit, he snagged

her hand and moved in front of her, guiding them through the maze of people until the penguin exhibit opened up in front of them. She pressed closer to his back, enjoying the way his cologne wafted up to fill her senses.

Once he nudged his way into an open spot closer to the observation area, he switched positions with her, shielding her with his body from all the other people trying to press forward.

As much as she loved watching the penguins waddle around and dive through the water, the only thing she could concentrate on was the feel of Tommy's chest pressing into her back. Her breath quickened and butterflies attacked her stomach.

His arm shot past her to the left. "Look at that one."

Inhaling, she followed to where he pointed, spotting the penguin that swam in front of the glass, bobbing up and down, entertaining the spectators. "That's so—"

The word "cute" was lost as his arms wrapped around her waist and he put his chin on her shoulder. "They're called *Jackass* penguins."

Julie stifled a laugh. He said that *every* time they came to the exhibit. The man just found the name hilarious.

"You mean like you," she responded as always, covering his arms with hers and leaning her head back against his shoulder. So this was what it was like being his girlfriend. She'd always wondered, imagined. He'd never actually dated anyone steadily, so she'd had no clue what kind of boyfriend he'd be. If he was a PDA sort of guy or if he preferred just holding a girl's hand. She liked that he was so willing to hold her in public, no hesitation about it.

His chuckle vibrated against her back, and she inhaled sharply as his lips found her neck and nipped. A delish thrill went through her. They'd done this routine many times, but he'd never responded to her quip like this—and she loved this way more than the elbow nudge she used to get.

"Be nice," he said against her ear. Oh yes, Tommy was shaping up to be pretty good boyfriend material.

Unfortunately, that realization was making her have X-rated girlfriend thoughts in a PG establishment. *Got to keep it light.* She craned her neck to look back at him. "The truth hurts."

He stared down at her, his eyes dipping to her lips. Tension filled the air between them. Would it always be like this between them? God, she hoped so.

"I think I'd like to see the whales."

"Okay." His voice was deeper than it had been before.

He recaptured her hands and led her to the Beluga whale exhibit. The large tank took up one whole wall, casting a blue hue to Tommy's face. When he found an open area, again he positioned her in front of him and cocooned his body around hers. He did the same thing through the next two exhibits, and as they watched a scuba diver feed all the fish in the largest tank. He never let her go, always had a hand on her somewhere.

He made her feel so protected. More so than he'd done when they were just BFFs—and he'd been pretty damn good at making her feel protected even then. She leaned back against his chest and let the back of her head rest against him, loving it when he kissed the top of her hair.

She loved this man. Wanted a future with him. *Saw* a future with him for the first time ever, with no doubt or trepidations.

"Can we see *Dolphin's Tales* before we go?"

An amused smile came to his lips. "Anything you want."

She believed he would try to do exactly that.

As they made their way back to the foyer, Julie said, "I need to run to the restroom real quick."

"I'll wait right here."

After she came out, she couldn't find Tommy. She finally spotted him in the middle of a group, signing autographs, smiling and laughing. As she moved toward him, his gaze connected with hers. He sent her an acknowledging nod, then glanced away again. Ice formed in her stomach. There hadn't even been any warmth in his gaze, not a smile, not even a wink. She'd been completely dismissed.

All the ugly feelings she had from the past bombarded her as she stood outside the circle, watching him.

My God. She'd been so wrong. Tommy *was* going to change again.

For ten minutes, she waited. Finally, he broke away from the group and sauntered over to her. He wrapped his arms around her waist and steered her toward the show. "Sorry about that. I'm all yours again."

But it was too late. The damage had been done, and she felt like crap.

Was he really all hers? Was he ever really going to be?

Judging by the evidence, the answer was a resounding no.

She tried shaking away her sour thoughts, but they kept returning, louder and more panicked than ever.

In the theater, they found a place to sit directly in front of the huge pool and stage. He put his arm around the back of her chair, his fingers playing with her hair. She instinctively leaned into his side, wanting desperately to banish her depressing worries. The chairs didn't have arms, so his body pressed into her from shoulder to knee. She felt the kiss he placed on top of her head, and she chewed on her bottom lip.

Was she overreacting? He *was* completely attentive to her now. Was she being one of those girlfriends who must have her boyfriend's attention at all times or she'd have a freak-out? She did not want to be one of those women.

It was one incident, she reminded herself, and their relationship was new. She needed to cut him some slack and remember everything else he'd done for her.

Because she *couldn't* think about being cut out of one of the most important parts of his life. Or having to decide whether to live with the hurt or having to leave him for good.

# CHAPTER 15

As Julie fastened her robe around her waist, she stared at the rumpled bed. When Tommy had carried her back to her room last night after his training, he'd spent the next few hours devoted to her body, touching and kissing. The intimacy hadn't diminished as they'd slept, either. Their naked bodies had stayed in contact, either with her curled up under his arm, against his side, or with him spooned behind her, his strong arms wrapped protectively around her waist and making her feel as if she was his whole world.

Just because he had a fight in a few days didn't mean he'd forget all that as soon as he stepped into the cage.

The last three weeks had flown by. Tommy had trained like a madman, and she'd kept herself busy at the clinic. All their spare time was spent together, either in bed, curled together on the couch, or actually attempting to have a date. Publicity for the fight was running at full tilt, so a fan or two always interrupted them. But since she was sitting there with him, she didn't feel as excluded as before, when she'd stood on the outside looking in.

So she'd relaxed some on that front. Thank God. The last thing she wanted was for her issue to be the reason she and Tommy couldn't be together.

She walked into the living room. A shirtless Tommy had his elbows propped on the kitchen counter as he ate a bagel with peanut butter and read the sports section of the newspaper.

As she watched the muscles of his back flex every time he brought the bagel to his mouth, she wanted to say screw work, and take him back to bed. She reached out to run her hand up his spine, but paused when she noticed he was reading an article with the headline, A HAS-BEEN'S RETURN TO THE CAGE.

Julie cringed. Oh, that wasn't good. What effect would that have on him? Would it mess with his head?

Inhaling, she stepped beside him and asked. "What's the verdict?"

Without a word, he handed her the paper. She scanned the article and winced. The reporter was not a fan of Tommy's, pretty much calling the president of the Cage Match Championship desperate for ratings if he allowed a screw-up like Tommy back in the cage when there were plenty of fighters who would give anything to be there. The reporter went on to insinuate that those who purchased the event to watch at home on TV were stupid because it was sure to be another letdown, like the previous fight.

"He didn't hold anything back, did he?"

Tommy shrugged. "I have a lot to prove. All this reporter had to go on was my last fight, and even I admit

I looked like shit. He has every right to doubt me. I'll get my satisfaction when I wipe that doubt out of his mind and he's forced to admit he was wrong."

At his confidence, she smiled in relief. When Tommy leaned over, kissed her, and whispered, "Good morning," she could've easily melted to the floor.

As he straightened and gathered her into his arms, she wrapped her arms around his neck and lifted up on her tiptoes, kissing his lips. His body relaxed against hers, and he held her tighter. He pressed his forehead to hers. "I wish we could spend more time together."

At the sincerity in his voice, her heart squeezed. "I do, too, but you're four days away from the fight. I do know what that means, you know."

He kissed her gently. "My time will be limited, but I get to come home to you every night."

*Coming home to me.* God, she loved the sound of that.

"I'll be training most of the day," he continued. "Then tomorrow the chaos starts for the rest of the week. What do you say about a lunch date? Around one, so we miss the lunch crowd? We haven't visited our bench in a long time. I hear it calling our names."

Flutters erupted in her belly. They'd eaten lunch together on that bench for so many years, but this was the first time he had ever referred to it as "theirs."

She loved the sound of them having someplace that was theirs alone.

• • •

Julie drew in a deep breath before she opened the door to Mike's gym, carrying a white paper bag that contained two chicken salad sandwiches and chips. The nerves that hit her as she stepped inside were ridiculous, considering she'd walked into this gym on numerous occasions in the past without a second thought.

But this time it was different. She was here as someone other than Tommy's friend. Before, she'd known exactly where she stood and had acted accordingly. Now she wasn't sure what her role was. She was his girlfriend now. But what did that mean? Was she supposed to go up to Tommy and lift her face as if she expected a kiss? Would he be okay with that?

She hated the fish-out-of-water feeling. It would probably be best just to take her lead from Tommy.

As she scanned the gym, she realized her anxiety was unfounded. He wasn't there.

Maybe he was in the locker room?

She spotted Mike at the back of the gym talking to a younger fighter. He glanced up, and his brows knitted together. He made his way over to her. "Hey, Julie. What's brought you to this side of town?"

"I'm meeting Tommy for lunch."

Mike glanced at his watch. "He's been with that reporter for more than an hour. He should be wrapping it up soon."

More than an hour? That was an awfully long interview. Most lasted twenty minutes tops.

"Okay. Can you let him know that I'm waiting for him when he's done? I'm going to go ahead down the street to where we said we'd eat."

"Sure, but you may see him before I do. They went outside to do the interview."

"Oh. Okay. I'll keep an eye out for him."

Nodding, Mike turned, then he looked back at her. "It's good to see you, Julie. Didn't realize how much you were around until Tommy left. Glad he didn't somehow fuck things up with you and you're still friends. Good that we get to see your pretty face again."

Her smile slipped. Had he not told *anyone* they were dating? He wasn't hiding it, or he wouldn't touch her in public. But it didn't sit well with her that the people he spent a majority of his day with, people he considered his team, didn't know about them. Was he *trying* to keep MMA and her separate?

"Thanks, Mike. It's nice to be back."

After she stepped outside, she veered to the left and made her way down the sidewalk. As she got closer to their lunch spot, she noticed a couple had already claimed the bench, and her steps slowed.

No, not a couple, because he was supposed to be *hers*.

Tommy was exactly where he was supposed to be—sitting with another woman on *their* bench—and he was smiling that smile she hated. The one that made women throw themselves at him, fight for his attention, and be proud to be the arm-candy of the week. The I'm-a-confirmed-bachelor-and-I'll-gladly-fuck-you-but-not-marry-you smile.

She fisted her hands, fighting the insane urge to storm over and whack him upside the head and make her presence known.

Julie glared at the woman. Gorgeous. Petite. Long blond hair. Tommy said something and the woman threw her head back on a laugh as she placed her hand on his knee and patted. Tommy didn't seem to mind the touch. If anything, that smile widened.

When he never took his eyes off the reporter, her jealousy grew. No wonder the interview had lasted as long as it had. That woman was the epitome of every woman Tommy had been with over the years. And he'd brought her to *their* bench. If the crumbled white bag sitting beside the reporter was any indication, he'd already eaten lunch, too.

Ass. Hole.

Taking a calming breath, she squared her shoulders. She wanted to see him squirm, to have to look at her after he'd ogled the woman sitting beside him.

She strode up to them. When she was just a couple of feet away, Tommy finally dragged his eyes off the reporter and looked at her. And the smile immediately transformed into one full of warmth and happiness. The real one. The one she loved.

Some of the fight went out of her. Until he stood and kissed her on the cheek. The freaking *cheek*.

"Hey," he whispered against her skin.

A kiss. To the cheek. What. The. *Hell*?

The reporter looked at Julie from head to toe. She knew that look. God knew she'd seen it many times in the past when she'd come up to Tommy and a new girl. She was being sized up, seeing what kind of competition she would be. Apparently, the woman saw something to be worried about because she stood, too, her fingers laying against Tommy's forearm as she breathlessly said, "Thanks for the interview." She cast a pointed look at the bag of food Julie was carrying. "And lunch."

"What?" Tommy finally looked back at the reporter. "Oh, yeah. You're welcome."

She squeezed Tommy's arm. "I'll see you around."

And with that she grabbed her briefcase and walked away. Julie hated the way the woman's butt swished from side to side, like an invitation for Tommy to pursue her. That if he did, she'd give him anything he wanted. When Julie glanced up at Tommy, all her anger came rushing back and she smacked the bag of food against his chest. "Here's your *lunch*."

Then she stalked off.

He hadn't even introduced her. *Again.* No, "This is my girlfriend." Or, "Sorry but I'm taken." Just a damn, "Hey." *Hey* could mean anything. She could've been his freaking *sister* for all that woman knew. In front of an extremely attractive woman, he'd treated her just as he always had—like a sibling.

After everything she'd allowed that man to do to her body, all she got was a fucking "Hey." She had the notion to grab a handful of cock right now, and *not* to give him pleasure.

She'd made it several strides away before Tommy grabbed her arm and spun her around. "What's the matter with you?"

She snatched her arm out of his grip. "Who was that?"

"A reporter. I was doing an interview."

"Yeah, that's what it looked like."

Confusion clouded his eyes as he drew back. "What's that supposed to mean?"

"You were checking her out."

"Holy shit! You're jealous!" Laughing, Tommy

grabbed her and hugged her close to his chest.

Seriously? He was *happy* about it while she stood there, a steaming pile of fury?

"It's not funny, Tommy," she ground out.

"You're right, it's not. I'm sorry." He placed his hands on her upper arms and gently pushed her back until their eyes met. "Yes, she was an attractive woman, Julie. But I wasn't attracted to her. There is only one woman I'm interested in. I go home to her every night, and I'm very happy to call her my girlfriend."

She bit her bottom lip, wanting to believe that—with everything in her. But she wasn't sure she could.

"Except you *didn't* call me your girlfriend. You ate lunch with her. You were supposed to eat with me." God, she was pouting! But she couldn't help it; seeing him with that other woman, and getting kissed on the cheek, had hurt.

His brows flicked. "I heard her stomach growling. And trying to be a gentleman while *selfishly* hoping to win some brownie points for a good interview, I bought her a sandwich. I didn't eat. I was waiting for you."

Her anger notched down a fraction. "You didn't eat?"

A small smile played at his lips. "No. I didn't. I've been looking forward to our lunch date all morning."

"Then why didn't you introduce me?"

He blinked at her. "I— It didn't cross my mind."

Dumbfounded, she stared at him. "It didn't cross your mind to introduce your *girlfriend* to a woman who was blatantly coming on to you?"

He tried tugging her forward. "I love it when you say girlfriend. Say it again."

She broke away, still mad. "Tommy, I'm being serious!"

"All right! I screwed up!" He threw up his hands. "I'm sorry. Jesus, Julie, I'm new to this relationship stuff, okay? I swear it didn't cross my mind. I was just happy to see you."

Some of her tension abated, but her uneasiness lingered.

"Please, let's not fight," he said. "I've been looking forward to seeing you all morning."

She wasn't sure if the unease was her heart trying to protect itself or her head seeing red flags she wanted to ignore. Him neglecting to introduce her as his girlfriend was not her imagination. Neither was that sisterly kiss.

When she forced a nod, he entwined their fingers. As he led them to the bench, she stared at their joined hands. He'd said she was the one he wanted. The one he came home to every night.

But she'd just had her second glimpse of the old Tommy.

And everything she'd been so sure of this morning was now one big uncertainty.

• • •

As Tommy rolled up his wraps and tossed them in the gym bag, he could no longer fight the smile that had kept creeping over him all afternoon.

Julie had been jealous—raging pissed jealous. When she'd slapped their lunch against his chest and stormed off, he'd been shocked, which had been replaced by a small amount of happiness as he watched her eyes spit anger.

Over him.

That had to mean something, right?

She'd never reacted like that before, and he'd had plenty of other women around her in the past. If she felt like she had a claim on him, then her feelings had to be growing.

Maybe she'd needed to feel the jealousy, to get a taste of what he'd felt when she'd been around Brody. God knew, watching her with another man had quickly opened Tommy's eyes. And maybe this encounter had opened her eyes, too. Maybe she'd be more receptive to hearing how he felt now—and would actually believe it.

It was time to tell her he loved her.

And he would. Right after he reclaimed his belt. When he said the words, he wanted to be 100 percent, to be the best he possibly could be, to feel like he was worthy of her.

In less than a week, he'd have everything he wanted.

Mac walked into the locker room, opened his locker, and grabbed his duffel bag. "You ready?"

Mac didn't need to elaborate. Tommy glanced at him. "As ready as I'll ever be, I guess."

"At least you don't have to go out of town for this one."

This was true. The fight was being held right here in Atlanta at the Philips Arena. A huge bonus, since he really hadn't liked the idea of leaving Julie for a week to fly off somewhere else.

"If Moon has any sense, he'll realize this won't be like the last time you guys met in the cage," Mac said.

"Moon has sense. He knows if Ethan actually gave me a chance to win my title back, that I'm back and gunning for him."

Tommy had spent the last three weeks studying Moon's fight tapes from every angle. The more he watched the man, the more certain he was he didn't want to go to the ground with him. But Moon was superior at the takedown. Mike and Tommy had worked really hard on his ground game, even bringing Dante in to help. Dante was a stand-up fighter like Tommy, but he'd beat by submission the guy who used to be the best ground fighter in the industry. The man's knowledge was priceless.

Dante's advice and coaching had made Tommy as ready as ever to face Moon again.

Now to just do it.

Tate strode into the locker room. "Hey, Tommy. A few of the guys and I are headed over to the Boot Scoot for a little R and R. You game?"

He liked that idea. Liked the idea of holding Julie close even more, taking their relationship public. It was time to do that. Past time.

"Yeah, count me in."

"Cool. Mac, you game?"

"Nope."

Tommy had to suppress a smile at the blunt answer. Tate had only asked out of politeness. Mac rarely said yes.

"Okay. Tommy, we're going to shower and head on over there."

"I'll go over with you guys then."

"I'm out," Mac said. "See you tomorrow."

When his friend walked away, Tommy dug into his pocket for his cell phone.

"Hey!" Julie's soft voice flowed through the phone. Oh yes, he'd love to dance with her tonight. Have her body pressed against his.

"Hey, beautiful. Some of the boys are going over to the Boot Scoot. Would you like to meet me down there?"

A lengthy silence followed his question before she parroted back, "The Boot Scoot?"

"Yeah, it's been a while since I've been down there. The next few days are going to be rough, so it'd be nice to relax some."

"Tommy, it's after eight. I'm in my pajamas."

"Come on, Julie. Throw on some clothes and meet me down there. Let's live it up a little tonight."

"Live it up. Right." She gave a long sigh. "All right, give me an hour."

He smiled. "Awesome. Can't wait to see you."

After a quick shower and changing into a pair of jeans and a T-shirt, he walked with the other guys the few blocks to the bar. Being a Tuesday night, the place wasn't as packed as on a weekend, but the atmosphere was just the same. Loud country music pulsed through the large speakers. The saloon-style setting embraced him. And he felt all the tension about his upcoming fight leave him in one quick whoosh.

The bar scene had always done this to him—filled him with a sense of belonging.

He and the guys found an empty spot at the end of the bar. Tommy leaned an elbow against the polished wood, nodding his head to the beat of the music. His upcoming fight became a topic of conversation, and one by one, as the other patrons noticed them, they gathered around, bombarding him with questions.

"Hey, Sparks, you ready for Saturday?"

"What's your game plan?"

"What's it feel like to be going back into the cage?"

As he answered each question, he gave that fan his undivided attention, making sure he or she knew he had heard the question and appreciated the support. He loved his fans, had always gone out of his way to interact with them. And the extra initiative had paid off. No one seemed to remember he'd been away from the MMA scene for months. Instead, it was as though he'd never been gone. He joked around, kissed cheeks, shook hands, and signed autographs. The bar melted into the background. All he focused on were his fans and their excitement.

The grin on his face started to hurt.

Tommy "Lightning" Sparks was truly back.

No longer eschewed by the fans, but embraced. Bodies pressed against him as the group surged closer. He thrived on the attention, loving how they hung onto every word. And when a shot was pressed into his hand, and Tate held up his glass in salute—"To victory on Saturday"—Tommy downed the amber liquid without a second thought.

God, it felt great to be back.

• • •

Julie leaned against the wall and tried not to burst into tears. For more than an hour, she'd watched Tommy schmooze everyone except her. How could she be jealous over everyone? But she was. Other than another quick kiss to the *cheek* when she'd walked in the door, he'd been whooping it up by himself—and his bevvy of followers.

He sent her an obligatory wave or smile here and there, but he was so lost in his good time that he didn't even pick up on her increasingly bad mood. That said something, right? The fact that he could so totally ignore her said something. And she didn't even want to think about what it meant.

"Hey, beautiful," a masculine voice purred.

Rolling her eyes, she turned to tell the ass off, then gasped with happiness. "Brody!"

Without thought, she hugged him, just happy to have someone to talk to. He squeezed her back. While they hadn't seen each other lately, they still talked on the phone from time to time and caught up. She missed hanging out with him.

"What are you doing off to the side by your lonesome?" he asked with a frown.

"My boyfriend doesn't seem to remember he has a girlfriend. This is the"—she faked a thoughtful expression—"*third* time he's done this in as many days."

Brody scowled. "Are you serious?"

"He's completely attentive at home, but we start getting into the MMA world and I'm put right back in friend territory." Bitterness crept into her tone. "Do you know that none of the guys even know we're dating?"

She'd learned that little factoid about thirty minutes ago when Tate had hit on her and mentioned he knew she was Tommy's best friend and all, but he didn't think he'd mind.

"Damn, Jules. I'm sorry."

She shrugged. That's how she felt right now. Defeated. Exhausted. Didn't care.

No, that was a lie. She did care. A lot. She glanced back over at Tommy. He was talking to some guy about a mile a minute. He hadn't even glanced over to check on her.

If he had, he would've seen her with Brody. Would've maybe at least come up to her then. She didn't understand how hard it was for him to understand that she didn't need much. She could be standing beside him right now and be happy as a lark. She'd tried that twice. Both times it was like he'd forgotten she was standing there and had just walked off. The embarrassment she'd felt had finally pushed her to stand against the wall.

The only thing he hadn't done was encourage any of the women who came up to him. That should've felt like a bonus, but it didn't. If he could remember he was in a relationship with her enough that he didn't flirt with other women, how could he be so thoughtless to not introduce her, to let her stand here all alone? Would it always be like this?

When they were together, everything was hunky-dory, but the moment he put on his fighter's cap, she became invisible again.

No. She couldn't do this. Instinct had always told her that she and Tommy would never work. They were too different. And she was living that difference right now.

Why hadn't she heeded her own warning? She'd be saving herself a ton of heartache now if she had.

"Brody, will you walk me to my car? I want to go home."

He put his beer down on a table. "Sure, Jules. Come on."

She started toward the door, waiting for Tommy to stop her. As she walked down the sidewalk to the parking deck, she expected to hear his voice at any moment.

Getting into her car and driving away, she anticipated the phone would ring. And as she curled up with the dogs and wept on the couch, she expected the door to crash open.

But none of those things happened.

And her world fell apart.

• • •

"Julie!" Tommy yelled as soon as he tore into the house.

Warrior and Lucy greeted him with excited yaps, but he ignored them, his gaze sweeping the living room and kitchen. Where in the hell was she? One moment she'd been at the bar, the next he'd been asking people if they'd seen her. When she hadn't answered her phone, he'd really started to freak out.

When he didn't see her, he hurried toward the bedrooms. "Julie!"

He'd just entered the hallway when she stepped out of his room, carrying a duffel bag.

As she neared, she tossed it at him. "Get out."

Blinking, he caught the bag. "What the fuck, Julie? I've been worried sick."

He'd never seen her like this before. So calm, collected, like she'd just told him the weather was sunny instead of trying to kick him out of the house. Then he caught a glimpse of her face. Her swollen, puffy eyes. "Shit. You've been crying."

"Of course I've been crying. I was dating a thoughtless asshole," she said as she stormed across the living room.

Panic closed his throat. "Was? What the hell is happening here?" When she kept on her forward trek, he yelled, "Look at me!"

After she reached the front door, she finally did. "Two hours, Tommy."

"W-What?"

"I have been home for *two hours*." She then opened the front door. "Get. Out."

His jaw hardened and he dropped the duffel bag on the floor. "Not a fucking chance of that happening."

"You don't get to tell me no. This is *my* house. Get the hell out of it."

"You don't get to dump me without telling me why," he yelled.

"Oh, *now* we're in a relationship? How convenient you suddenly remembered."

He didn't even know how to argue with her right now. She was making no sense. "Of course we are. What have we been doing the last month?"

"Hell if I know." Her shrug even had a cold edge to it. "Fucking? That's all you said you were capable of, and tonight you proved it in spades."

Of all the men he'd ever taken a punch from, Julie's words had the power of all them combined. Dazed, he stepped back. "What the hell did I do that has you so upset?"

"The fact that you can't even see it is the issue, Tommy. How long did it take before you realized I was gone?"

"I tried calling—"

"Thirty minutes ago! I'd been home for an hour and a half. I left, and you didn't even notice. Not that you noticed me before that, mind you."

Had she really been gone that long?

"Did you know I talked to Brody?" she asked.

"What the fuck was *he* doing there?"

When her shoulders slumped and she closed her eyes, he realized that had been the wrong answer.

"Get out," she whispered.

"Julie, just listen."

Opening her eyes, she charged forward, her calm appearance shattering, and he finally saw just how angry she was. Her chest heaved and fury jerked her motions. "No! I'm no longer going to listen to you *or* my stupid heart. The one time I let it take control, the one thing I knew would happen, sure enough, it happened." She pointed her finger at him. "I allowed you to hurt me, just as I always knew you would. I told myself not to trust you, but did I listen? Oh, hell, no."

"What are you *talking* about?"

"For a fighter who makes his living anticipating his opponent's next move, you're pretty damn clueless, you know that?"

He flinched back. He didn't know this Julie, who was so hurt she was going out of her way to hurt back.

She laughed, a short, hollow sound as she raked her hand through her hair and stared at the ceiling. "I am *such* a fool. I thought you'd changed. But no, you're still the same old good-time Tommy. The man who gets so wrapped up in the lifestyle, he only thinks of himself."

"I *have* changed."

"No, you haven't." The words were said so calmly, with so much conviction behind them, he realized that whatever he'd done tonight had destroyed everything.

"You're the same Tommy, and I'm the same idiot Julie. The little fool in love with a man who has always put the party before anything or anyone else. I've already gone down that road with you once. I refuse to do it again."

He felt like he'd been slammed to the ground. Stunned. Unable to breathe. "Y-You love me?"

She sent him a disgusted look, but if the disgust was meant for him or herself, he couldn't tell. "I've been in love with you since we were ten years old, Tommy Sparks. It's only taken twenty-three years, but thank *God* I'm finally *over* you. Thank you for helping me move on." She stepped back to the door and motioned with her hand. "Now get out before I call the cops."

He took a step forward, swallowing hard. "Julie. I love you, too."

"Yeah, well. You have a real funny way of showing it." Dead eyes met his. "Did you even really want me there tonight, or did you feel obligated to ask me because you had secretly started calling me your girlfriend?"

"I wanted you there. I wouldn't have asked you if I didn't. What's this shit about secretly? You're my girlfriend. Period."

"Really? Is that why you hadn't told Mike…or anyone else at the gym we were even dating? Is that why you spent the entire night totally ignoring me instead of being proud to have me by your side? Is that why it took you an hour and a half to realize I was even gone?"

Silence descended between them. Tommy struggled to find words. But it all came down to one thing: Julie was right. He'd been completely submerged in the moment. He'd been entirely content just knowing she was there, having no clue that, with his inattention, he was hurting her more and more with every passing second. And his utter

failure rang clear. He'd made her feel totally unwanted—
when nothing was further from the truth.

Julie jetted out a breath. "That's what I thought."

"No. You don't understand."

"I understand perfectly. I'm not telling you again.
Get out. I don't even want to see your face right now."
She stared straight ahead, her jaw taut, her arctic eyes
unblinking.

Even though she stood only a few feet away, she had
never been further from him. Nothing he could say right
now would help. She was so fucking angry. Rightfully so.
She needed time to calm down, so they could talk rationally.
Then he'd get her to see what *he* now understood perfectly.

She was the love of his life. Not the partying, not the
fans, not even fighting. She was.

He swallowed and bent to pick up his duffel bag, then
snatched Warrior's leash off the hook by the door. After
he connected it to the dog's collar, he stopped in front of
her. She refused him eye contact, staring straight at his
shoulder.

"This isn't over, Julie."

Her eyes snapped to his. "Yes, it is."

He stepped out onto the porch, and she slammed the
door behind him. The sound made him jerk and his grip
on Warrior's leash tightened.

She'd loved him.

Past tense.

Seemed unfair, since he'd just learned about it in the
present.

But what he'd said was true. This wasn't over. Not by
a long shot.

He made his way down the steps to the front yard, then froze as he looked around the quiet neighborhood.

Julie had kicked him out, and he had nowhere left to go.

# CHAPTER 16

Julie looked through the peephole in her front door, saw Brody standing on the stoop, and breathed a sigh of relief. Over the last two days, Tommy had knocked on her door more times than she cared to count, sometimes yelling for her to answer the damn door. The neighbors were surely getting an eyeful, but she didn't care. She never responded, and he didn't dare use his key. Smart man.

She didn't want to see him. Probably for the rest of her life.

When she opened the door, Brody stepped inside.

"Hey," she said. "What are you doing here so early?"

He'd been lucky he'd caught her. She was just about to leave for work.

"Mac got in touch with me."

She waved her hand and retreated to the living room. "I don't want to talk about him, Brody."

He grabbed her upper arm. "Jules, you need to listen."

"Listen to what?" She yanked her arm out of his grasp. "How Tommy misses me? How he's hurt and can't understand why I won't talk to him? How—"

"He's canceling the fight, Jules."

That slammed her mouth shut. The last bit of the anger she'd clung to since she'd watched Tommy completely exclude her evaporated as Brody's words sunk in. "What? Why?"

"He's got it in his head it's the only way you'll forgive him."

She stepped back. "He can't do that. He can't put that on me."

"Well, he is. This morning, unless you stop him."

At a loss for words, she dropped her gaze to the floor. Tommy was willingly giving up his chance for redemption in the ring, for her? He'd worked so hard for this fight. Him giving up fighting had never been an option. Never even entered her mind.

Her gaze shot to Brody's. "You can't let him do that."

"No, *you* can't. So go stop him."

With a curt nod, she grabbed her purse and was out the door within seconds. As she sped down the highway, she realized she wasn't sure where to go. Should she go to Mac's, where Tommy'd been staying? Or Mike's, where he was training?

The gym would be the best bet. If he wasn't there yet, she'd wait for him.

After she found a place to park, she ran down the sidewalk. She spotted Tommy with his head down, shoulders hunched, just as he was pulling the gym door open.

"Tommy!"

He froze, his head slowly turning in her direction. then he spun and started walking toward her. "What are you doing here?"

"You can't do this."

"Fucking Mac." Tommy thrust a hand through his hair, his jaw clenching. "What'd he do? Wait until I was asleep and come to you?"

"He contacted Brody."

"Brody?" A forced laugh came from Tommy's mouth as he placed his hands on his hips and looked skyward. "Shouldn't be surprised, should I? That asshole has stuck his nose in my business from day one."

"You can't cancel the fight."

"You won't talk to me. It was the only thing I could think of to get your attention enough to know I'm serious."

"Fine. We can talk now," she said, crossing her arms.

"Okay." He reached for her hand, but she couldn't bring herself to touch him, fearing if she did, she'd lose herself in him again. Right now, she had to stay focused on herself, on what was best for her…and that wasn't Tommy.

When he realized she wasn't going to take his hand, hurt shone in his eyes and he dropped it. "How"—he cleared his throat—"how about we find a place to sit?"

"Lead the way." She followed him down the sidewalk, thankful he'd gone in the opposite direction of "their" bench. About half a block down, he finally found another bench under a tree, and sat.

Neither of them spoke, the silence between them tense, thick. Finally, Tommy whispered, "I'm sorry."

The sincerity in his voice caused tears to sting the

backs of her eyes. Julie dropped her head to hide them. "I know."

"I *did* get caught up in the moment. I was Tommy 'Lightning' Sparks again. The superstar. It felt good." He paused as he shifted on the bench.

She'd known this, but hearing him confirm it sent another shot of hurt winging through her. She'd been scared to death of this outcome, had tried to protect herself from it. But the man had made her believe. Believe in *them*…only to turn around and jump right back into the lifestyle the second he stepped foot in it again.

"But you were wrong about one thing," he continued. "I did think of you…looked for you. All it took was for me to see you, and I was at ease. But when I couldn't find you—" He pinched the bridge of his nose. "Julie, I felt lost. I was filled with so much panic. Nothing means more to me than you. My life is with *you*." He shifted again, taking her hands, squeezing. "Julie. I love you."

It was the second time he'd said those words in a way she'd waited a lifetime to hear. And a flare of hope budded in her chest, but it quickly wilted as she remembered how happy he'd been. The grin on his face. The twinkle in his eye. And no matter how much he said he loved her, wanted to believe he'd never do it again, had looked for her, he *had* forgotten her. He hadn't noticed her absence for an hour and a half.

She tugged her hand from his.

"Julie—"

"Let me speak now." A sad smile came to her lips. "You've been my best friend for so long. But you've also been so much more to me than that. The other night, I was immediately back in the past, watching from the sidelines, reliving all those years when you never noticed I'd left a party because you were too busy *with* the party…too busy with your women to realize that I was no longer there."

"Oh, God, Julie," he said, voice hoarse, his eyes stricken. "I swear, I didn't know."

She waved his words away. "No you didn't, because I didn't want you to. I never once thought we could ever work. Besides, all you'd ever seen me as was your best friend…until you didn't." She paused, the thickening in her throat making it difficult to speak. She swallowed. "We had a great time these last few weeks. It was more than I'd ever imagined it would be. But you forgot me, Tommy, when all I wanted was to be by your side. I *wanted* to be introduced as Tommy Sparks's girlfriend. Not kissed on the cheek, then pushed aside…just like you did when you thought of me as your sister."

"We were doing great until the Boot Scoot—"

She shook her head. "No, Tommy, we weren't. It's been building for a few weeks now. First at the aquarium, then the reporter, and now this."

"I don't have to go back. I can cancel the fight. Get a desk job. Prove to you that it's *you* I want."

"And then what? You'll grow to resent me because you're no longer doing what you love? I can't risk that, either."

He gazed at her, his eyes filled with apprehension. "What are you saying?"

She clasped his hand in hers and met his gaze, no longer caring if he saw her tears or how hard this was for her to say. Letting Tommy go *was* the hardest thing she'd ever done. "I want you to go into that cage on Saturday and kick Moon's ass. I want you to get everything you've fought so hard for. But I can't go down that road again, Tommy. I can't go back."

"So...this is it?" His voice cracked, and he cleared his throat, glancing away as he swallowed.

"Yeah, this is it."

Before she broke down, she placed a light kiss on his cheek and walked away. Each step harder than the last, but this was the right thing to do.

He was free now. She was free.

So, why did she feel more bound to him than ever?

• • •

As Julie waited for the popcorn popping in the microwave, she puttered aimlessly around the kitchen, opening cabinets, straightening the silverware, restacking the bowls. Anything to keep her busy.

The house seemed too quiet. Empty.

It had been two days since she'd left Tommy sitting on that bench. Two days of trying to get through the day as if there weren't a gaping hole in her life. Tommy had been such a constant for so long, it was like a piece of her was missing now.

After she'd kicked him out, and she'd had her anger to hang onto, it had been easy to ignore his absence. But now...now with all her feelings spilled to him and her anger gone, she was faced with how big a mark Tommy had left in every nook and cranny of her home.

The couch was the center point of so many memories, she was going to have to burn it.

Who was she kidding? She could burn down the entire house, and just seeing a couch would still trigger thoughts of their first real kiss, and of where he'd shown her how much he'd wanted her, and of him taking her for the first time bent over the arm of it, or of how he'd tug her down to lie beside him after a long day.

The most needed piece of furniture in a home—a constant reminder.

Even her dog, who also seemed to be grieving, reminded her of him.

Lucy moped around the house, sending Julie accusing looks, as if she'd been the one to send her best friend away.

And she had.

Sighing, she returned to the microwave when it beeped. As she poured the popped kernels into a bowl, a knock came on the door.

"It's unlocked," she called. "Come on in."

A few seconds later, Brody appeared in the kitchen doorway. "You really shouldn't do that, you know."

"I knew it was you by the way you knocked." She frowned. "Why are you wet?"

He cocked an eyebrow. "It's raining."

She listened, and sure enough she heard drops hitting the roof. Funny how she hadn't heard that before. Only the silence in the house.

Brody studied her. "You okay?"

She sent him a strained smile. "Wonderful."

"We don't have to do this."

"Yeah. I do, actually." She passed him the popcorn. Brody had forgone going down to the arena with his team to instead curl up on the couch here with her. Even though she tried to convince him she'd be fine, he'd refused to leave her alone tonight.

Tommy would be fighting any minute. Here in Georgia. And she wouldn't be there.

She'd missed his fights in the past, but now she knew she'd never be ringside again. God, why did that hurt so badly?

Brody sat on the couch while Julie grabbed the TV remote and turned it on. She normally didn't miss a fight in the lineup, but tonight she hadn't had it in her to watch the hours of matches preceding the main event. As it was, both men were already in the cage as the announcer introduced the headline fighters. Tommy and Ricky Moon.

She couldn't tear her eyes off of Tommy. Black and teal boxing shorts rode low on his hips, and his chest was bare. He had his gloved hands resting on his hips as he slowly scanned the arena. What was going through his head right now?

Was he worried? Energized? Normally, she could tell, but not tonight. He just kept looking. Then it hit her. It was the deafening roar of the stadium. The chanting of his name she could hear among the screams of Moon's fans. It had to be a special moment for him.

No matter how things had ended with them, pride expanded her chest. He'd worked so hard for this return — so deserved this moment.

"How much of a chance does he have?" she asked.

"From what I've heard, a pretty damn good one. A lot of it will depend on if Moon takes control in the beginning."

"I want him to win, Brody. I really do."

Brody leaned forward and grasped her hand. "I know you do. You never would've gone after him, convinced him not to cancel, if you didn't."

She squeezed his hand as she turned her attention back to the TV. Tommy and Moon tapped gloves, signaling the start of the fight.

As the men circled each other, a vise tightened on Julie's chest, making it difficult to breathe. She took a shaky inhale, trying to calm the nerves attacking her body. Releasing Brody's hand, she settled on the couch with her feet tucked up under her, and pressed her laced fingers to her mouth, muttering, "Please. Please. Please."

Moon wasted no time charging Tommy, grabbing him around the waist and driving him into the cage. Moon landed multiple body shots. Each fist that hit Tommy's torso made her body tenser, until she felt as though she'd explode from the pressure.

Brody sat forward, a vehement *"Shit"* spewing from his mouth.

*Shit* was right. Moon had taken control and had Tommy against the cage within seconds—the exact same way he'd beaten him the first time.

"He's got to get out of the clinch!" She shifted on the couch until she was perched on her knees. "Get out of the clinch, Tommy!"

When Moon grabbed the back of Tommy's head and yanked it down to meet his knee, Julie screamed, "No!"

It was like watching history repeat itself. At any moment, Tommy would crumble. The match would be lost. And his chance at reclaiming his title would be gone for good.

But unlike before, the knee to the face didn't take him down. Tommy came up with an uppercut and caught Moon square on the chin. His opponent stumbled back, and Tommy straightened, chest puffed out. He advanced, not giving Moon a moment to recover, landing punch after punch.

Brody was on his feet, yelling at the TV. Julie was standing on the couch, jumping up and down. "Come on, baby. Come on!"

Now Tommy had Moon up against the cage with relentless jabs, making continuous connections with his sides and head. All Moon could do was bend over and protect his chin with his gloved hands. One blow to the temple stunned Moon and his hands dropped down a few inches, exposing his chin. Tommy brought his arm back, and with one right hand, Moon was on the mat, the umpire covering him, waving his hand.

And the fight was over.

In less than two minutes. Just as that article had predicted…but with a totally different outcome.

Screaming, Julie jumped around and cheered, then launched herself at Brody, hugging him.

"He won! He won!"

Brody laughed, and he was about to say something when the announcer interrupted with, "Ladies and gentlemen."

She waved at Brody. "*Shhhh*! Here it comes."

Tommy and a now recovered Moon stood on either side of the announcer. "This fight has ended one minute and forty-two seconds into the first round by knockout, declaring the winner and new Middleweight Champion of the World Tommy 'Lightning' Sparks."

The referee lifted one of Tommy's arms into the air. The belt came out, and her happy grin started to fade. She stepped away from Brody and moved closer to the TV, gazing longingly at Tommy.

She wasn't there with him.

Her eyes were drawn to the photo hanging on her wall from a couple of years ago, where Tommy held the belt over his head, sweat coating his body, just as he was right now. The only difference was, in the picture she was beside him, smiling up at him.

"You love him, Jules."

"I know. I've never denied that," she said, turning back to the TV where his team was surrounding Tommy.

Twenty-three years of friendship flashed before her eyes. Even if at times they'd been in different states, they'd always had the other's back, facing the world together. And now that friendship was gone.

As much as she'd prepared herself for this moment, spending years knowing one day their relationship would change, nothing had readied her for the pain that engulfed her.

Tears burned the backs of her eyes and she hugged her arms around her torso.

"Brody. I need to be alone."

He sighed. "Okay." She felt him come up behind her, and then he kissed her cheek. "Call me if you need to talk."

As soon as the door clicked shut behind him, the first hiccupped sob shot past her lips. She pressed her hand to her mouth as she turned her attention back to the TV.

Tommy's face was overjoyed, his eyes and smile bright with happiness.

The same look he'd had two nights ago at the club. If only his career inside that cage had stopped, maybe they would've had a chance. But the reality was, it hadn't. At least not for Tommy.

She had to move on, no matter how much it hurt to do so.

Julie picked up the remote and turned off the TV. She knew what came next. He'd interview, leave the cage, and the partying would start. He was free to do as he pleased. No worries of her disappointment. Her judgment.

Would he embrace it? Maybe not at first, but once the atmosphere got to him, excited him, he'd find his groove again—just as he had the other night. And then he'd realize she'd been right, and had done them both a favor by ending things between them.

She laid the remote down on the couch and straightened. Then she stood there, the silence closing in on her again. She wrapped her arms around herself.

What now?

Change clothes.

Yes, getting into her pajamas sounded like a good idea. She walked back to her room.

No, not a good idea.

The bed was as imposing as ever, screaming Tommy's name. Lucy lay on the rug and lifted her head, that accusing look back on her furry face.

"Lucy, I'm sorry. I did what I needed to do."

The dog made a whiny sound and lowered her head to her paws, those chocolate brown eyes latched onto Julie as she backed out of the room and retreated to the living room. Was there nowhere to go to escape him?

Would it just take time for his memory to fade from this house?

All she knew was, she couldn't think anymore. If she could have thrown herself into her work, she would have, but she had to settle for cleaning an already spotless house. When her phone rang, she froze, only to be disappointed to see it was Brody. After the third time, she'd set her phone to go directly to voice mail, not needing the constant roller coaster of emotions.

For two hours, she concentrated on killing every dust bunny she could find, which wasn't many, but the hunt kept her occupied. She'd just cut the vacuum cleaner off when she realized someone was knocking on the door.

She sighed. She should've just answered the damn phone.

As she opened the door, she said, "I'm—" The words died on her lips, and her heart skipped a beat.

*Tommy.*

He stood on the porch, drenched from the pounding rain. Blond hair plastered to his head, water dripping off the tip of his nose. The baseball cap gripped tight in his hands.

She swallowed, a thousand emotions crowding her heart. "What are you doing here?"

"You didn't call."

She blinked.

"I looked for you," he said. "Before the fight, after the fight, hoping you couldn't stay away, hoping I hadn't really fucked up the best thing that ever happened to me. But I didn't find you, and I felt empty, Julie. Totally empty."

Her stomach fluttered. She'd been wrong. He hadn't been enjoying the crowd's cheers. He'd been looking for her. She tightened her grip on the doorknob.

He'd felt empty. So had she. But that didn't change things.

"You didn't call," he whispered hoarsely. "I waited and waited, but you never called. I went back to Mac's, paced around his place, and waited some more. I couldn't believe you wouldn't call. So I got in my car and came here. I've been stalking back and forth to my car trying to convince myself to leave for the last hour."

She stared at him. "Tommy, you should know I was proud of you. You didn't need me to call to know that."

Hurt seared across his face as he jerked back. "Jesus, Julie, did I fuck up so badly you didn't even watch the fight?"

"Of course I watched the fight."

"And that is all you have to say?" Again hurt flared sharp.

"I'm not sure what you're looking for. Congratulations?"

"I tell the entire arena, and millions watching at home, how much I love you, how much you mean to me, and congratulations is all you've got?"

Gasping, she clamped her hand over her mouth. Her eyes stung. "You did *what*?"

His gaze narrowed. "I thought you watched the fight."

"I did, and I did *not* see that."

He stepped forward, crossing the threshold, an almost frantic expression on his face. "During the interview. You didn't see it?"

"No. I—I turned off the TV after you won."

He shoved his hand through his drenched hair. "Fuck. I can't even make up with you right. No wonder it was so easy for you to let me go."

At his words, pain compressed her chest. "Easy was the last thing it was," she whispered.

But he wasn't listening; he was messing with his phone. After a few seconds, he tried to hand it to her. When she hesitated, his eyes pleaded with her. "Please, Julie. I need you to hear this. I need you to know."

Hands shaking, her heart pounding, she took his phone to find a YouTube video pulled up. The title read MMA FIGHTER %^$%S UP, BEGS FORGIVENESS.

She pressed play.

Tommy took the mic from the official. "But there is someone even more important I need to thank. A woman I realized too late I've never thanked or even mentioned, though she has been there for me every second of every day. Stood by me when *bleep* got real. Never wavered in her support of me. I never thanked her. I took her for granted. And now I've lost her."

He looked into the camera. "Julie, baby, I love you. You have been my world since we were ten. You are my everything. I have never met a woman I wanted to hold hands with. Hold. Wake up beside every morning. Until you. I *bleep* up. I made you feel unwanted." He looked around the arena. "I *made* the woman I love feel unwanted." Boos came from the stands.

"Yes, I'm a complete *bleep* for doing so." He looked back at the camera but was motioning with his hand to someone in the background. A second later, the Braves cap was thrust at him. Tommy held it up. "The moment I realized all the things you'd given me were about to be destroyed in that fire, I rushed headlong into the flames to save them. No hesitation. No thought. I couldn't lose everything I had of you. That was *before* I knew I loved you, Julie. I failed in saving that box of memories. I lost every cheesy gift you've ever given me, and it was one of the most painful moments of my life. Then you gave me this hat"—he held it up—"and that's the night you became more to me than just my best friend."

He tugged it on his head. "That's the night I realized that, yeah, it sucked losing the little mementos of our friendship, but as long as I have *you* I don't need a damn box of...things." He stepped forward, his face tight with emotion. "I'm *so* sorry. If I have to walk through flames again to show you how much you mean to me, I will cross hell and back to prove it. I *bleep* up. I'm still new to this relationship stuff, Julie, but *you* are the one I want to make mistakes with. *You* are the one I want to become *great* for. I want a future with you. I want you by my side. I want the entire world to know you are the woman I love, and who I want to make a whole lifetime of memories with. And most important, at the end of each and every day, I want to come home to *you*. Please let me come home. My life is empty without you."

Tears swam in her eyes as the video ended. After all these years, not only he'd finally mentioned her in a speech—and so beautifully—but he publically expressed his love for her in front of millions. Confirmed bachelor Tommy Sparks had told the world he was in love...with her.

When she glanced up, he stepped forward and said, "I know they are just words and I have to prove myself, but I swear to you, I will spend the rest of my life making up for this. You will never doubt again that I want you by my side. No one will ever question what you are to me. All I want is to come home." He took her face between his hands, pressed his forehead to hers, and whispered, "Can I, Julie?" He closed his eyes momentarily before opening them again, and she was shocked at the moisture that glistened in his gaze. "Can I please come home to you?"

He loved her. Truly, deeply loved her. She saw it in his gaze. Felt it in the tremble of his hands against her skin. Yes, he'd screwed up, had hurt her. But she was certain the man before her now would never leave her standing alone again, because he knew the emptiness of being without her. And he would do everything he'd vowed to never feel it again.

She nodded, a shaky "Yes" stuttering from her mouth.

The tension released from his body as he pulled her into his arms, muttering, "Thank God."

Then he kissed her, a frantic kiss that spoke of the level of fear he'd had about losing her forever. She clung to him, the emotions and desperation she'd experienced for days nearly overwhelming her.

He lifted her into his arms and kicked the door shut. She thrust her fingers through his damp hair, not caring that the moisture from his shirt was seeping into hers. All that mattered was that she wanted to spend her life wrapped in his arms, wrapped in the certainty that he was truly hers.

He broke the kiss. "Where to?"

"Our room."

He smiled that heart-stopping smile he saved for her alone. "Man, I love that."

She brushed his hair back. "I love you."

It was the first time she'd said the three words to him without a "but" following, the first time she'd allowed all the feelings she'd kept hidden for years to free themselves in her eyes and heart.

Seriousness stole over his face. "Say it again."

She cupped his face in her hands. "You're my best friend, my past, my present, and now my future. I love you, Tommy 'Lightning' Sparks."

Blinking rapidly, he cleared his throat. "I won't screw up again, Julie. You have my word."

She pursed her lips. "Oh, you'll screw up. It just better be more of the feeding your dinner to the dogs variety from now on."

He chuckled, hugging her closely as he walked into their room. She couldn't believe it had only been weeks since she'd given Tommy a place to live, never imagining that his home catching fire would finally lead to a lifetime of happiness for both of them.

After he laid her on the bed, she took the baseball cap from his hand and gazed at it. "It really meant that much to you?"

"The first time you gave it to me, I went home and cried like a fucking baby. It was my first real present, Julie. I kept all your gifts, but that hat was always the most special one."

Tears blurred her vision and she cupped his cheek. "I never knew that. That's why you ran back inside to try and save it."

He kissed her palm. "No. I was trying to save the past. The only times in my childhood I knew happiness was with you. But I don't need to look back at the past anymore. We have a future to build now."

Love expanding her heart, she tugged the hat on the head of her best friend and lover. "Oh, we don't have to completely shut out the past." She looped her arms around his neck and tugged him down. "I love you, Green Knight."

Unshed tears brightened his green eyes and he took a moment before he spoke. "I love you, too, Lady J," he said, his voice deep and rough. "From this day forth, I dedicate my life to protecting you."

And he did.

# ACKNOWLEDGMENTS

When I turned Fighting Love, I was happy with the story. I really believed it was Tommy and Julie's story. Then I received the revision letter from Liz and her assistant, Allison.

It was a grueling process that included sleepless nights, extremely early mornings—especially for this hates mornings author—lots of caffeine, very, very understanding roommates and two exceptional children that knows when mommy's hair starts sticking up like that its best to go play in their room. But I powered through. My editor, Nina, was assigned the task of editing—I prayed for her. Nina did her wicked editor magic, marked some places I needed to work on, and sent me back the edits. This was when I saw the story for the first time with fresh eyes.

This was Tommy and Julie's REAL story. It had been there all along, but I'd focused on the wrong things, when what I should have focused on was the friendship that

Tommy and Julie had shared since they were ten years old. Their history. Liz and Allison saw that and I can't thank them enough for pointing that out.

Then the amazing Nina came in and her edits helped me write one of the most emotional endings I've ever written. Because of one comment she left during the Valentine's Day scene, the perfect ending for Tommy and Julie bloomed in my mind.

How did I know this was Tommy and Julie's real story? Because I didn't cry when I wrote the ending to the original. As I revised the new ending, I sat there and wept. In fact, I still get chocked up thinking about those last lines, because it is the epitome of their relationship. And it is perfect.

I have those three ladies to thank for helping me shape this book into something I am immensely proud of.

I also need to thank Candy and Stacey for jumping on QA and CE as quickly as you did. One thing about Entangled, these editors jump in without hesitation and it's awesome.

The art department did another banging job on the cover. I love it.

My publicists, Dani and Anjana, who are waiting for so much from me right now it's not even funny. But they are on the ball! And I thank them for getting Fighting Love out there!

To my roommates: can't believe this will be the last book I'll be editing with you guys around. Are you relieved? LOL. Seriously though. Thank you for dealing with my stress-swings for the last year. It's going to be weird living apart. I'll miss you guys.

To my parents for jumping in to take the twins and understanding I could not come to Sunday dinner.

To my readers: All of you rock and I love you all.

And last, but never least, my kids: I love you, and thank you for thinking it is soooo cool your mom is an author and don't blink when I tell you I have a deadline. Mwah!

# HEAVY METAL

*By Natalie J. Damschroder*

All Riley Kordek wants is a chance to figure out her new ability to bend metal's energy. When a hot guy who knows more than he should helps her escape attackers, she thinks she might've found someone who can lead her to answers.

When Sam Remington takes Riley to the Society for Goddess Education and Defense, the stakes rise beyond what either of them could have imagined. Riley uncovers a plot with disastrous ramifications not only for herself, but for Sam and the people he loves—and potentially every goddess in the country.

# DEEP RISING

*By N.R. Rhodes*

In his nine-year stint with the CIA, Jared Caldwell thought he'd seen it all. But when his latest mission instructs him to apprehend the beautiful scientist Lana, who's allegedly linked to a devastating new form of warfare, he isn't prepared for the prospect of battling man-made tsunamis—or the misplaced feelings he harbors for his number one suspect.

But time is running out and Jared and Lana must work together to protect the mainland. As the heat between them—and the threat of mass destruction—rises there is more at stake than just their hearts.

# DEEP IN CRIMSON
*By Sara Gillman*

Kidnapped by humans and raised in a research facility, Jett was taught to believe his own race of demons to be insidious and violent. Jett wants to bring his captor to justice, so he joins forces with the demon Guardians, and the demon child's older sister, Lexine.

Irresistible attraction grows between Jett and Lexine, but if Jett goes through the all-consuming process of becoming a Guardian, he may forfeit any chance they have of being together.

# HEAVEN & HELLSBANE
*By Paige Cuccaro*

Someone's murdering angels and turning the half human, half angel illorum warriors against their angelic supporters. No one's more surprised than Emma Jane Hellsbane when she's called in to find the killers.

But when her own angelic mentor—and off-limits hottie—Eli is targeted, Emma takes it personally. Now Emma isn't just fighting off demons, rogue nephilim, and Fallen angels, but she's defending her honor as well.

It's all in a day's work as Heaven's ultimate bounty hunter.

# WAKING UP DEAD

*By Emma Shortt*

When her best friend, Tye, disappears hunting for food, kick-ass Jackson Hart's 'head south to safety' plan looks like it's dead before it's even begun. But then she meets ex-mechanic Luke Granger, who offers her protection against the zombie hordes.

But the flesh eaters are getting smarter and the bunker is compromised, so Jackson and Luke travel for thousands of miles looking for other humans. On the way, they discover that even if flesh eating zombies are knocking down their door, there's always time for sex and even love.

# MALICIOUS MISCHIEF
## *By Marianne Harden*

For twenty-four-year-old college dropout Rylie Keyes, keeping her job means figuring out the truth about a senior citizen who was found murdered while in her care. The late Otto Weiner was not a liked man and his enemies will stop at nothing to keep their part in his murder secret.

Forced to dust off her old PI training, Rylie must align with a circus-bike-wheeling Samoan while juggling the attention of two very hot cops. She has no idea that along the way she just might win, or lose, a little piece of her heart.

# CINDERELLA SCREWED ME OVER

*By Cindi Madsen*

Darby Quinn has a bone to pick with Cinderella. Burned one too many times by ex-boyfriends, she's sworn off love, Prince Charmings, and happy endings. Or at least she did…until she met Jake.

Charming, fun, and unwilling to give up on her, Jake doesn't fit any of the profiles Darby has created from her case studies of ex-princes-gone-bad. Finally presented with her own Prince Charming, Darby learns that sometimes the perfect love, like a perfect pair of shoes, is just within your grasp.